RIVER
OF INK

GENESIS

Also by Helen Dennis:

River of Ink 2: Zenith

And coming soon …

River of Ink 3: Mortal

The **Secret Breakers** series:

The Power of Three
Orphan of the Flames
The Knights of Neustria
Tower of the Winds
The Pirate's Sword
Circle of Fire

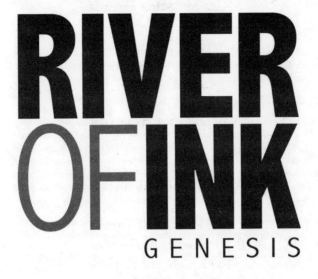

RIVER OF INK
GENESIS

HELEN DENNIS

Illustrated by
BONNIE KATE WOLF

Hodder
Children's
Books

An imprint of Hachette Children's Group

First published in Great Britain in 2016
by Hodder Children's Books

4

A Catalogue record for this book is available from the British Library

ISBN: 978 1 444 92043 7

Typeset in Adobe Garamond by Avon DataSet Ltd, Bidford-on-Avon, Warwickshire

Printed and bound in Great Britain by Clays Ltd, St Ives plc

Hodder Children's Books
An imprint of
Hachette Children's Group
Part of Hodder & Stoughton
Carmelite House
50 Victoria Embankment
London EC4Y 0DZ

An Hachette UK Company
www.hachette.co.uk

For Meggie Rose:
daughter, supporter and best friend.
And because you are my greatest inspiration!

'The time will come when diligent research over long periods will bring to light things which now lie hidden. A single lifetime, even though entirely devoted to the sky, would not be enough for the investigation of so vast a subject . . . And so this knowledge will be unfolded only through long successive ages. There will come a time when our descendants will be amazed that we did not know things that are so plain to them . . . Many discoveries are reserved for ages still to come, when memory of us will have been effaced.'

– Seneca, *Natural Questions*

DAY 1
28th February

Some people believe that when you drown, your whole life flashes before you. The boy in the river saw only bottles, driftwood and the dented licence plate of a foreign car. Not his life. But he knew for certain that he was drowning.

He wanted to swallow, but the muscles in his throat constricted. His whole neck and jaw, vice tight. He was pretty sure his lungs were ripping open. A searing pain pierced his nostrils and his eyes were grazed with grit. He was heavier now and the surface was retreating every second, so the light that rippled in circles over his head was getting further away.

His time was up.

But this wasn't how the boy had planned to die. In fact, he was certain he hadn't planned to die at all. Ever.

So he fought.

He punched his hand through the surface. He forced his chin up into the light and gulped. River waterfalled into his throat. He was sure his chest would explode. A wave dragged him under again and flung him hard against the bank. His shoulder buckled and in the darkness he scrambled to push himself up again for air.

He fingernailed at the brickwork. Certain his arm would break, he held on. Because he didn't want to die.

Another wave flung him hard and this time he got a tighter latch on the wall. The muscles down his arm spasmed. He kicked against the bricks, hauled himself in closer and strained his head upwards.

The third wave lifted him higher. Air tipped into his lungs and drilled inside his nose. He hung on to the lip of the wall and heaved himself clear, his legs and arms splaying, weighed down by his waterlogged clothes.

And the river fell away behind him, clinging to its cargo of bottles, paper and cans, carrying them down towards the sea.

He was on dry land. This fight was over and, for now, the boy had won.

He lay with his face pressed against the pavement.

He could still hear the river. And he could hear the sounds of a city moving all around him. But he had no idea where he was.

And he realised in that moment, there was something else that was incredibly important that he didn't know either.

Kassia was talking to a dead person.

She wasn't in the habit of talking to the dead. But she came on Saturdays to the City of London Cemetery to talk to one in particular. Her dad.

Her mum came too, but she'd given up talking to Kassia's dad while he was living and felt it was hypocritical to talk to him now he'd passed on. She visited the grave each week with her daughter because certain things were expected.

Dante never came. Kassia didn't discuss this with her brother. It was one of the things they didn't talk about.

'I'm going to take my GCSEs early, Dad,' Kassia mumbled down to the grave. 'Mum's done the paperwork. It's a great idea to get them out of the way. Focus on my A levels sooner.' She folded last week's flowers and wrapped them in a sheet of newspaper laid out by her knees. 'I'm excited about it. I really am.' A rose thorn caught the heel of her thumb and a streak of blood cried on to the newspaper. She folded the page and then sucked the nick on her hand.

'Kassia, please!' Anna Devaux's voice was pinched and her face creased like a gourmet chef who'd just witnessed a customer adding tomato ketchup to a finely prepared roast beef dinner. 'Think of the germs!' She took a small bottle of hand sanitiser from her handbag and passed it to her daughter. Kassia squirted the gel into her palms and rubbed them together. The cut stung.

'I'm going to raise this with the groundsman,' her mother continued, unsheathing a pair of scissors from her bag and brandishing them in the air so the sun glinted on the points of the blades. 'I fail to understand why they can't run the lawnmower round this gap.' She bent down and snipped at the edging of grass running like a collar between the headstone and the marble slab covering the ground. 'The amount we pay in fees each year, you'd think they would have someone on this.' With her plastic-gloved fingers she scooped up the grass cuttings and tucked them into a small white bag she'd brought along for the purpose. Then she dropped the bag on to the folded newspaper that still lay on the memorial slab and stripped the gloves from her hands so they made a noise like an air gun being fired.

Kassia tucked the bag of cuttings into the folds of the newspaper and then unwrapped the new flowers and stood them in the vase.

'Finished?' Her mum slipped the scissors into their plastic blade protectors and dropped them back into her handbag.

Kassia moved closer to the gravestone. 'You think getting on with my exams early is a good idea, don't you, Dad? No time like the present, Mum says.' There was, of course, no answer, just a silence that seemed to extend for ages.

Her mother reached down and plucked a browned petal from the edge of the nearest bud. She looked at it doubtfully, unsure what to do with it, and then tucked it into the folds of newspaper Kassia carried, before gelling her own hands with the sanitiser. 'We need to try another florist,' she added. 'These flowers are sub-standard.'

'Mum. I wanted to talk to you.'

'So you have the history essay and two books to read for English today, yes? And then I've found some past papers online.'

'Mum. I was wondering about school.'

'I need the history done by Monday if I'm going to get it marked on time,' Anna Devaux continued. 'And it's best you do as many dry runs of the final papers as possible. I'm thinking twenty for each subject.'

Kassia calculated the time it would take to do this many tests online. 'I wondered if you'd thought about me going back?'

Kassia's mum stopped walking. She pulled the sleeve of her jacket away from her wrist and looked down at her watch. 'If we catch the 8.17 you could get three hours' work done before lunch.'

'Mum. About school? If I'm taking the exams then isn't there a Year 11 class that I could go to for a few months? Part-time even, if you thought that was better.' Her mother had started walking again and she was finding it hard to keep up. 'Mum?'

'This isn't the time, Kassia.'

Kassia thought of lots of smart answers in her head but she knew better than to say them aloud. 'Could we just talk about it?'

'There's nothing to talk about. Although,' Kassia waited for her mother's next words, like a dog waiting expectantly for its owner to throw a stick and shout 'fetch', 'I *do* need to have serious words with the groundsman before we leave.'

Kassia pushed her hands into her pocket. The cut on her thumb caught on the zip of the pocket and the pain made her eyes smart.

* *

Reverend Solomon Cockren was ready for the day. He loved Saturdays. People flocking in their masses across London to visit St Paul's. The cathedral full of visitors.

He walked briskly towards the East Door, looked down at his watch and, despite the fact it was still a little early, he turned the key in the lock and pushed the door open.

The sound was, for a moment, overwhelming. Reverend Solomon took a second or so to adjust but he didn't mind the noise. It meant the city was alive.

He liked to watch people. He enjoyed working out their stories. Looking out on the street outside the cathedral was like looking at the shelf of a busy bookshop. Tens of stories packed together, none of them connected to each other, some big, some small, some easy to read and some much more of a challenge. 'Guessing the story' was his favourite game.

This morning there was a gaggle of sightseers. Early risers, he presumed, keen to tick St Paul's off their To Do lists. There were some party goers who'd obviously been out all night and were wearily making their way home. And there was a girl hurrying along behind a woman who was clearly her mother. The girl clutched a crumpled newspaper under her arm, a bunch of dead flowers poking out the top of the folds. She must have been to a graveyard, he figured. That's the only place he could think of where dead things tended to outnumber things that were alive. This guess made sense of her story and he was proud of himself for thinking of it.

The girl and her mother were in a hurry. As they passed the door to the cathedral, a tall black boy, with buzz cut hair, rounded the corner. The girl sidestepped and the dead flowers fell from her hands. The boy bent down to pick them up. The girl's mother was snapping and snarling, the girl looked embarrassed but the boy was unflustered, the woman's words running off him like water, as if he'd heard such ranting a million times before. Maybe he was used to things much worse than dead flowers. An unhappy home perhaps. Another story successfully deciphered. Reverend Solomon was doing particularly well today.

He made a mental note to add the two youngsters to his prayer list. He was just debating whether to add the mother too, in spite of her snapping, when he saw a story he couldn't read.

There was a teenager making his way shakily up the steps to the cathedral. He was smartly dressed. A suit of sorts, although slightly old fashioned. His red hair was long, curled around his face.

None of this was especially remarkable. Reverend Solomon was used to seeing all types of dress and outfits in the city. Someone had once described London as a melting pot and not much of what bubbled away in the stew here could really surprise him.

But he was surprised. And confused. Because despite the fact the sun was blazing in the sky and it hadn't rained for days, the boy was soaked to the skin, his clothes dripping into a pool of muddy water at his feet.

'Are you OK?' Reverend Solomon fussed, steering the boy towards the open doorway. 'Are you hurt? Do you need help? How did this happen?'

'I don't know.'

Reverend Solomon glanced down the road at the Thames. It was the only explanation. 'You've been in the river? Why?'

'I don't know.'

The boy looked like he would fall and so Reverend Solomon helped him sit down on the steps of the cathedral. He stared into the boy's eyes and held his hand tight. 'What's your name?' he said at last.

The boy took a long time to answer. 'I don't know that either.'

DAY 4
3rd March

Three days later the boy from the river still had absolutely no idea who he was.

Doctor Nat Farnell had been on duty when they'd brought him into the hospital. Unlike some of the other doctors and nurses, he didn't seem to be cross about the boy's inability to answer the most simple question of all. Everyone had asked the boy, as if perhaps they'd have a magic way of phrasing those three words that would make the answer suddenly appear. It didn't matter how the question was asked, though. 'Who are you?' always got the same answer. Silence.

'So it seems you're still a bit of a puzzle,' mused Doctor Farnell, sitting down heavily on the end of the boy's bed. 'And I'm afraid our attempts to try and draw out members of the public who recognise you, has rather backfired.' He passed the boy a copy of the day's newspaper.

The headline read: *Do you know the River Boy?*

The boy stared at the photograph they'd taken. His long red hair was wild around his face and the flash had caught the whites of his eyes, making them look pearly, like the inside of a seashell.

'A puzzle and now a bit of a celebrity, I'm afraid.' The doctor took back the newspaper and folded it so the photograph disappeared. The headline was still visible.

The boy felt a wave of panic, like he'd done in the river. He'd climbed out of the water, but all the memories of who he was had drowned. This didn't scare him as much as the idea that no one was coming for him. Why hadn't his parents seen the news reports? Why hadn't any friends come forward? He was totally alone.

The doctor sensed his discomfort and put the newspaper on the floor out of sight. 'Look, memory's a complicated thing. It can be lost for all sorts of reasons but we have to believe there's absolutely no reason why things won't come back to you. Like a hungry dog coming home for its dinner,' he proposed, 'we just have to find a way of tempting it back. Offer it beef and gravy and not just healthy

11

kibble, if you know what I mean.'

The boy ran his fingers through his hair, as if he was digging for solutions. He wasn't sure at all what the doctor meant. The man seemed to be comparing his lost memory to a stray dog.

Doctor Farnell adjusted the knot of his tie as if it had suddenly got very hot. 'Look, the truth is, things would really work out for both of us if we could unlock that memory of yours. The head of department's breathing down my neck. Seems he can't quite get over the fact I put plaster cast on an unbroken arm last week, so my job's on the line to be honest. Unlock your memory and we are on to a win-win.'

The boy rubbed his arms rather nervously.

'So I'd like to try something with you, if that's OK.'

The doctor passed the boy a pad of paper and a thick black pen.

'I want you to write something. Anything really that comes to mind. Words, pictures, it's up to you. I don't want you to think too hard about what you're doing. Don't try and force things. Let your mind steer your hand and bring to the surface whatever's lying just below. Can you do that for me?'

The boy tightened his grip on the pen.

'Use as much paper as you want. And don't self-check whatever comes. It should be like water really.

Just let the memories flow. I'll wait outside so you don't feel self-conscious. Agreed?'

The boy nodded. He'd no idea how this would help. He had nothing to say, so how could he have anything to write? But the doctor had been kind compared to all the others. And he really had nothing to lose.

So he waited until the doctor moved out of the room into the corridor and then he pressed the nib of the black pen against the clean white page.

His heart beat like a metronome, speeding up as if needing music to play faster and faster. At first the pen was tight in his hand, the marks on the page small and jagged. But then his hand began to loosen, the pen leaning lightly against the fold where his thumb and forefinger met. He watched the marks on the page darken. There were no words yet, but maybe these would come. The doctor had said he shouldn't self-check so he let his hand keep moving, the white of the page eaten up by the dark of the ink until the first sheet was nearly covered. He pulled it free of the pad and pressed the nib against the second page and his hand moved again, faster now, in time with his heart.

As he finished each page he let them fall to the floor and as his hand moved backwards and forwards, the ink flowing now so it covered the page, he realised his eyes were prickling.

He'd no idea who he was. For three whole days no one had come forward to claim him. And the pages that were supposed to help him were covered now in thick black lines. But he kept on moving the pen. And as the final page fell from the pad he noticed the corner had been made damp by a single tear.

He let the pen fall. It clattered on to the floor. There had been no great unlocking. He still knew nothing. Except that he was terrified.

The lights were so bright they were burning his eyes. And outside his window he could hear the reporters who'd collected to cover his story, chatting and laughing. If he really was a puzzle, who was going to help fit the pieces back together again?

He rolled on to his side so all he could see was the wall. And then because there was no one to hold him, he wrapped his arms around himself and held tight.

When Doctor Farnell came back to check, the floor was littered with paper covered in scribbles and the patient, who'd no idea who he was, had fallen into a fitful sleep. 'Splendid,' the doctor muttered through clamped teeth as he scooped the pages up from the floor. 'That went well, then.'

* *

The lights went off, and stayed off. Kassia moaned as she stepped uncertainly downstairs to open the front door. 'Really not funny any more.'

Uncle Nat grinned. 'Have to disagree with you! It's always funny.'

When they first moved to Fleet Street, Kassia's dad had kitted the flat out with all sorts of devices intended to make things easier for deaf people. The doorbell not only rang but made all the lights flash on and off. This way her elder brother Dante would know there was someone at the door despite not being able to hear the bell. Also, for as long as Kassia could remember, her uncle had thought it funny to keep his finger on the doorbell every time he visited, so the lights remained off. He insisted the joke never got tired.

'Tell him he's late!' Kassia's mum's voice thundered down the stairs.

Kassia looked up at the clock in the hallway. It was three minutes past six.

'Good day?' Uncle Nat said, nodding his head towards the stairs.

'One more Victor Hugo book to go – *The Hunchback of Notre Dame*,' winced Kassia. 'But I've done the history. And four past papers.'

'So you're definitely taking your GCSEs this year then? She likes to get on with things, doesn't she?

And more than one book by Victor Hugo? Will you be tested on all of them?'

'No. The Hugos are for *fun*. To broaden my mind.'

'Oh.' Her uncle shrugged.

There was the sound of heavy footsteps from above. 'And this dinner will be ruined unless he gets a move on!' came her mother's voice again.

'What she got in store for us?' grimaced Nat. 'Not sushi. Tell me it's not sushi.'

'Superfood pasta,' grumbled Kassia. 'With extra pomegranate. Does something to your IQ, apparently.'

The stairs shook as Dante raced down to join them. Her brother crashed his hand against his uncle's in an exuberant high five. 'You got a death wish?' Dante signed, glancing over his shoulder back up the stairs.

'It's *three* minutes,' groaned Nat.

'That's how long it takes to drown,' laughed Dante with his hands. 'She's not happy.'

Nat's face seemed to say something along the lines of 'is she ever?' but he didn't bother putting his answer into words.

'Got the tickets?' pressed Dante.

His uncle pulled four tickets for the 'Climbing the O2' experience out of his inside pocket. 'You can go any day in April. There're details on the back.'

'You got four?'

16

'Ah, yes. Part of the master plan. One each for us three and then one for your mother.'

'But she won't come!' exclaimed Kassia.

'Exactly. But she'll feel so bad we bought her a ticket, she won't be able to moan about us going.' He winked conspiratorially.

'Nice,' signed Dante. 'It'll never work. But it's a great idea.'

Suddenly a voice pierced the air like a needle bursting a balloon. 'It's on the table!'

Dante snuffled the tickets into his pocket and led the way up the stairs taking them two at a time.

Nat kissed his sister on the cheek before sinking into a chair at the head of the dinner table.

'Shoes!' she barked at him.

'Anna. I work in a hospital. My shoes can't possibly be dirty.'

Anna put the plate down on the table without looking at him. The plate rocked on the place mat. Nat slipped off his shoes and carried them to the plastic matting at the top of the flight of stairs. He winked again at Dante before returning to his chair.

'Bad day?' Dante signed.

'Confusing.' Nat made sure he signed his answer too. Everyone in the family always did. Dante just used sign but it didn't mean his opinions were 'quieter' than anyone else's. When Dante got cross or excited the shapes he made with his hands got larger and filled more space.

'River Boy?' Dante asked, his signs already quite big. 'He's got to be faking it, right?'

'I don't think so. It's been too long. He'd have weakened in three days, surely? Let something slip to give us a clue. Can you imagine how much energy it's taking for him to keep pretending, if that's what he's doing?'

'I couldn't keep up a lie for even a day. Far too difficult,' Kassia said, before passing the jug of kale and nettle smoothie to her uncle. He poured himself a glass and flinched as a splash of juice leaked on to the tablecloth.

Anna jumped up and grabbed a wet sponge from the sink.

'I'm sorry,' Nat whimpered quietly.

'It doesn't matter,' snapped his sister, rubbing vigorously at the stain in a way that confirmed it definitely did. She took the sponge back to the kitchen. 'I won't be able to tell if we caught it in time until it's dry.'

Kassia watched as her mother sat down again. Anna's jaw was locked tight. She pushed the food around her plate as if she was trying to kill it.

Kassia pulled a face at her brother and he rolled his hands, encouraging her to keep talking. 'Maybe he's scared to death. No one's come for him, right?' Kassia ploughed on. 'I mean, where're his mum and dad? How can *nobody* recognise him?' She looked across at her uncle. 'You've been nice, right? Made it clear he can tell you anything?'

'We've been *more* than patient. Tried to make him feel as comfortable as possible. But I don't know how long the hospital's going to stay safe.'

'The Press, you mean?' asked Dante. 'Bet they're desperate for answers.'

Nat finished his mouthful and took a swig of his smoothie. 'I'm worried it's getting out of hand. Reporters being there every minute of the day and night. It unsettles the other patients. The story's on every news network in the country and overseas as well. There's even a news team flown in from France.'

'But that's exciting,' said Kassia, looking hopefully at her mother. Her mother speared a sprig of broccoli with her fork. 'It's a great story.'

'Which is why the guy's got to be faking it. Dragging it out for as long as possible,' signed Dante, stretching the words dramatically so his hands were wide apart.

'Then why hasn't someone come forward to claim

him yet?' said Kassia. '*He* could be pretending, but someone out there must know who he is, so why haven't they made contact?'

'Exactly. The boy's not faking. He's lost his memory, that's all, which is why being in a hospital isn't helping him.' Nat twisted a length of pasta round his fork and looked over at his sister. 'He needs to be in a home, Anna. The hospital's not right for him. He won't get better there.'

Kassia watched her mum dab a white serviette to the corner of her lips, before slicing a circle of courgette into quarters. What was her uncle doing? Was he asking what she thought he was?

Nat put down his fork. 'He needs to be with a family if he's ever going to get better.'

Her mother spiked the first quartered ring of courgette and nibbled silently, her nostrils still flared, her gaze still locked on the wet patch on the tablecloth.

Was her uncle asking them to have the River Boy stay with them? What was he *thinking*?

Nat leaned back on his chair. 'Look, Anna. This is awkward. I've kind of agreed to something with the hospital.'

Oh my life! He wasn't asking. He'd actually arranged it already. Kassia looked across at her mother. She'd speared the second quarter of courgette and was raising it to her mouth. Her uncle definitely had a death wish. Kassia could hardly bear to watch. It was like seeing a kitten mistaking a coiled snake for a ball of wool.

'You see, the thing is, the psychiatrists think he would be best in a family setting. More chance of his memory returning that way. And it needed to be an approved family, with people in the house regularly. Say, a student who's being home-schooled. That would work.' He nodded at Kassia. She tightened her grip on her fork. Anna ate the third quarter of courgette. 'And the clincher is really some sort of link with a social worker already – like you have with Jacob.' This time he nodded at Dante. 'And then, of course, the third requirement was some sort of medical connection. A doctor who was prepared to visit every day and check in on things.'

Anna swallowed the fourth quarter of courgette.

'So I volunteered you.'

Anna rested her fork on the edge of the plate. She locked her hand vice-like round the serviette. The white fabric spilled between her fingers like foam on a wave.

Kassia hunched her shoulders protectively. Her mother was going to blow. There was no way this would end well.

21

'Look, I know I should have cleared things first and everything. But I didn't have a choice, Anna. It's the boy's only hope.' Nat swallowed. '*You're* his only hope.'

Kassia put her hands flat against the table and braced herself.

Her mother's eyes widened. When she spoke it was in a voice that seemed a bit too high. Her signs were as sharp as knives. 'You. Here. The boy. Here. My house. You.'

'Anna, look. It's not all bad. There's payment. No one expects you to do it for nothing. And you could use the money. And it would make things so much easier for me at work. You know. After the broken arm thing.'

Dante choked a little on his smoothie.

'It could have happened to anyone,' Nat said defensively. 'The woman's arms were wonky. But the point is, if I do this. Well, I mean, if *you* do this, then the consultant will be off my back. There might even be a promotion in it for me.'

Kassia could tell her mother was trying to make sense of this information. The thought of her uncle being promoted seemed to produce a sparkle in her mum's eye, but it was no way a closed deal. 'You expect me. To take in a boy. Who doesn't even know who he is. And stay here. Are you insane?'

Kassia was pretty sure all the evidence of the last ten minutes suggested her uncle was exactly that. Totally bonkers.

'Anna, please. I can't have him at my place and you fit all the criteria. It's perfect.'

'It's ridiculous! It's crazy! It's not happening!' She took her plate to the sink and then returned to the table and began to tug at the tablecloth. 'I need to wash this. If I put it on at forty degrees there's a chance we can get the mark out.'

Kassia scrambled to pick up her plate and made a grab for her brother's. Her mother was so angry she'd stopped signing. Kassia carried the plates to the sink and scrambled the last few moments into signs. 'Mum has turned down the chance for us to look after River Boy.'

'Shame. Would have been cool,' signed Dante, standing tall so his signs could be clearly seen. 'Kind of thing Dad would have done.'

Kassia looked across at her mother.

Anna let the tablecloth crumple to the floor. Her eyes were drawn together and Kassia had no idea whether she was angry or sad. It was impossible to tell. 'But we know nothing about him,' groaned Anna.

'That's the point!' Dante's signs were huge.

'He could be disturbed. Dangerous, even.'

Nat shuffled awkwardly in his chair. Kassia sensed her uncle had more to say and she was sure her mum could sense it too. There was no way this was going to end any way less than really horribly now.

'See. I *knew* it!' Anna's eyebrows were so far up her forehead they looked as if they might escape. 'You've made arrangements for some headcase to stay here and you didn't think for a second about checking things first with me! And there's obviously even more stuff you're not telling us!'

'OK. OK.' Nat opened his hands in surrender. 'I should have checked. I should have asked. But it won't be for long. And I can tell you everything I know.' He watched as his sister stuffed the tablecloth into the washing machine, jabbing the controls like she was hoping to blast it off into space.

'So go on then!' She slammed the washing machine door shut.

Nat reached for his briefcase. 'There is *something*,' he said at last. 'I asked him to write. Or draw. It can sometimes open up all sorts of locked-in memories.'

'So? What did he write?'

'Nothing.'

'Draw then?' pressed Kassia.

'Nothing.'

'So what's the problem?' signed Dante.

Nat took the wad of papers from his case and put them on the table. 'He just scribbled. On and on, for pages and pages. I've got no idea what it all means.'

Kassia took the top piece of paper. It was nearly black with pen marks. The one below almost identical. In places the pen had almost scored through the paper. 'He did this to every page?'

'Pretty much. There're some gaps on some. Some lines on others. But most of them are completely black.'

'Why?'

'No idea.'

Anna took the pages from her daughter. 'And you want me to have . . . this . . . here. In our family?'

'Yes.'

Kassia had to admire her uncle's bluntness.

Anna shuffled the papers.

'He's on his own, sis. He's got no one and I think being here could help him. If I get this right, then the broken arm thing's history.'

It wasn't enough. There was no way her mum was going to cave.

'And the money you'd get. It would cover everything you'd need for Kassia's exams.'

Anna pressed her fingers to her temples. 'All the books?'

Nat nodded.

Kassia watched her mother.

Anna took a deep breath. 'Dante, go and sort out some old clothes for the boy to wear. Kassia, load the dishwasher.'

Dante thumped his hand on to the table. 'Nice one. Should be a laugh.'

'It's not a laugh,' spat Anna. 'It's an inconvenience. And a complete cheek. And your uncle had no right.' She folded her napkin and slid it inside the silver napkin ring. 'But if it improves things for him at the hospital.'

'And the money for Kassia doesn't hurt, does it?' said Dante, and his signs were very small.

'Kassia's future is important. If she wants to be a doctor too then getting to university early is the way to go. It will save her years. We have to take this chance.'

Dante sniffed. His signs were awkward. 'You want to be a doctor, Kass?'

Kassia felt the blood rushing to her cheeks. Anna reached out for her son's arm but he walked towards the door. Kassia could hear him opening and closing drawers in his bedroom as she loaded the plates into the dishwasher.

'Not like that,' snapped Anna, her attention suddenly pulled back to the kitchen. 'How many times have I told you? The plates have to face *this* way. They won't fit otherwise. It's like a puzzle.'

Kassia watched as Anna repositioned the plates. The way her mum had them arranged didn't look any different from the way she'd done it. But she and her mum had the same discussion every day. 'Like a puzzle, Kassia. Think like you're completing a puzzle.'

Kassia stood up straight.

'Well you can still help,' screeched her mother. 'There're the saucepans. And the cutlery. And there will be a billion things to do to get ready for someone to stay here.'

'Anna, the flat is more than ready,' sighed Nat.

'Well there'll be the bedding issue and—'

'Puzzle!' shrieked Kassia. 'Like a puzzle.'

Her mother looked up, the empty smoothie jug balanced in her hand.

'Supposing the pages the boy drew fit together like some giant puzzle. Did you try that?'

'Of course we didn't try that,' grinned Nat. 'It's genius. We didn't think of genius.'

Kassia grabbed the blackened pages and spread them across the table. They made her feel uncomfortable. It was easy to see from the way the paper curled with the pressure of the scoring, that the

River Boy had been frantic. Desperate somehow. But to do what?

Dante stood in the doorway.

'Move that page back a little,' Kassia suggested.

'What are we supposed to be seeing?' Dante asked, in a failing attempt to look like he wasn't that interested.

'That line. The page is almost black except for the top corner. If you fit the edge of that paper with the one beside it, you get a white stripe. See?' Kassia shuffled the two pages so they connected together, the white stripe lined up across both. 'Get it now?'

'I see it,' said Dante. 'What about the next one?' He shuffled a third page in line with the first two. It was possible to extend the white stripe.

Kassia moved the first interconnecting three pages down the table and then moved the remaining paper into space so they could be seen more clearly.

'So you're not supposed to look at them alone,' signed Dante. 'It's one big picture broken into pieces.'

'One big picture of what?' urged Nat.

No one answered and so they worked without talking or signing, sliding paper across the table, connecting edges and extending lines.

By the time they'd finished, the washing machine had reached the spin cycle.

But on the dinner table, made from pages of paper fitted together like pieces of a jigsaw, or bricks in a wall, was a completed picture.

The bank of reporters outside the hospital had thickened. Lights fixed to huge poles made it seem like daylight when in fact it was nine o'clock in the evening. Nat explained he'd called the press conference so quickly because he hoped the item would make the ten o'clock news as well as the morning papers.

'Has someone come forward?'

'Have you found River Boy's parents?'

'Has he got a name yet?'

'Do you know who he is?'

Kassia stood behind the reporters and watched her uncle raise his hand to silence them. There were several sound-recordists with microphones jostling for the best position in front of him.

'There *has* been a development,' Nat began.

'Are you going to tell us who he is then?'

There was a general rumble of disapproval at the interruption and one of the reporters nearest to the back called out, 'Let the doctor speak.'

The crowd hushed.

'As of eight o'clock this evening,' Nat went on, 'despite extensive press and public interest, there's still been no positive identification of the boy who's become known as "River Boy". He has, although being to all intents and purposes, medically well, continued to remain silent. He's not uttered a single word about who he is or where he's come from.'

Nat took several sheets of paper from his briefcase. Dante had scanned in the images the boy had made, fitted them together on the computer screen just as they'd done on the dinner table, and then reproduced the single image the puzzle had created for copying.

'We gave the boy pieces of paper and a pen and asked him to share with us in whatever way he could. And this is what he drew.' Nat held up the paper and flashbulbs from cameras clicked repeatedly. 'I'll pass out copies of the image for you all in a moment. We're hoping that someone will see it and they'll understand why the boy felt compelled to draw it. We hope this symbol will help solve the mystery of the boy's identity.'

'Can you describe the image for audio listeners?' asked a reporter who held a microphone heavily branded for BBC Radio Four.

'It's an ouroboros,' said Nat. 'A circular dragon drawn in segments. And the dragon's eating its own tail. It's a classic symbol used in alchemy to represent the idea of life being like a cycle.'

'So why'd the boy draw that?' asked the radio reporter.

'We're not sure yet. We've asked him. He seemed shocked to see the symbol made from his scribblings, which suggests the image came from his subconscious. But this is common with memory return in cases like his. Patches of information might come back and initially make no sense to the patient.'

There was a squeezing forwards of reporters then, and a clamouring for copies of the reproduced image as they began to be passed out.

'One final thing,' Nat said, rubbing his arms against the cold. 'We've decided to move the boy from the hospital to a more suitable facility in the hope of aiding his recovery.'

'Where?'

'When?'

'Will there be a photo op?'

'How can our viewers track his move?'

Nat held up his hands again. 'We understand the interest. And we appreciate all your coverage. Let's hope your running of the symbol unearths a lead. But no, we won't be releasing details about where the boy is moving to. Any information should still come to the hospital or police email address as previously issued. For now, his new location will be undisclosed.'

Kassia stepped back from the crowd and looked up at the hospital. There was a movement at one of the windows and she was pretty sure she could see the River Boy peering down at them. The curtain flickered and the face from the window was gone. But not before Kassia had noticed how sad he looked. And how scared. And suddenly, she was scared too. She couldn't remember the last time they'd had a guest to stay in their home. She hadn't had a sleepover since before her dad had left. Her mum didn't do visitors. Guests meant mess. Guests meant changes in routine. These things were to be avoided at all costs. Like germs.

She turned back to see her uncle move away from the crowd and into the foyer of the hospital. She counted to a hundred in her head, just to be sure she wasn't too quick, then she walked inside, over to the lift and pressed the button for Level Seven. Her uncle was waiting for her as the lift door slid open and he now held, instead of a briefcase, a huge bunch of helium balloons.

'Ready?' he said.

'Not really.'

'Well, it's time for action anyway.'

The plan was simple.

'The poor kid's got the most famous face in

London,' said Nat, striding along the hospital corridor, clutching the helium balloons which streamed in front of him. 'I saw this in a film once. With Sigourney Weaver. Worked a treat.'

Kassia was struggling to keep up. She carried a bag containing some old clothes from Dante and it was banging against her leg as she hurried. 'The River Boy's OK with all this, is he?'

'Ah, about that,' said Nat. 'Surprises are good. Everyone like surprises, right?' He passed her the strings and the bunch butted together above her head.

'You haven't told him! Haven't warned him what he's getting in to!'

'I thought it best your mum came as a lovely surprise.'

Kassia blew out a breath. 'I bet he'll get his memory back just to escape us,' she said.

'So it's a win-win,' grinned her uncle.

Kassia felt the same way she did before an important exam. Her mouth was totally dry. She was desperately wishing Dante had volunteered for this part in the plan, but Nat had said that might be too complicated. So it was down to her.

Her uncle opened the door to room 696 and they stepped inside.

The River Boy was sitting on the end of the bed. He looked older in real life but his face even sadder than his photo. His hair was auburn, a shock of colour around a ghostly pale face, and his eyes a vibrant blue like the brightest balloon she carried.

Kassia tested a smile to see if he'd return it. He looked too shocked.

'I know. Crazy idea,' said Nat, batting the balloons away. 'But we've got to get you out of here without being seen. We've just told the press we're moving you and you can bet some of them will be stalking the doors to try and get a close-up.'

Kassia watched as the boy tried to process all this. He looked as if he was trying to work out a really complicated maths problem and was forgetting what number he'd got up to.

Nat hopped anxiously from foot to foot and then seemed to remember Kassia was with him. 'This is Kassia,' he said. 'My wonderful niece. Plenty of time for proper introductions later but for now we need to get you out of here as quickly as possible. Put these on.'

Kassia wondered how you welcomed someone who didn't speak and didn't know who you were, or even worse, who they were. A handshake seemed the sort of thing an adult might do, so she thrust out her arm and the balloons clashed awkwardly, bumping on the River Boy's head. 'Oh I'm sorry. I—' She pulled her hand out of the tangle of strings and did a sort of awkward bow instead, closing her eyes as she looked down in an attempt to hide her embarrassment.

Something like a smile was playing across the boy's lips when she looked up. The balloons bobbed around her head like a thunder cloud. He took the heavy coat Nat passed him, slipped it on and bent down and put on the shoes.

'Here.' Kassia passed the boy a baseball cap, making herself focus on all the aspects of the plan her uncle had gone over with her in the lift. 'Pull it down as far as you can. Nat says we don't want anyone to see your face.'

The boy did as he was told, tucking as many stray strands of red hair as he could manage under the cap. He looked across at Kassia, maybe seeking her approval. 'Nearly,' she said and without thinking, she reached out and smoothed away a coil of curls which had fallen free by his ear. 'That's better.'

He nodded and she pulled away as the balloons bumped between them.

Nat reinforced the plan. 'Whatever happens, you can't let them recognise you. Keep the balloons as close as you can. Understand?'

The boy hung tightly to the strings.

'Don't stop for anyone. Just keep going.'

Kassia's pulse was racing. It had seemed so easy going through things at home but now she'd seen the photographers and reporters in action, she'd begun to be less sure this would work. The boy had pulled the balloons down to hide his face so she'd no idea how he was feeling.

Nat opened the door and glanced down the corridor. It seemed fairly clear. 'OK. This is where I leave you. The press know me now so I'll be a marker for them. Kass, it's down to you. Remember the route?'

She nodded, then looked across at the River Boy and, through a chink in his balloon armour, she gave him a look she hoped told him they should go. She pushed her way out of the door. River Boy followed, the balloons thudding together like a pulse. Only when they were nearing the lift did Kassia risk looking back. Her uncle had gone in the other direction. His white coat was billowing out behind him like a sail.

Kassia steered the River Boy into the empty lift and helped bundle the balloons in front of him. She pressed the button but just as she was beginning to congratulate herself on how well their escape was going, two nurses appeared from the opposite side of the corridor waving for Kassia to hold the doors.

'Thanks so much,' the first one said, laughing as her friend stepped inside. 'We're off to see if we can get our fifteen minutes of fame before it's too late.'

Kassia didn't answer. She glanced to her side. The River Boy's eye sparkled behind a gap in the helium protection. She tried to make her face look reassuring but she was scared it might look more like she'd got very bad tummy ache and was about to throw up.

'TV stuff,' the nurse continued, undeterred. 'They're asking anyone they can get hold of about this River Boy. It's trending on Twitter 'cos there's been a development. Esther from paediatrics has been on Sky News twice. Don't see why we shouldn't have our shot at stardom.' She moved deeper into the lift and checked her lipstick in the mirrored wall at the back. The highest balloons thumped against the ceiling, filling the space between them. Kassia glanced in the mirror and, reading her warning expression through the glass, the River Boy looked down at the floor and pulled the balloons in tighter. 'I'm going to tell 'em, #RiverBoy's got to be some Russian prince or something, seeking exile. That's what me and Chloe figure, don't we, Chlo?' She pressed her jaws together and scraped at a smudge of lipstick on her top tooth. 'You?'

Kassia glanced at the display on the lift. Three more floors to go. 'Sorry?'

'Who d'you think he is, then?'

Kassia could feel the balloons bobbling behind her. She was sure she could hear the boy's breathing. Two more floors to go.

The nurse flicked her hair dramatically behind her shoulders. 'You know Maternity is floor eight, don't you?'

Kassia had no idea what she was on about.

'The balloons. New baby. You should be going up in the lift, not down.'

Kassia looked at the bunch of helium camouflage. It was the first time she'd noticed that several of them had '*Congratulations. It's a Boy*' printed all over them. She tried to think of anything coherent or sensible to say but the nurse didn't allow her time to attempt an answer.

'I think boys are a whole load of trouble, don't you, Chlo?' she giggled as the lift bell sounded and the doors slid open. 'Watch for us on the news tonight,' she called over her shoulder, steering her friend towards the exit and the bank of reporters.

'You OK?' Kassia asked.

The balloons moved a little in answer. She guessed perhaps the River Boy was nodding his head. She took a deep breath, and then grabbed the arm of his coat and steered him out of the lift and into the corridor. This one was busy, the main door and the wall of reporters only steps away. But that's not where they were heading.

Nat had sketched her a map on an envelope. She desperately hoped she was remembering the route correctly. The boy hurried beside her. Right and then right again she turned, past the waiting room for X-rays and then down the corridor and past the plaster room. Was it left or right now, she wasn't sure? She glanced up at the signs on the walls. Something about radiotherapy and palliative care. Her mum had made Nat explain those things to her. All part of her preparation to be a doctor. But just because she knew what those departments were, didn't mean she knew her way past them and on to the street.

'I'm lost,' she mumbled. 'I'm sorry, I've messed this up.'

For a second the balloons moved a little to the left so she could see the River Boy's face. And everything in the way he looked at her told her it would be OK.

Kassia took a deep breath and pushed on with renewed confidence. A turn in the corridor led towards the fire exit. The cold air from outside hit her like a wall and caught in her throat. But her mum's car was there, the lights blazing, the engine purring.

Dante leaned across from the driver's seat and opened the back door so they could climb inside. He pointed meaningfully up the street.

Kassia saw a man poised, camera around his neck, notebook ready. But he didn't turn and look in their direction. He was too busy interviewing one very chatty nurse and her rather less chatty friend about Russian princes and conspiracy plans.

Kassia bundled into the car beside the River Boy and, before she'd even done her seatbelt up, Dante floored the accelerator and began to drive.

A single blue balloon had slipped free from the bunch. It drifted up into the London night sky, the word *Congratulations*, bobbing up and down as it rose.

Half an hour later the boy sat on the edge of the settee, his boots left neatly on the square of plastic at the top of the stairs. The woman who'd let them in stood awkwardly beside the fire place. She was wearing an apron and bright yellow gloves. She was wrinkling her nose as if she was checking for unpleasant smells or about to sneeze. The room was totally quiet except for the balloons thudding the ceiling, like the sound of a ticking clock.

Suddenly the lights went out.

'It's OK. It's because of Dante,' the girl explained. The boy didn't think this was much of an explanation.

After a while the lights went back on again and the boy heard muttering in the hall and then footsteps on the stairs.

'You made it.' Doctor Farnell was accompanied by a tall black man with broad shoulders, dressed in combat trousers and a tight fitting T-shirt. He had a laptop tucked under his arm. The boy was sure he'd never seen the man before and was just wondering whether he was someone else from the hospital when he realised Doctor Farnell was talking to him. 'So you've met my sister, Anna, then. She couldn't wait to help out by taking you in.' He punched Anna playfully on the arm. 'And I guess you know Kassia now.'

The boy looked at the girl who'd led him out of his prison. She was blushing, her long hair tied in a tidy plait, her eyes the colour of wood made wet in the rain.

'And your getaway driver was Dante. Hope he kept to the speed limit.' Doctor Farnell began to move his hands around and the boy guessed he was making the shape of words.

The boy was pretty sure he'd never met anyone who was deaf before. He felt a little awkward but Dante was smiling, his hair the same black as his sister's, and longish too, curling around his face. His eyes, though, were darker than hers, the colour of soot.

The doctor pointed to the tall man who'd entered the room behind him. 'And finally, this is Jacob. He's a social worker, attached to this lot. He comes to visit Dante every week. Thought it best you got to know him, as having him on board was one of the reasons this arrangement seemed like a good one.'

Jacob stepped forwards, reached out and pumped the boy's hand in an enthusiastic handshake. A ribbon of tattoo circled the man's arm, disappearing under the cuff of his T-shirt.

'So this is us,' Nat concluded. 'Well, this is them, really. Anna's totally fine with you staying here for as long as you need, aren't you sis?' The woman's nose wrinkled so much at this point, the boy couldn't help thinking she looked a little like a tortoise. 'And I'm available any time. Anna can get hold of me, even if I'm at work, you know.' He pointed to a phone clipped to his belt.

The boy smiled. He thought this was the best way to say thank you. For the moment, anyway.

Jacob sat down on the edge of the settee. He

switched on the laptop and angled the screen so the boy could see. 'We haven't got much to go on to find your story,' he said, and his dark black eyes danced in the folds around his even darker skin, 'but the symbol you drew has got to be a start.'

The boy looked at the screen as an image of a dragon appeared. It was eating its own tail.

'Ouroboros. A symbol for everlasting life. Quite common in ancient writing and alchemy books. Like a phoenix coming back from the flames. Kind of an epic symbol. But I take it you've no idea why you drew it.'

The boy had no idea about a lot of things. Pictures of tail-eating dragons didn't really seem to him to be the thing they should be focusing on, but he had no way of telling them that.

'I was in a graffiti crew back in the day,' Jacob went on. 'I wondered if this was a tag you'd drawn.' Everyone around the room looked more than confused. 'Graffiti artists "tag" their work. Sign it off, so you know who's done what. Perhaps this everlasting dragon is your tag? Mine was an angel. Because of the Bible story about Jacob and the angels.' The confusion intensified. 'Anyway. Let's not get bogged down. That idea might have been a stretch.'

The boy stared down at the carpet. The strands on the edge of the rug in front of the fire were so straight they looked like they'd been brushed into place with a toothbrush. He was finding it hard to think about the symbol. When he'd scribbled on those pages, he'd no idea he'd even drawn a dragon eating its tail. And he didn't think he had any idea what an ouroboros was. The image unnerved him and he could feel perspiration prickling on his forehead. There was banging in his head and the room suddenly seemed too hot.

The doctor seemed to notice his discomfort. 'We've got plenty of time,' he said quietly. 'No need to rush anything now you're here. There's an old saying. If at first you don't succeed . . . then don't try parachuting.' He laughed weakly. 'We'll get the answers in the end if we try and try again.'

Jacob took the hint and closed the laptop. 'Yeah, we've got time, mate. As much as you need.'

There was silence then, except for the balloons marking the time with their thudding bounce.

'I should show you to your room,' said Kassia, obviously picking up on a signal from her uncle. 'It's my room actually and I'm going to sleep in the loft.'

The boy stood and followed her down the hall. This family had obviously gone to a lot of trouble to have him here, but everyone seemed so nervous he couldn't be sure they were honestly as thrilled with the idea as the doctor made out.

'It's a bit untidy,' she apologised, opening a door and straightening a purple notebook on the desk inside the doorway, so its edge lined up with the end of the desk.

The boy stood still for a moment. The room reeked of organisation. It made the hospital ward look untidy. The walls were papered with charts and timetables. Pages and pages of highlighted lists. A calendar of the year took up as much space as a window. Books were displayed neatly on shelves and the boy could tell without looking too closely that they were arranged not only in subject areas but in alphabetical order. There was a pot of pencils on the edge of the desk. Each one was sharpened to a point like a spear.

There were no soft toys. No fluffy cushions or posters on the wall. There were no photos except one. It was free standing. Propped on the dressing table, angled slightly away from the door. The girl and her brother were both in it, although they were obviously much younger when the photo had been taken. The woman too, her face unlined and laughing. And there was a man. He was tall and had his arm protectively around the woman as she laughed. He had the same black hair as the children and was laughing too, his shirt neck open, a golden medallion glinting at the base of his throat.

'My dad,' Kassia said quietly. 'He's not with us any more.'

The boy guessed from the way she spoke that the man was dead and he was sorry.

'So this is it,' Kassia said. 'I know it's a bit much. My mum likes me to use my time well. I'm going to be a doctor, you see.' She seemed embarrassed by the montage of timetables on the wall and steered him towards the window. 'You have a nice view, down into Fleet Street, and if you crane your neck a little you can see St Paul's Cathedral.'

Her final words seemed too loud. Something about them made him feel uncomfortable again and he put out his hand towards the bed to steady himself. Kassia looked embarrassed, but the boy nodded to reassure her. He wanted to say thank you. But he wasn't ready for words. So he just smiled.

Kassia smiled back awkwardly. 'There're some more of Dante's old things,' she said, pointing to a stack of clothing on the chest of drawers. 'And the bathroom's just down the hall on the left. You should make yourself at home.'

The door clicked behind her as she left and the boy stood in the centre of the room. He knew one thing for certain. This wasn't the hospital. But it wasn't home.

He sat down on the edge of the bed, strangely aware that he shouldn't crease the bedspread. He looked up again at the walls. The charts and tables were overwhelming, like a patchwork blanket pressing tight across his chest making it difficult to breathe. The photo on the dressing table bothered him too. Everything about the room was neat and precise but the photo was facing the wrong way. Anyone sitting at the dressing table would see only the velvet stand which propped up the photo. Maybe it was set that way so Kassia could see the picture from her bed. He rocked back slightly where he sat. That didn't work either. So the boy reached out and turned the frame towards him.

The effect was immediate. A surge of static, like an electric shot, spiked up his arm. He pulled his hand away, his arm flexing sharply at the elbow. The shock wave stretched into his stomach as if his belly button was being pulled back tight against his spine. The photo wobbled on the dressing table and then clattered backwards so the image stared up like a corpse, at the ceiling. But the boy could still see the picture in his head. It was glowing just in front of his eyes, like a copy of the image had lifted from the frame. Around the edges of the photo something circled and pulsed. A snake-like dragon just like the symbol he'd drawn. It was spinning frantically, its jaws pressing hard around its tail, circling and spinning, scoring the image deeper into the boy's mind. And the man from the photo was smiling. But his eyes were the saddest the boy had ever seen.

The boy pressed the heels of his hand against his eye sockets, trying to force the picture from his mind. And within the circling of the dragon, the man with the sad eyes reached out and blood trickled slowly from his lip.

For a second the boy thought he was going to be sick.

His head thumped. Noises like car tyres squealing pummelled his ears. Then the man in the picture closed his eyes, and the dragon thinned like smoke, drifting and stretching until it disappeared.

Maybe the dragon was important after all.

'Why d'you think he doesn't talk?' Kassia asked her uncle after Dante had gone to bed and her mum was seeing Jacob out. 'Do you think he still can?'

'A reaction to the trauma, probably,' Nat explained. 'He did speak, when he first came out of the water, but only to say he had no idea who he was.'

'And there's been nothing since?'

'Not a word.' Nat leaned back in his chair. 'My

guess is something terrible happened to him, and his voice and his memory have just shut down.'

'But how can he remember some stuff?' Kassia pressed. 'Like how to walk and how to drink and things like that?'

'The brain's like a huge blanket,' explained Nat. 'Folded and pleated. And some of the memories are where the boy can still find them. And some of them are hidden, in the folds.'

'But he will be able to get to them, won't he? Eventually?'

Nat steepled his fingers together as if he was about to say a prayer. 'You know what to do when life gives you lemons, Kass?'

'Sure. You make lemonade.'

'Or you could take the lemons back to the shop and demand you have oranges like you ordered.'

Kassia had no idea what his uncle was on about.

'It's bedtime, Kass. It's been a long day. You should get some sleep.'

'Will he get his memory back?' she pressed again.

'I think a lot of that will be up to him. And us,' said her uncle. 'You did well earlier by the way. Great execution of a brilliant plan.'

Kassia knew the conversation was over.

* *

49

The boy sat on the end of the bed, and slid his fingers in front of his eyes so they blocked out the light. Nothing. He saw nothing. The circling dragon and the man with the sad eyes had gone. But his head throbbed with noise. Words that made no sense, floating like flotsam in the river of his mind. *Water. Time. Fire.* Over and over again, the words banging together and scraping against the inside of his skull. Why wouldn't they stop?

He stared up at the wall and the lines of schedules and timetables papering it. Dates seemed to glow and stretch in front of him, burning his eyes as if he should remember. *January 14th.* Was this his birthday? *December 23rd.* Was this more than a day close to Christmas? And numbers. 1926 and 1933? Were these part of his address? Digits from his phone number?

And why the dragon circling and circling, its six-segmented body squeezing the pictures he saw in his mind?

That night the boy dreamed of a road far away. The car was getting closer and closer and the headlights were so bright they were almost blinding. The boy woke with a start and his bedclothes clung to him, greased with sweat.

Outside the door to his room, Kassia stood listening.

She'd heard the boy crying.

And the boy didn't know that she listened.

There was a lot the boy didn't know.

Etkin House was registered as a Care Home. This was exaggerating things a bit. The idea of care. And the idea of home. But Etkin House was where Victor Sinclair lived. He'd been there for nearly five years. People weren't too keen on adopting orphans once they were over ten, so the Care Home had been the best option.

Victor lay on his bed and stared at a poster of the constellations stuck to his ceiling. The poster had been a present for his fifteenth birthday – from himself. That had been a week ago. Or sort of.

Victor was a 'leapling'. He was born on the 29th February in the millennium year. That meant he'd had three proper birthdays since then. On the years in between, when there'd been no February 29th, he'd celebrated his birthday on the 28th, as he'd done this year. 'Celebrated' was pushing it a bit. No one did much celebrating round here on any occasion, least of all birthdays.

Etkin House was OK. Some of the other kids who lived there were OK too. But it wasn't home and Victor had no intention of staying long. But then he'd never had any intention of being here in the first place. But life had definitely given Victor lemons.

He was just trying to work out where on the poster the phoenix constellation was when he heard the voice of Mrs Shortt the house parent through the closed door. 'Visitor for you. Waiting in the common room.'

Victor never had visitors.

But he made his way to the common room anyway. He'd nothing better to do.

A woman stood gazing out the window. She looked like a grandma. Not his grandma because he didn't have one. But the sort of woman who should be a grandma. She had grey hair, and was soft and blurred round the edges like she'd been left in a steamy room and puffed up a bit in the heat. Victor fiddled awkwardly with the hem of his T-shirt, stuffing it into the waist of his jeans. He ran his hand over his buzz cut. The woman peered over the frame of her glasses and there was the tiniest trace of a laugh behind her eyes. 'Pleased to meet you, Victor. Take a seat.'

It seemed odd to be offered a seat, as if the grey-haired woman in the long spotty dress had suddenly converted the space into her own front room, but Victor did as he was told, settling on to the settee and taking a floral patterned cushion and holding it in his lap.

'Martha Quinn,' said the woman. 'Good to meet you again.'

Victor presumed he should recognise her, but as far as he could remember they'd never met.

'I've been looking forward to this day for quite a while.'

'Is this my Harry Potter moment?' Victor asked. 'You've come to take me away from this place?'

'It's good you're a reader, Victor. Though I'm afraid I'm not here to open a world of magic for you. My interest is definitely in the world around us. But you're right. I *am* here to offer you an escape from this place.'

Victor felt his breath flutter a little. He'd been making a joke, but this woman, in her spotty red dress, seemed deathly serious.

'Let's start from the beginning, shall we? The fact is, I knew your parents.'

Victor began to feel a little queasy. He'd hardly met anyone who'd known his mum and dad. They'd died so long ago he was sure there were hardly any links left to that part of his life.

'And I hate to continue the Harry Potter analogy too long, but I was actually godparent to your sister.'

Violet had died before his parents. He only had a very few memories of her, but they were mostly happy ones. Until the ones in the hospital.

Martha Quinn wrinkled her nose and ran her finger along the top of the mantelpiece. A cloud of grey dust lifted. 'I'm so sorry it's taken us so long to come for you. We had to wait until you were fifteen, you see. Your time under the care of the state is nearly over now, and the chances of being taken in by a family with only a year of governmental care left is really very small. So your father, wise and thoughtful man that he was, sent me to collect you.'

Victor felt even more queasy than before. This woman knew his dad was dead. What was she talking about? How could his dad have sent her?

'I'm sorry Victor. I'm probably not making myself clear.'

That was a bit of an understatement. Like saying turkeys weren't that fond of Christmas.

'In your dad's will, he made provision for you. Once the state began to relinquish your care then we, as his past employers, were to take over responsibility for your welfare. It's an unusual arrangement, I'll grant you. To live in a place of work. But your father's workplace is a little on the exceptional side.'

'You want me to come and live in an office?'

'I think you'll like it, Victor. Your schooling can be arranged from there. All your financial needs are

54

covered. Our only problem, of course, is if you'd rather stay here.'

Victor plumped the cushion vigorously. He had little idea who this woman was. He had no idea where she was taking him. But she'd been sent by his father. And as far as Victor was concerned, that was all that mattered. 'Took your time, Dad,' Victor mumbled.

'I'm sorry?'

'Oh, nothing. I was just wondering if I have to sign anything before I leave?'

Martha Quinn picked up her newspaper from the table, her finger lingering just a second on the picture of the River Boy, who was featured once again on the front page. She sniffed and folded the paper in half, scoring down the fold on his face. 'No. No, Victor. There's nothing to sign. Everything is in place. Your life is about to change.'

Conspiracy London @Consp
I have my theories. #RiverBoy

Tiffany Harrison @Tiff92   17h
UNREAL. **#RiverBoy** #LDN #hot

NOAH @NOAH   20h
#RiverBoy ! _,-9+3

Metro UK @MetroUK   20h
Young boy discovered at St Paul's #Ri

Joeseph Albright @BeastyJoe   20h
Fell in a river. LMAO. #N00B **#RiverBoy**

flood @flood   21h
#unicornprotocol #activate **#RiverBoy**

Climb
an icon

Climb experience for one

DAY 9
8th March

There was a routine at Kassia's house. It was simple. Kassia worked on her schooling projects. And prepared for exams, which everyone seemed to think were important. Dante went out to work. Anna monitored things. And cleaned. She did lots of cleaning.

Each day was marked with a number. The boy recorded them. Days since the river. His stomach twisted every time he saw the number increase. He tried to see them as footsteps nearer to answers. They stared back at him like scratches on the wall of a prison cell. Each one seemed harder to write. He was aware of the clock ticking as he made each mark. Every day the ticking grew louder.

The doctor arrived each morning. He checked the boy over, took his temperature and blood pressure and then he asked questions. The boy still gave no answers. He didn't know any. But he *did* know how to talk. He remembered that. He was nervous now, though, about breaking the silence. It had gone on too long. And everything here seemed to be adapted for silence so it wasn't a problem.

Dante never spoke either. He made noises sometimes, when he was thinking, or as he walked around. And sometimes, when he signed, tiny vocal sounds accompanied the movement of his hands. The boy from the river was fascinated. He watched as the family turned all they said to each other into swift and fluid shapes with their fingers. They changed their faces too, to fit the signs, and when they were especially happy or especially serious the signs grew or shrunk in size. It was like watching water ripple and flow. The signs were there, strong and powerful and then they were gone, not even a trace remained. The boy from the river watched carefully. He was trying to learn. When he wasn't trying to remember.

Doctor Farnell had several strategies for trying to prompt the return of the boy's memory. He offered more paper and asked the boy to draw again. Nothing. He played music, hoping the boy would relax and the memories would fall into place. Nothing. He showed the boy photos, mainly of places in London, hoping for some recognition. Nothing.

And so each lunchtime, Doctor Farnell packed up his bag and returned to the hospital for his shift. 'It's OK,' he said one day as he left. 'Like my mum always used to say, the early bird might get the worm, but it's the second mouse who gets the cheese. We'll get there. We just have to be patient.'

The River Boy wasn't quite sure what the doctor meant about the cheese. Neither was he sure how much patience he had left.

Jacob, the social worker, came to the flat each afternoon. Kassia was allowed precisely thirty minutes break from her school work then, as long as she marked it on her time chart. The three of them would sit round the computer. If there was nothing from the past to work with they'd try and deal with the present.

First, they checked the news sites. Occasionally, there were updates on the River Boy. These were bizarre because there was no more information to share but the media was still trying to get to the bottom of the mystery. Often, there was a lonely reporter standing by the Thames wondering aloud or in print what had become of him.

Next, they searched Twitter and YouTube for the

latest videos. Most theories seemed to be leaning very much towards the boy being mad.

Finally, they tried to find out more about the ouroboros.

The press were all over the idea of the weird symbol, and every morning there was some new theory about it, usually hidden towards the back of the newspapers among the gossip columns. Kassia didn't know anything about alchemy, and if the River Boy did, then he didn't remember, so they sat together and searched online to find out more about the theories suggested.

It seemed alchemists were like ancient scientists. They had tried to turn lead into gold. Some of them had even looked for an elixir of life to make people live for ever. They were mad, of course. That much seemed pretty clear. If not mad, then just mistaken. But they certainly loved their symbols. There was a whole language of signs and pictures they used to explain things to each other to keep their ideas secret. The ouroboros was one of these symbols. It still made no sense why the River Boy had drawn it. Alchemists lived in the past. They didn't climb out of the River Thames not knowing who they were.

When Jacob left because he had clients to visit, and

Kassia went back to her work, the boy had little idea what to do with his time.

He tried to read but his mind couldn't really focus. He looked at a guidebook on British Sign Language for the Deaf and when no one was looking he practised talking with his hands. He watched TV every so often, flicking through the twenty-four-hour news sites. He hated seeing the picture of himself filling the screen and hearing no one had come forward to claim him. But he knew that anyway. Doctor Farnell had 'that look' each morning when he arrived announcing it was time to mark down a new day of not knowing. The doctor's face said he was sorry. And embarrassed. And the circle of searching for answers began again, leading, it seemed, absolutely nowhere.

The boy from the river had so many questions. 'Who was he?' was the big one. 'Why had he drawn the symbol?' was another. But what had happened when he'd held the photograph of Kassia's family was the question that bothered him most. Why did the dragon symbol twist in front of his eyes? Was this a memory? Part of what was lost, spinning forwards in his mind, trying to work itself out?

The thought terrified him.

And there was something else. Even more scary.

A bigger question that choked his breath every time he thought it.

Why had no one come for him?

Had he done something so bad that no one wanted to say they knew him? When his mind dwelled on this, he did anything he could to keep busy. Running up and down the stairs; sit-ups in his room; testing himself on sign language shapes. In fact, anything to stop his mind focusing on the huge and gaping hole that was him.

And that's why he'd picked up the box.

It was hidden by coats and jumpers in the bottom of the wardrobe in Kassia's room. He hadn't gone looking for it. His hand had just brushed against it when he was packing his clothes away. And it smelled like a memory. The seaside perhaps.

So the River Boy sat on the floor and put the box on his lap. Then he lifted the lid.

Inside was a finger painting of a puppy, a necklace made of pasta, a Christmas angel with crooked wings; a tiny turtle made of modelling clay, a toilet roll snowman covered with cotton wool and a crayon drawing of a mountain. There was an origami pelican, a fan made of tissue paper, a silver pocket watch and a pom-pom made of scraps of multi-coloured wool. And there were notebooks. Lots of them, crammed with pages and pages of writing. Stories. By Kassia and her dad.

The box was her childhood. The River Boy could see that. A fragment of time, shut away under a thick wooden lid and smothered by jumpers. As he turned the pages of the stories, it was as if time had rolled backwards and he was inside another person's past.

It felt overwhelmingly happy. And safe there. Until the River Boy looked up and realised he was no longer alone.

'What the hell are you doing?'

The notebook he held tumbled to the floor.

'They're my private things! You're reading my . . .' Her words merged together to form something like a howl.

The boy grabbed for the book. It had fallen, facedown on the carpet, the pages splattered and crumpled. He tried to smooth them shut; tried to wipe away all traces of him having looked. He could explain. He really could.

'I don't know what they do wherever you come from but people here don't read other people's stuff!' She lurched at him and tugged the book away, holding it to her chest. 'Why would you do that?'

Answers bounced around his head like the balloons they'd used in their escape from the hospital, which hung, deflating now, in the corner of the room, their strings tangled around the metal headboard of the bed. He'd looked because it was her life. And because he could find no pieces of his own life he just wanted something, *anything*, to hang on to.

He knew it was wrong. He'd known as soon as his fingers had lifted the lid that this wasn't anyone's to share. But he wanted a story with a beginning and a middle he could claim as his own. And if not that, then any story. He wanted . . . Now his words were a jumble of balloon strings in his head. He wanted to remember and nothing before had been any help.

He looked up and she was still there in the doorway and her eyes were the colour of deep, dark mahogany. 'None of this is our fault,' she spluttered. 'We're trying to help you.'

And she *had* helped him. But he couldn't look at her.

'You're unbelievable,' she mumbled. And he knew that was true too. He was scared of what he'd forgotten and scared of what he was starting to remember. He was a boy who had no life of his own; trying to steal from someone else's.

* *

Kassia sat slumped against the wall of the corridor, her head in her hands, like she was trying to hide from him.

'I'm so sorry.'

She looked up, her eyes wide with anger and surprise. 'What?'

'I'm so sorry.'

'You can speak now?' Her words punched like rapid gun fire. 'You stay here all this time and you say nothing. Then you look through my things and suddenly you can speak?'

'I had nothing to say before,' the boy mumbled awkwardly.

Kassia linked her hands together and pressed her locked knuckles against her teeth. 'I don't get you. I really don't.'

The River Boy kneeled down beside her. A silence stretched thinly before he spoke again. 'I don't either.'

The space separating them was so small he could have reached out and touched her.

Everything in her eyes told him she was searching for something else to say. Anger fighting surprise. Maybe pity winning through. 'Those things were private.'

'I know. I'm so sorry.'

'Especially the stories. You shouldn't have read them.'

They sat for a moment in the silence. Time marked its progress as the light faded.

'How can I make you believe I'm sorry?' he said at last.

She rocked her head back against the wall. 'Well, you can make sure you don't stop talking again. That was annoying.'

'So it was worth it?'

Her body tensed. It was too soon to joke.

'I'll put everything back. I'll do your chores in the kitchen. I'll do anything to make it better.'

'Dishwasher,' she smiled. 'I hate doing that.'

'OK.' He stood up. 'I'll empty the dishwasher. You'd better supervise where I put stuff though. I'm thinking a saucepan out of place might be more stress than your mum can cope with.'

She followed him into the kitchen and watched as he put things away, nodding and pointing as he held things up for guidance.

'Does it feel weird, speaking?' she asked eventually, as he lined the forks carefully in the segmented drawer liner.

He nodded. 'I was afraid to. Before, I mean. At first I was too scared that I couldn't. Then I was too scared to try and then . . . Well, it would have been a big deal. And like I explained, I had nothing to say.' He slid the drawer shut noiselessly.

He took an upturned jug from the dishwasher and reached for the highest cupboard. Kassia leaped up. 'Not that one!'

'What's in there? Gold?'

Kassia batted away the question like it was an annoying wasp. 'Cake stuff. My mum doesn't use it, you know. Cakes aren't really her thing.'

'So this was your dad's cupboard?'

Kassia opened her mouth to reply and then closed it again.

The River Boy nodded. 'I think I might like making cakes.'

'Seriously?' Kassia looked at her watch. 'Mum's out for another hour. I have two more past papers to do before she gets back. She'd be so cross if there was mess.'

'I'd clear up. You could check things. We'd be careful.'

She bit her lip.

'It's OK. I don't know if I do really like baking. It just felt like something I should say.'

'Like sorry?'

He nodded.

'So you should try. We'll just be careful. OK?'

She reached up and opened the cupboard. It was full of cake tins and trays, flour and baking powder, sugar and spices. The River Boy reached for a tub of cocoa powder, opened the lid and drank in the smell.

'You should check all the dates,' said Kassia quietly. 'Things might be older than they look. Mum never checks in here.'

The River Boy rolled up his sleeves. Then he went to the oven, pressed the ignition button and watched the flame burst into life.

It was the first time in weeks he'd felt properly alive. Up until now he was sure a part of him had been pulled away under the waters of the Thames. He opened packets and weighed ingredients, whisked and poured. He didn't need to look at a recipe. He just *knew*. And it felt amazing.

He spooned the mixture into a baking tray and then watched through the glass of the oven door as the cake fluffed and rose. And Kassia watched him. And they talked. About nothing in particular. And it wasn't awkward or strange. It was as if the time of silence had slipped away and been erased.

After about half an hour, he slid the metal skewer into the sponge and pulled it out clean.

He knew the cake was cooked. The transformation complete.

He waited a while, the cake resting on a wire rack. Then he slid it on to a plate and used a spatula to spread the buttercream evenly across the top. He took a tub of decorations – golden stars – and sprinkled them on to the cake as dusting.

'You're good at this,' Kassia said. 'Maybe you're a baker?'

He laughed. 'Maybe I am.' Then he formed his right hand into a fist and rubbed it in a circular motion in front of his heart. He hoped this was the right sign. He hoped she really understood that he was sorry.

Later that evening, Kassia knocked on her own bedroom door. The River Boy was lying on the bed looking up at the ceiling. His face glowed in the shine of the electric light. He scrambled to sit up when she came in.

'I'm sorry she was cross. I should have known she wouldn't want the egg shells in the regular bin. I should have checked that.'

'I don't mind about your mum. It was a relief, really. Almost like she was treating me normally and that felt good.'

'It was a lovely cake,' she said.

He moved along the bed a little so she sat down beside him, keeping one hand tight beside her so he couldn't see what she held.

'It's been a weird day, hasn't it?' she said. 'Nat's thrilled about the talking thing. And he said there's a chance the memory will follow. But he said we weren't to get too excited. And so about my mum . . .'

He reached out as if he wanted to stop her saying sorry again, but she carried on anyway.

'It's just that she worries. About me and about my future. And there are things we've planned for me to do. And I mustn't waste time. That's all.'

He nodded. 'The stories you wrote with your dad were good, you know.'

'Why would you bring that up?' She couldn't believe he'd mentioned it. 'Do you want me to get angry again?'

'I just wanted to tell you they were good, that's all.'

'Yeah, well they were from a different life. I don't write stories now. I want to be a doctor.' The clasp of a thin silver bracelet caught on her skirt as she moved and the chain fell open. They both watched it fall to the floor, but as the River Boy bent down to pick it up, she reached out to stop him. She knew he saw the book she held. 'I can't bake with you again. But I've been thinking. I know you want to remember your name and everything, but perhaps it would help you if we called you something. I mean you can't be River Boy for ever, can you?'

He took a deep breath, as if inhaling the idea, and she hoped he realised she was trying to make a joke.

'There're thousands of names in here so I thought perhaps you could choose one. It might not be your real name but it would do for now. You could be anything you wanted.'

She passed him the book and he looked surprised at how heavy it was.

He flicked through the pages then he nodded. And she knew his smile was a way of saying thank you.

The boy lifted the silver bracelet from the carpet and put it down on the dressing table. The length of silver looped into a circle. It still felt warm from Kassia's skin.

He climbed the step ladder slowly up to the loft. It was difficult with the huge book of baby names tucked under his arm. He wanted to be sure his feet made as much noise as possible. He didn't know if there was a door to knock on and he wanted Kassia to know he was coming.

She looked up from the chair in the corner. She was reading, her feet tucked underneath her, a blanket draped across her knees. 'Hi,' she said and put the book down in her lap.

He finished climbing the steps and stood, bending slightly because of the way the roof sloped above him.

She got up nimbly from the chair. 'Bit tight up here, isn't it?'

'You should really have your own room back. I could sleep up here, you know.'

'I like it. It's cosy. I've got everything I need. And I've got the best view of the cathedral. You don't have to crane your neck at all, see?'

She steered him towards the window. St Paul's was lit blue in the darkness, the top of the dome glowing. His stomach clenched for a moment and his eyes burned as if he'd looked too long in the direction of the sun. An image spun round and round inside his head. The circling dragon again and in the centre of the circle, the dome of the cathedral cut sharp against the sky. Then the words crashing in his brain. *Fire. Time. Clock.* Another number. 1951. And a date. 15th August. He bit his inside lip and pressed his eyelids tight shut. He hoped desperately that Kassia hadn't seen his reaction. He wanted to be brave but

73

she was gazing down at the floor as if she was scared to look at him.

'Jed,' he murmured.

'Pardon?'

His heart was thumping and he gripped to the window sill to keep his balance. 'I've decided on Jed. It's the name I've chosen.'

That night, for the first time, there were no dreams. No car headlights blazing. Just darkness. And it was overwhelming. Jed jolted upright. The alarm clock beside his bed was ticking so loudly the beat drilled into his skull. The number six glowed on the clock face as if it was on fire. He crashed his hand out. The clock skitted across the top of the unit and thumped into the wall before tumbling to the floor. The glass face shattered and the clock hands fell free.

Jed fumbled in the darkness, scooping up the shards of glass so that one pierced the end of his finger. The blood dripped on to the broken hands of the clock.

He could hear Kassia standing outside the bedroom. Her breathing was shallow in her throat. He must have called out. He'd no idea what he'd said.

'Are you OK, Jed?'

He held the fractured pieces of the clock in his

hands. Wet with blood they felt like they were made of water and that time was running through his fingers.

'I'm fine,' he lied.

'Are you sure?' Kassia's voice was shaking. He'd scared her. But she'd still come to check on him.

'I'm fine. Honestly. Go back to sleep.'

But neither of them slept again that night.

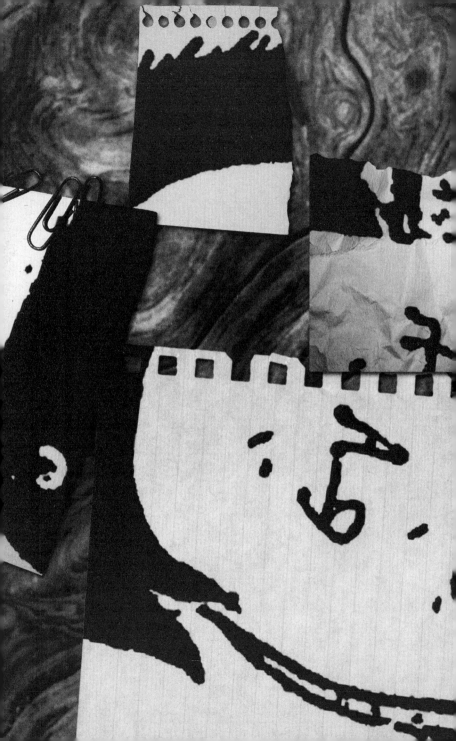

DAY 17
16th March

It was moving day. Victor Sinclair could hardly believe it had finally arrived. Apparently there was lots of paperwork to complete before the transfer of his care from the state to his father's place of work could be made official. He didn't worry about why it had taken so long. He just wanted it to be over.

'Seven schools, Victor,' said Martha Quinn from her seat beside him in the back of the taxi. She was holding a copy of his school records.

'Yeah, well, I like change.'

'It looks to me as if you like to get into trouble.' She was flicking through the pages and her eyes were widening with each turn of paper.

'You don't want to believe everything you read,' he said. 'Teachers exaggerate. I may have got a bit angry once or twice.'

Martha snapped the folder shut. 'I suppose you had a lot to be angry about,' she said more quietly. 'But no matter now. This is a time for a new beginning. We can forget your old life and move on with the new.'

Victor liked the old lady. She had style.

The taxi pulled to a halt in front of a huge glass building Victor recognised as The Shard. The entrance was tucked away in a tunnel under London Bridge Station. The designers claimed the building was a vertical city. Martha had been sure to impress Victor with all the details after she'd explained his father's office was housed inside Europe's tallest building.

Standing over three hundred metres tall, there were seventy-six floors with offices, apartments, restaurants and hotel rooms. Covered in windows, and like a skinny pyramid in shape, the top of the building was jagged and open, stretching into the sky. It looked like the broken neck of a bottle.

'Woah. Seriously. I'm going to live here?' he said, as they took the ride in the lift up to the observation desk on the seventy-sixth floor. Martha watched as Victor took a walk round. 'What exactly did my dad do?'

Martha Quinn's eyes were fixed firmly on the red ribbon of car tail-lights snaking into the distance. 'Plenty of time for that later. You just need to know that this is your home now.' She rubbed her hands against the cold. 'So, enough of the view. Let's show you your new room.'

They travelled back down towards the fiftieth floor.

As the lift approached the fifty-fifth floor it slowed a little. A red light registered on the display panel. Victor looked across at Martha Quinn.

'Restricted access,' she said in answer to his silent question. 'A place like this can't be open to everyone.'

'So what's on that floor?'

'Department Nine,' she said dismissively. 'Nothing for you to worry yourself about.'

The lift doors slid noiselessly open and she stepped out briskly and led the way along Floor Fifty to his room.

His bedroom at Etkin House could have fitted into the far corner of the suite Martha unlocked the door to. 'Seriously? This is all mine?'

'We'll give you a few weeks to settle in and then we'll sort out a system for your schooling.'

Victor's stomach fell a little at the thought of work, but he tried not to let it show on his face.

'I'm sure things will work out well for you here,' Martha said, closing the door behind her.

Victor was pretty sure she was right. He went into the ensuite bathroom and checked out the shower, opened all the drawers and chuckled as they slid noiselessly back into position, then lined up his shoes in the bottom of the wardrobe and attached the poster of the constellations to the ceiling above his bed.

Finally, he made himself a hot chocolate, took a bag of crisps from the mini-bar and went over to the bookcase. There were all sorts of books on science. He could barely understand the titles of most of them. He scanned along the line of book-spines. He was tired and he wasn't really in the mood for anything too heavy. He took out a slim red book with a thick cardboard cover, and then lay back on the bed. He flicked it open and turned to the first page.

A Story of Unicorns

In a time that is long forgotten, when the world was young, God looked down on his creation and was sad. He decided that he would destroy all living things on the earth because of the wickedness and violence that he saw. But God felt sorry for Noah. So God told him to build a huge boat in which to keep his family safe when the time of punishment came.

Noah set to work building an ark. It had three decks and was covered inside and out with pitch. In one side of the ark, Noah built a window and in the other side he put a door. Then God told Noah to take two of every sort of animal into the ark with him. And He told him to take some of every kind of food that was eaten. And He prepared Noah and his family for the flood that he would send.

The skies grew dark, and the clouds grew thicker. Noah and his sons herded the animals on-board the monumental boat that they had built. But they forgot about the unicorn.

The unicorn was the most beautiful of all God's creations. A silver-white horse with a single spiralling horn that ended in a red tip. He was strong and graceful and his horn was a thing of great power. When the waters of a pool grew old or poisonous the unicorn simply dipped the end of his beautiful spiralled horn into the water and the waters ran clean again. So powerful was the horn of the unicorn that many believed it held the spark for eternal life.

But Noah forgot the unicorn.

And it began to rain.

It rained for forty days and forty nights. All the fountains of the great deep were broken up and the windows of Heaven opened. The waters swelled and lifted the ark above the earth.

But the unicorn was left behind.

He struggled over the rocks and clambered across

the higher ground, all the while straining his horn into a darkening sky. And the rains fell. And the floods rose. And as the ark drifted on the waters, with the beasts of the air and the land locked safely inside, Noah remembered about the unicorn. But the animal was seen no more.

The storm raged but God thought about Noah and every living creature with him in the ark. He caused a wind to pass over the earth and to quieten the torrents. The waters receded for a hundred and fifty days so that on the seventh day on the seventeenth month the ark came to rest on the top of Mount Ararat.

Noah opened the window of the ark and he saw that the ground was dry. And so he led the animals he'd saved out of the ark and he and his family stepped again on to the surface of the earth.

And new trees sprouted and new grass grew and a new earth was born from the waters of the storm. And Noah and his family lived long and happy lives on the earth that had been cleansed.

And they never saw a unicorn.

But he was there. Tossed and turned by the waters, he'd struggled and he'd fought against the punishment that God had sent. And he had won.

He had survived the worst that God could send and he was alive.

And so it was that the days of all those that had journeyed with Noah on the boat, were numbered. But not so the days of the unicorn. For he'd battled death and been victorious. With his spiralling horn, he'd taken the poison from the waters. He lived. And he lives now. Unseen.

Victor closed the book. OK. That was weird. But he liked weird. He lay back on the bed and threw a crisp up into the air and caught it in his open mouth.

And he thought about the story he'd read.

But another thought burrowed in his mind. Level Fifty-Five. The restricted floor. Interesting. He wondered if that was where his dad had worked. And he wondered how long it would take him to get the truth out of Martha Quinn, about what exactly happened in Department Nine.

DAY 18
17th March

'You're going to tell me I still can't go out, aren't you?' Jed was standing by the window looking forlornly down into Fleet Street. His arms were folded. In most conversations he tried to add a few signs so Dante could keep up. But he was pretty sure it would be entirely obvious to Dante how he felt at this moment.

The research on the ouroboros had led them only to dead ends. Even the papers were running dry on theories about what the symbol could mean. And there were no other clues. No more flashes of memory. Nothing.

Nat shuffled the paper in front of him awkwardly. 'I just think the whole reporters thing could be difficult. It's better that we wait.'

'*I* wait, you mean.' Jed may have stopped referring

to Nat as Doctor Farnell now, but it was obvious the medic still thought he was in charge.

Nat's face took on the kind of gentle awkwardness doctors usually reserved for patients who claimed to be on a diet but admitted to eating twenty bars of chocolate a day despite weighing more than a small car. 'If you go out there too soon and blow your cover, then we'll have to find a whole new place to hide you. This is Fleet Street, Jed. It's where stories are made.'

'*Were* made,' corrected Kassia. 'The newspaper business moved to Canary Wharf years ago. You know that.'

'And you know what the Press can be like. And how they can find whoever they want if they're given a tiny lead.' He took a newspaper from his briefcase and passed it over.

Kassia scanned the article on the front page. '*River Boy must have a broken heart.* Where are they getting this stuff from?' she groaned.

'That doesn't matter. The point is, the story hasn't gone cold yet. Which is good,' he added, 'because if we want people to come forward with information, we need as much interest as possible. But it means people will be watching. And so we have to be careful.'

Jed took a deep breath. 'It's OK. I appreciate all you've done for me. Everything you've *all* done. I'll do as I'm told. I'll stay where I am.'

Nat took the newspaper back. 'It's for the best.'

Jed nodded but his hands were still tight in his pockets. Kassia was looking at him so he turned away as the doctor and Dante left the room.

'I'm going outside.' Jed was still at the window. Fleet Street was bustling with people.

Kassia was at the dinner table, her books neatly stacked in a tower. As far as Jed could tell, she hadn't got beyond lesson one of the day. She dropped her pen and it rolled across the table and on to the floor. 'What? You told my uncle you'd wait.'

'I know what I said.'

'Are you sure? I mean, what about the reporters and being seen?'

'I could use the balloons,' Jed joked.

'Or you could just do as you've been told and not go out there!'

He moved to stand beside the table. 'I can't wait. Not any longer. I feel like I'm locked inside a cage.'

Kassia looked at him oddly.

'Supposing there's a time limit. On how long

memories stay before they're lost for ever? I feel like there's this giant clock ticking and I need to know things soon or it's going to be too late.' He was silent for a moment, waiting for her reaction. 'Does that make sense?'

She didn't say anything for a while either. Then she closed the books she was working on and tidied the pile on the table. 'We'd have to disguise you. And we couldn't go far. Just a little walk. To be back before my mum gets home.'

'You'll come with me?' Jed felt almost giddy with nerves. 'Are you sure?'

'No, I'm not sure. I've got seven more pages of algebra to do; an essay on the Russian Revolution; a book review of *The Hunchback of Notre Dame* and three past papers to do before my mum gets back from her meeting.' She chose her next words carefully. 'But I'm not letting you go out there on your own.'

'This could be worse than misfiling egg shells.'

'It could.' Her mouth twitched awkwardly.

'OK,' he said almost too loudly in his enthusiasm to thank her. 'Let's do this.'

She brought him the coat and the heavy shoes he'd worn on his escape from the hospital. He already had the baseball cap. She helped him smooth his hair away inside. It was less awkward this time. Then she brought him big sunglasses and a long scarf which he wrapped around his neck several times, before bunching it across his chin and mouth.

'What d'you think?' His voice was muffled in the scarf.

'Good, if I could hear you properly.'

'We – can – sign.'

She giggled. '*I* can. You're still learning.'

He made a jokey sad face but it was hidden by the scarf. He was very hot. He pulled it away from his chin so he could breathe more easily but he kept the glasses on.

'We should leave a note. In case my mum comes back early,' Kassia said.

'Really? You sure you want to commit the crime to paper?'

'I need to give her the least amount to be cross about as possible.' Kassia took a page from the notebook and wrote something neatly. Then she signed her name and added 'and Jed' next to it.

Jed looked at the page. Was that really him?

'OK,' she said, slipping on her own coat. 'Let's get out of the cage.'

* *

The noise hit him like a wall. Jed swallowed hard and rearranged the scarf.

'You OK?' Kassia had an anxious expression on her face, like she was scared again that this wasn't such a good idea.

Jed wondered how many times he'd been asked that question over the last few days. And how many times he'd lied.

But he said he was fine. And he was. More than fine. The noise was loud after so long inside such a well-managed home. It didn't scare him, though. It made him feel alive.

People were hurrying in all directions. It seemed incredible more of them didn't crash into each other. It was like an elaborate dance and the only music was the ticking of the clock as they sped along. The air was cold in his lungs and smarted his eyes, but suddenly all Jed wanted to do was laugh.

'Seriously, Jed. We can go back. We don't have to do this.'

'No way. This is incredible.'

Now it was Kassia's turn to laugh. 'It's a busy street. Rush hour in London. There are lots of words for this. I'm not sure incredible's the best one.'

Jed spun round where he stood. 'Well I love it!'

Kassia beamed. 'That's good. So, where do

you want to go?'

'Erm. Surprise me.'

She squinted at him in the sunlight.

'Yeah,' he continued. 'Where would you take me if I'd just come to visit, like a proper guest?'

And so she took him around the places she called home. But in reality it was as if he was sharing his home town with her. At his suggestion, they bought bags of coconut ice fudge from Hardys Original Sweetshop; he led the way as they walked through the gardens of the inner temple and it was his idea to buy mugs of hot chocolate from a street vendor just outside St Clement Danes church. 'What will your mum say?' Jed asked as he filtered the lumps of chocolate through his teeth and warmed his hands on the mug.

Kassia flinched. 'I'll explain I was trying to help you find your history.'

'And where d'you think it is?'

Kassia pulled the edge of his scarf. 'No idea yet,' she confided.

They finished their walk at Somerset House. Jed stood in the courtyard of the huge building and watched as the fountains built into the ground of the courtyard spurted water up at unsuspecting visitors who crossed their path.

'They ice this over in winter,' said Kassia. 'It becomes a rink and you can skate here.'

'D'you do that?'

'Me?' Kassia said incredulously. 'No! Skating's dangerous! You could break an arm and be out of action for six weeks. Longer if there're complications. It's an unnecessary risk.' Jed couldn't help noticing that she sounded like her mother.

'So it would be bad to lose six weeks of life then?'

'Obviously.'

Jed looked sad.

'I'm sorry. I didn't think—'

'Let's come back in the winter and skate here,' he said. 'When I know who I am.'

Her mouth twitched awkwardly again. But she didn't say no.

They watched the fountains, and the sky above them was streaked with white clouds like ribbons.

'Do you want to go down to the river?' Kassia said at last. 'It's where this all began for you, so maybe . . .'

Jed felt a bead of sweat prickle just above his eyes. He loosened the scarf around his neck again. 'Sure. Let's hit the river. I've got nothing to lose.'

They made their way through the South Wing of Somerset House and out through the river entrance and turned left. Jed tried not to look at the water. It made him feel uncomfortable. They headed past Temple Underground Station and then veered into Temple Gardens to walk through the park before rejoining the Victoria Embankment. From there they walked along the river until the Millennium Bridge stretched in front of them. It was thronged with people. Kassia steered Jed to the left and a wall running along the side of the river. There were steps leading down into the water. 'So it was here, you think?' said Kassia, pointing down at the steps.

Jed gripped his hands tightly around the railings. He focused on the flow of the water and suddenly the noise of the city which had been so reassuring and life affirming became stifling and oppressive.

'It's OK,' Kassia whispered and they stood together watching the river ebb and flow, a bottle tossing back and forth on the waves. 'Shame there's not a message inside,' she added quietly. 'Telling you what you need to know.'

Jed looked down at the bottle. It rose on a wave and then, caught somehow by the change in the current, it was pulled below the surface, its end bobbing for a moment before being submerged. Jed's hands tightened even more. His breath caught in his throat. The sweat prickled on his brow. The world began to swirl and the noise of the city punched his head relentlessly.

He saw the dragon again, circling closer and closer in his mind's eye. And hands reaching out from inside the space made by the dragon as if they were stretching to be held. To be clutched tightly and pulled to safety. And the wind whipped at his face and the air burned like it was on fire.

He was aware Kassia was talking to him though he had no idea what she was saying. Her mouth was moving but the words were lost on the wind.

He slid to the ground and rested his head on his knees as if he was going to be sick.

She kneeled down beside him. 'What is it?' she insisted, her voice breaking through his confusion like sun through cloud. 'What do you see when that happens?'

'A dragon,' he murmured. 'The ouroboros spinning round and round. And stuff which could be memories or nightmares. I can't tell the difference yet.'

She eased him up to stand. 'Come on. Let's get you away from here.' She turned him from the water and began to lead back up Peter's Hill. The City of London School was on their left. A place of answers. Jed and Kassia had none.

People were hurrying and rushing around them.

But the two of them moved slowly, as if Jed was a man of at least a hundred years old.

'You would have walked up here, look,' she said, guiding him up the steps past the headquarters of the Salvation Army. 'Is there anything you recognise?'

He squeezed his eyes hard together to try and see. And his hand brushed lightly against the wall.

There was a surge of static again. Like electricity, pulsing through his arm so his fingers recoiled.

'Jed?'

He clutched at his hand, nursing the scalded tips of his fingers as the image of the black dragon coiled and circled in front of his eyes. The dragon spun and spun. And in the centre of the curl, as if the body was a frame, Jed could see the door to St Paul's before his eyelids pressed shut and the image fragmented like shattered glass.

The memory was from the day of the river. He remembered that he'd *known* where to go after he'd clambered out on to the land. Something that was churning inside of him now, had pulled him towards the cathedral.

'I needed to be here.'

They were on the steps of St Paul's. Kassia was

sitting and Jed had been too, but now he was standing and looking up at the huge frontage of the great building. He peered at the circle on the side and wondered if there'd once been a clock there which had since been removed. Again his eyes burned as if he'd stared at the sun. What was it about the top of the cathedral that made him feel so unwell? He swallowed hard, shook his head and looked at Kassia, as if she was an anchor to keep him from being thrown about in a storm.

'I got out of the water and I knew I had to come here. Why's that, you think?'

Kassia didn't answer. Jed could feel his mood moving backwards and forwards like the waves they'd watched on the river. His scarf had slipped down around his neck and he knew his face was barely hidden apart from the sunglasses and the baseball cap. 'Sit down,' Kassia urged. 'We should be careful.'

Jed was barely listening. He began to pace. He sensed people were starting to notice. He felt a lock of hair tumble free from the baseball cap and bounce on his shoulder but he didn't have the energy to readjust the cap.

'I think we should go back now,' Kassia begged. He could tell she was panicking. 'People are watching.'

And they were. A group of people sitting to their left. One of them had a newspaper rolled up on his lap. Jed could see the photo from here. It was smaller than it had been when the story had first broken, but it was still there, on the front page. His face framed by red. He could feel more of his hair loosening from the baseball cap but he did nothing to stop it.

Kassia stood up and tried to steer him round the corner, reaching to push the fallen hair under the cap. 'We need to be careful, Jed!'

'We *need* to go inside. This place is important, I know it is.'

'I'm not sure. I think we should go back.'

He turned to look at her. 'Please.'

She jogged behind him as he hurried up to the front door. The family on the steps were whispering. One had taken their phone out. He saw Kassia looking around. So many people with cameras. He knew she thought this was a bad idea. A really bad idea. But something was pulling him towards St Paul's like a magnet.

They'd entered an anti-porch. There were all sorts of signs about audio guides and tours. And the pricing. Kassia rummaged in her bag for her purse. It was so expensive, but there were signs explaining that too. The upkeep, the restoration. It was all listed. And next to that was another notice. As Kassia read it, he saw her let the purse fall back into her bag.

She pulled Jed out of the queue.

'What are you doing?'

She pointed at the picture. It showed a baseball cap with two thick lines scored though it. 'You'd have to take your hat off.'

'So?' he reached up and Kassia grabbed his arm and pulled it down.

'You can't, Jed.'

'Of course I can.'

Kassia was pleading. 'We can't let people recognise you. Your face is everywhere. Has been for a month now. It's what my uncle warned us about. If people see you, then they might follow you. Then all the Press who've been camped outside the hospital might find us and they'll be outside our home and it will be awful for us and—'

It felt like she'd thumped him hard in the gut.

'I didn't mean…' She was searching for the right words, not to sign this time, but to say. 'I know it's awful for you already.'

'No you don't.'

'What? How can you say that?'

'You can't possibly know what it's like.'

Kassia bit her bottom lip as if she was desperate to stop it from shaking. 'I'm trying to.'

'And I'm trying to find answers. And they're in that building. I know it.'

'But you can't!'

Jed stared at her. He was going to turn away, take off his hat and go inside.

But he didn't. 'I'm sorry I've made things difficult,' he said at last.

'Let's go home,' she said.

'I don't know where my home is.' He pulled his scarf up around his face and walked slowly back out of the cathedral entrance and down the steps.

'You are grounded for ever!' Anna stood at the top of the stairs, her arms folded, a vein throbbing on the left of her temple and looking as if it was going to burst at any second.

'I'm sorry.' Kassia looked down at her socks.

'Sorry? How can sorry ever win back the time you need to prepare for your exams? You must be focused and committed and determined. Every second counts, you know. Every single second!'

'It's my fault, Mrs Devaux.' Jed risked lifting his gaze from the floor, but only slightly.

'Of course it's your fault. Everything here's your fault. The state of the kitchen. The water mark on the side table in the lounge.'

'Mum, we cleared up. He used a coaster.'

Anna took a deep breath. 'Look, we knew this wasn't going to be easy. For any of us. And I'm incredibly sorry about your memory loss and all that means, but you cannot stay here and lead my daughter astray.'

'We went out for fudge, Mum. We didn't leave the country. And we left a note.'

'You were supposed to be working!'

'I'll work now. I'll work all evening. And I won't stop for dinner.' She hesitated. 'You said my marks were improving.'

'They are. And that's down to hard work and commitment and following a plan. And plans are made to be kept.'

'I promise I won't have any more time off unless you schedule it in. I'll work harder than ever.'

Mrs Devaux's face softened slightly.

'Fine. Make sure you do. And if there are any errors in your Russian Revolution essay then you can write me an extra essay on social order in Korea. Understand?'

It was clear from her face that Kassia didn't

know much about social order in Korea, but she nodded anyway.

'And you,' she said, turning towards Jed. 'I think it's best you spend some time on your own, thinking.'

Jed smiled nervously. If that's what it took to make the woman less angry then he'd do it. But Jed was pretty sure he'd had his fill of thinking for a while.

Physician's Evaluation

Physician's Evaluation
(continued)

t / Mental Health:

a memory impairment or mental health disorder? Yes ☒ No ☐ DX: _____

of memory impairment or mental disability does   Mild ☐ Intermediate ☐ Advanced ☒

ervision to help keep them safe and to protect them from the ordinary   Yes ☒ No ☐
onment?

ts regarding patient's need for help with ADL's: _____

ted age 16-18; bruised finger _____
clambering from the water of
_____ scratches on his body and
_____ to his knees again from
_____ from the water.

Physician's Signature: *Nat Farnell*   Date: 01/03/201_
(Must be signed by a Physician - M.D. or D.O.)

cian's Name (please print): NAT FARNELL

cian's Address: 221C Amherst Street   Phone: 0781696 18_
SW3 1/2/c

itional supportive documentation as appropriate)

Name:
Date of
Age on
Gender:

Name of
Date of las
Hospital:

Are you cur
If YES, plea

MENTAL ST
Please check i
sad ___anxious ___depressed ___frightened ___guilty ___angry

BLOOD TYP

A H

Describe any im
may be affecti

This very rare phenotype is
generally present in about
0.0004% (about 4 per
million) of the human
population.

DAY 25
24th March

For the next seven days Jed and Kassia barely saw each other. Kassia worked long into the evenings. She left her books only for meals.

Anna supervised the household with the precision of an archer. Any scrap of paper out of place, bottles incorrectly aligned in the fridge, scatter cushions incorrectly angled on the settees – she was on it. Jed found it all totally exhausting.

'I'm going round to talk to Nat,' Anna said at last, one evening. 'I want to come up with a strategy for your A Levels. We need to get resources. No need to waste the summer while we wait for your GCSE results.'

Kassia swallowed her response about how it would be nice to have a summer holiday. 'I'm working as hard as I can,' she said instead.

'Yes, well, the grades will tell us that, won't they?' Her mother grabbed her coat from the hook in the hallway.

'She still isn't happy,' said Jed, as the front door banged shut behind her.

Kassia sighed. 'She hasn't been happy for years.' She crossed the room, took up her regular seat at the table and opened her history textbook. 'What are you going to do while she's gone?'

Jed laughed. 'Well, a walk's a no-no after nearly being recognised. So I guess I'd like to do something to say sorry.'

'Sorry for what?'

'Everything,' he said, walking into the kitchen.

He took the eggs and broke them one by one. He cracked each shell and let the contents run across his fingers. The white slipped through the openings he made and the golden ball of the yolk stayed in the cup of his palm. He set the yolks aside in a small dish then he took the bowl of egg white. Then he took a whisk and began to beat.

Jed knew there was a food processor. It was on the counter top smothered by a protective cover. He was sure Anna only ever used it to pulp vegetables for smoothies so he thought it best not to use it. And this way was better anyway. He beat the mixture again and again, angling the bowl to the side and arcing the whisk through the air so as much air as possible could fill the bowl. He beat the mixture so hard it formed high peaks. And the rhythm of the whisk was reassuring. It drowned out the ticking of the clock and was the only noise he heard. Until the front door opened and there were footsteps on the stairs.

He tipped in the sugar. It fell like snow. He folded it into the egg white and then poured the mixture slowly into rough piles on the hot baking tray. Then he slid it into the oven, turning the flame down to the lowest heat. The best meringues took the longest time.

He wiped the counter and rinsed his hands before he turned towards the doorway. Kassia was standing there, clutching a small brown paper bag.

'You're supposed to be working,' he said.

'I know. And I will. But while Mum's at Nat's, I asked Dante to bring home something to be *my* way of saying sorry.'

'What are you sorry for?' he asked.

'Everything that's happened to you,' she said, suddenly business like.

'Are you sure you want to do this?' Kassia still had the brown paper bag in her hand, but now she also had a huge pair of shiny silver scissors.

It seemed obvious. Whoever Jed was, he was recognisable. His hair was such a giveaway. His photo had been shown so often, everybody thought they knew him, even if he didn't know himself.

'If we do this, and we get my mum on side, then we can go back to St Paul's. We can go anywhere we need to. You won't be "you" any more.'

It seemed a ridiculous thing to say. Perhaps the idea of getting Anna on side being the most tricky part of the plan. And then there was the problem of him not being himself when he'd no idea who that person was in the first place. But Kassia knew she was right. He had to look different. Had to *be* different. Before he could be him. And this, it seemed, was the only way.

'Have you done this before?'

'Never.'

Jed groaned.

'But there're instructions. And pictures, look.'

Kassia took the packet of hair dye out of the brown paper bag, undid the box and slid out the pamphlet.

'It's a *wash-in* thing. Not permanent. Dante said those ones had warnings all over them about skin rashes.'

Jed groaned again.

'It can't be that difficult. Lucy Miller's mum has dyed hair and Lucy used to do it for her.'

'What colour was Lucy Miller's mum's hair?'

'Purple. But that's not the point.'

Jed lowered his head into his hands, but Kassia tilted it back and turned on the mixer tap over the sink.

It was weird. There was nowhere to look except into Jed's face as she tipped the dye on to the soaked hair and ran her fingers through it. At first it was awkward and she felt herself blushing. But after a while it was OK and she began to think about how she needed to make things even and spread the dye carefully. She didn't want his hair to be patchy.

After a while she stood up and blotted his head dry with a towel.

'Well?' Jed's voice was a little higher than usual.

'You'll have to wait,' she said. 'I've got to cut it now.'

She was sure Jed groaned again but she tried to ignore this. She combed the hair straight. It looked kind of OK. Definitely black and not red any more. But still too long. She reached for the scissors and they fell to the floor, clanging on the bathroom tiles.

'Oh, fantastic. Totally brilliant. You can't even hold them.'

'I'm nervous.' She picked up the scissors.

'*You're* nervous?'

'Sit still and just let me do this.'

She combed his hair again and then took a section and squeezed it between her fingers like she'd seen the hairdresser do a hundred times before. She wished she'd paid more attention. Did you cut below the fingers or above? She couldn't remember.

Suddenly Jed's hand was on top of hers.

'You don't want me to do this? I won't if you're not sure.'

He squeezed her hand gently. 'You can do it. I trust you.'

'You do? *Really*?'

A tiny smile flickered over his lips and then he shut his eyes. 'Just do it.'

Ten minutes later, Kassia put down the scissors. She flicked the strands of hair from Jed's shoulders and stood back to admire her work. 'It's not bad,' she said.

He stood up from the chair and turned slowly to face the mirror and for a second she saw his eyes widen.

'You don't like it?' she panicked. 'I've taken off too much. It's too dark. Not really *you*?'

'It's perfect,' he said. 'It isn't really *me*. And that's exactly what we wanted.' He hung the towel over the rail and grinned again at his reflection. 'Now as long as we win over your mum we can get out there and start to find out who *me* is.'

DAY 26
25th March

Dante made a sound like a can of fizzy drink exploding. His hands carved the air and his eyes were so wide they looked as if they were going to pop out of his head.

Jed looked across at Kassia, obviously hoping for a translation.

'He likes your hair.'

'Really? All *that* was to say he *liked* it?'

Kassia shrugged. 'Dante doesn't really do subtle.'

'Because of the not hearing thing?'

'Because of the being a complete pain thing.' She scowled at her brother and made small signs close to her body that Jed had no chance of understanding. Whatever she said caused Dante to nod and the smallest hint of colour rushed to his cheeks.

Nat looked up from the settee. 'It's good. I like

it too,' he grinned.

'Good enough for me to go outside?' Jed said hopefully.

Nat took a while to answer. 'A short walk, maybe. Not too far. But I don't think you should go alone.'

'Well, Kassia's not going with him.' Anna was standing in the entrance to the kitchen, her rubber gloved hands raised almost as if she was preparing to box.

'You can't really ground her for ever,' signed Dante.

'Just watch me.'

Dante looked across at his uncle and angled his head as if prompting him with forgotten lines from a play. Nat lurched forwards on his chair. 'Oh yes, of course. I've been meaning to say. Things are looking good at work. Seems the consultant has forgotten the little broken arm issue so that's good.'

Anna looked confused.

'He was talking to me about that in the conversation we had all about the value of fresh air. Brain enhancing, you know. New study just confirmed it's even better for brain architecture than first thought.'

Kassia tried to stifle a smile. She could see what her brother and uncle were trying to do.

'Makes such a difference to exam performance, apparently.'

Anna's nose wrinkled once again in that tortoise-like way it did when she was concentrating. Kassia held her breath. 'Two hours only,' Anna relented. 'A second over that and the essay on Korea is back on the to-do list.'

Kassia tried hard to stop herself from grinning. 'Totally. Two hours only. You'll hardly know we've gone.'

Anna's answer wasn't a word. She flicked the ends of her gloves and droplets of soap suds rained down on the carpet.

Jed shot a grateful look across at Kassia. 'You ready?'

She barely had time to ask him where they were going before he was out of the door. 'What about breakfast?'

They ate croissants on the way, the butter melting as they walked. Kassia's fingers were sticky and Jed laughed as she licked each one clean.

'I'd like to go back to St Paul's,' Jed said. 'There's something about it. Something I recognise, maybe. And I don't know if it's a memory of before or after the river. So I want to see the guy who found me.' They were hurrying down Fleet Street by now. Jed was dressed in the long coat and scarf from before and below the black dye of his hair his eyes looked wilder than ever. 'I've been thinking, maybe there was stuff he noticed; things I said, that he didn't tell reporters but he might tell us.'

'So we'll check,' said Kassia, hurrying to keep up.

They reached the steps of the cathedral and Jed rocked a little as he looked up towards the dome.

Kassia wasn't sure if she should hold on to him to keep him steady so she let her arm hang close to his, the fabric of their coats touching. She could see his eyes were narrowed. From concentration, pain or confusion, she wasn't sure. 'Another vision of a dragon?' she asked quietly.

Jed shook his head. 'No. Not this time.'

Kassia didn't know how to answer. 'We should ask someone where the chaplain is,' she said.

Jed nodded. She could tell he was struggling.

She steered him towards the Information Desk where they bought tickets. 'I wonder if you can help us,' she said. 'We wanted to have a chat with Reverend Solomon Cockren.'

The woman behind the counter rolled her eyes. 'You're not from the newspapers, are you? Surely you're too young. The Reverend has said all he can about that River Boy incident.'

Kassia could feel Jed trembling beside her. 'No. We're not from the paper. We're doing a school project. For History. And we were told Reverend

Cockren was the one to ask.'

'Oh, you'll be interested in his dad then, I suppose. OK. I'll see if I can call him.'

She fiddled around rather incompetently with a walkie-talkie and, after much beeping and crackling, she looked over again at them. 'He's on his way.'

'*His dad?*' Jed whispered. 'What d'you think that's about?'

'No idea,' said Kassia. 'But at least she's going to let us see him.'

The chaplain, when he arrived, was dressed for early morning communion; a long stole flying out behind him like a wake. 'You're doing a project,' he beamed, shaking first Kassia's hand and then Jed's. 'On our wonderful St Paul's.'

Kassia nodded vigorously.

'Well, of course, there've been several versions of the cathedral. There's been a place of worship on this site for four thousand years. The one you stand in today was finished in 1710 and was built after so much of London was destroyed in the Great Fire. I like to think of the cathedral as being rather like a phoenix, rejuvenating itself time and time again. That's why I think the name is so appropriate, don't you?'

Kassia wasn't sure why the name St Paul was relevant.

'It's because of the disciple Saul, who changed his name and his allegiance after receiving a sign from God,' he explained. 'Sorry. I'm confusing you. There're questions you needed answering?'

Kassia felt a little buffeted by the deluge of information. 'Erm, signs,' she blurted, catching on to the chaplain's last statement. 'Signs. We were interested in signs and decorations here. Paintings and stuff. You know.'

She could tell Jed hadn't expected the conversation to go in this direction, but if the chaplain thought they were doing a school project on the cathedral, she couldn't plough into River Boy questions straight away. They had to keep Reverend Cockren on side.

'Ah well,' said the chaplain, his smile widening. 'It was once said that this building was a picture book of signs. You only have to look around to see all the coded references and symbols.'

Jed stepped closer as if his movement would encourage more explanation.

'The Cornhill Pictures, of course,' he said, waving towards paintings in the huge dome of the building. 'Stories told in images. And the ornaments along the aisle are signs of the journey of life, from the front door to the cross at the altar. Nothing in this cathedral is here by mistake. Every image and sculpture has been chosen to "say" something. It's up to us whether we hear or not.'

Kassia felt the explanation was in danger of turning into a full blown sermon, especially when she saw the chaplain's eyes begin to roll upwards slightly. 'Of course my favourite sign here, and your teachers will love this one, is how the whole building is a symbol in itself. The cathedral measures three hundred and sixty-five feet from the top of the dome outside to the ground. It represents a calendar year, you see.'

Kassia could see Jed was unsteady again on his feet. And she realised now her idea about building up to the proper questions was just wasting time.

'Your best bet is to take an audio-guide,' urged Reverend Cockren. 'I'm sure it will give you enough extra details to keep your teachers happy.'

Kassia was aware they were losing him. They couldn't risk waiting any longer. 'River Boy!' she yammered, pulling a newspaper cutting from her pocket. It showed the ouroboros Jed had drawn and the initial photo snapped on the day he'd come from the river. 'You found him. We just wanted to ask about the symbol. And if you knew any more about him and what he drew.'

The chaplain's face darkened. Behind the windows of the great cathedral, the sun had slipped behind a cloud. He took the newspaper cutting and his eyes flashed.

Jed ruffled his newly cut hair and smiled hopefully. 'I just wondered if there were things you could tell me. Anything to make sense of the symbol – or me?'

'It's you!' gasped Reverend Cockren, peering at Jed nervously and passing back the paper as if it had dirtied his hands. 'You said this was a school project. You said—'

'Please,' Kassia grabbed his arm impulsively. 'Please. If there is anything you can tell us to help us find out more. Anything at all.'

The chaplain seemed barely able to speak. 'You shouldn't have involved me. I want nothing to do with this!'

'Please. If you—'

'You need to go,' he said sharply, pulling his arm away and striding down the aisle.

'Reverend Cockren?'

He turned. His eyes wide, his face lifted, focusing on the roof. 'The answer is in the building,' he said and then he turned and fled.

'What happened in there? He took you to the hospital so why the major freak-out when he realised who you were?'

Jed was slumped on the steps of the cathedral. His fingers were plunged deep into his hair, raking lines and revealing streaks of ginger.

Kassia was panicking.

Jed had hurried down the aisle, pushing through the crowds. Everything they'd done before leaving the house had been about not drawing attention to themselves. Now he was sitting, head on his knees, looking like he was going to be sick.

'He's got to be hiding something,' insisted Jed. He pulled his hands across his face, took a deep breath and sat up straight. His hair was still raised in messy clumps. 'Something about that building freaks me out. And obviously something about *me* freaks out the chaplain.'

'How does St Paul's freak you out?'

'I knew I had to go there and I don't know why. And whenever I look up at the dome something feels wrong.'

'In what way?'

'I don't know. It just makes me feel uncomfortable. Weird. But I think I have to be there.' He thumped his hands down on the railings. 'I don't get it. I don't get any of this.'

'It's OK.'

'It's not OK. That's the point. *I* am not OK. And I

have no idea what to do about it.'

'What's he doing in there?' Dante's signs pointed to the kitchen. 'And how did you get Mum to agree to him doing it?'

Kassia drew her legs up on to the settee and rested her chin on her knees. 'He's baking something. It relaxes him, I suppose. Mum saw he was in a state and for once she didn't argue. She's given him strict clean up instructions though.'

'D'you think he's going to be all right?'

Kassia watched her brother's signs. They were small. He was nervous. 'I don't know. It was all so odd. The chaplain's reaction when he realised who Jed was. The stuff he said about answers. And there's something about St Paul's that makes Jed feel weird.' She wrapped her arms around her knees. It was her way of saying she didn't want to talk any more. Hands folded away would make it impossible. She looked into the distance too. No eye contact with her brother and the silence was unbreakable.

Dante wasn't ready for silence. He thumped his fist down hard on the coffee table. 'We can't just do nothing. He could stay like this for ever.'

Kassia felt the panic rising in the back of her throat. 'So what's your big plan?'

Dante opened the laptop his uncle had been using earlier, and pulled it across the coffee table towards him. He clicked the touchpad to reactivate the screen then angled it in Kassia's direction.

'You want me to read this?' quizzed Kassia. It showed an article on something called Dissociative Fugue. She read a few paragraphs but couldn't make sense of much.

Dante turned the screen back towards him. 'I've read it,' he said. 'And it's about what Jed's got,' he said. 'Loss of identity. Not knowing who you are. It's an actual disorder. Says here the writer Agatha Christie had it. She completely forgot who she was for eleven days and was found miles from home, staying in a hotel.'

'OK. So what?'

Dante fumbled his hands as if selecting his next signs carefully. 'The article says sometimes the memory just returns. But if it does, it usually takes just a few days.'

Kassia didn't like where this conversation was going. 'You really think he might never get his memory back?' she sighed.

'No. Yes. I don't know. It's been nearly a month now and he's spent so long trying to remember stuff and maybe that's not the way to go. Maybe he should just try and live a bit.'

'He's living with us.'

'Yeah. And that means watching you study and helping Mum realign the cocktail sticks in the holder.'

Kassia could see her brother's point. The occasional walks outside weren't enough.

Dante reached into his pocket and pulled out four strips of card. He put them on the table. 'What d'you reckon?'

About twenty minutes later, Jed came in from the kitchen. He carried a plate of biscuits fresh from the oven. The room smelled of toffee and cinnamon. But when Kassia took a cookie from the pile, she saw the edge was burned and as she bit into it, a cascade of charred crumbs sprinkled on to the floor.

She nodded at her brother and then spoke in signs just small enough for only him to see. 'I think we should try it.'

ST PAUL'S
EXIT

HONNEUR UNITÉ

FRÈRES D'HÉLIOPOLIS

DAY 30
29th March

'It's risky.' Nat was pacing round the front room.

'It was *your* idea. You got the tickets.'

Nat threw a glare in Kassia's direction but did not stop his pacing. 'For us. And your mum.'

'And you knew she'd never go,' signed Dante. 'Which means there's a spare.'

Nat stopped pacing and took a deep breath. 'When I said the consultant was over the broken arm thing, I lied. If I do *anything* that messes up the boy's recovery, any hope of keeping my job will be out the window, let alone a promotion.'

'It won't mess anything up,' urged Dante. 'It's just a chance for him to do something. Have some fun. Maybe even build some new memories worth having. Come on, Nat.'

Kassia did her best pleading face. And her brother

held his hands out as if waiting for an answer.

'OK. OK. We'll go and climb the O2 together,' said Nat. 'But who's going to tell your mother?'

'Well she's not going to go with anything I suggest, is she?' Dante's face looked suddenly more pinched than normal.

'And she's got a whole new list of things for me to get through this week,' said Kassia. She looked at Nat.

'Me. Why me?'

'Because you'll be able to blind her with science,' laughed Dante. 'Give her some technical reason why it's a good idea. We haven't got a chance, but if it comes from you then we're sorted.'

DAY 34
2nd April

Anna insisted they ate soup. It was made of lentils and contained extra omega oils. She said it would help prepare them. 'I'm working on the basis that fresh air and a change of scenery will adapt the architecture of your brain,' she said, as she ladled extra into Kassia's bowl.

Nat winked across the table at his niece. 'Architecture of the brain. Good one, eh?' he mouthed surreptitiously.

Kassia stared hard into her soup as her mother carried on talking.

'And I've timetabled this period of recreation into your master schedule. You'll see it highlighted in pink.'

Kassia nodded.

'Nat has suggested a chance to build new memories

might be useful for you too,' Anna said, angling the ladle into Jed's bowl with the precision of a fly fisher. 'Back by four, though, everyone.'

Nat took it upon himself to reassure her they wouldn't be late and bundled them out of the door as soon as the soup was finished.

They travelled on the Underground, taking the Jubilee line, and got off at North Greenwich Station. The O2 Arena sat on the edge of a peninsular of land, bulging out towards the River Thames. There were shops and restaurants lining the route and signs leading to ferries that promised to take you down the river. The arena itself looked like an enormous grey pillow, secured to the ground by yellow spears.

Jed had agreed to the whole idea because of Dante. Apparently he'd wanted to make the climb for a while and Nat had offered tickets for his birthday. It seemed rude not to join in, and if Anna was OK about them leaving the house, then it seemed too good an opportunity to miss.

The air was cold on his face. The smell of the river hit him in waves. He was strangely excited. Today wasn't going to be about finding links to the past. This was to be an experience just for itself. Something fun. And he felt the same way he'd done when he and Kassia had sipped hot chocolate on their first escape from the house. He wondered if this was what *normal* felt like.

Dante was in charge and led them into the base camp experience. It was all decked out as if they'd be climbing a mountain.

Their guide was called Bobby. He was a university student working to earn cash as he studied. He talked about his shared house and his late night the day before. Then he let them watch the safety video before launching into an explanation of what was in store.

'You OK?' whispered Kassia.

Jed nodded. And this time he wasn't lying. He really was OK. The sun was shining, his fingers tingled with the cold and nothing mattered except the climb. Things felt good.

'OK, peeps,' began Bobby, in a voice that was gravelly and a little too loud. 'You might not know this about our mighty beast the O2, but she was actually built as a monument to time. Sounds impressive, don't you think? Nothing's a mistake here. The architects were dead clever and made sure every feature of this site had a purpose.'

Jed's mind sped back to St Paul's and Reverend Cockren's warning that nothing in the cathedral was there by chance.

'You can read this place like a book,' went on Bobby.

Reverend Cockren had said that too. The cathedral was a picture book of signs.

Bobby pointed up to the strange grey structure that looked as different from St Paul's cathedral as it was possible to be. 'Ladies and gents, I give to you the Millennium Dome. Built for the year 2000. There's a time capsule hidden in the foundations, of course. People like to leave records of the past behind.'

Jed wished someone had hidden a time capsule for him. Buried treasure to explain who he was. He shook his head and tried to concentrate. This wasn't supposed to be about him. This was Dante's day. If only he could switch off his wondering and just enjoy this for what it was. An adventure.

'So, let's see if we can read the monument's meaning, shall we?' Bobby went on. 'I had a group last week who were useless, but you lot look like you might actually have brain cells.'

There was a ripple of laughter. A large American woman shouted out a suggestion. 'Do the twelve yellow masts represent the twelve months of the year?' she asked.

'Well done,' encouraged Bobby. 'That's our easiest sign to read. The rest are more tricky.'

Jed's mind pulled back to St Paul's again. Why was it doing that? This was supposed to be a day off from puzzling. But something else Reverend Cockren had said gnawed at the back of his mind. 'Height,' he stammered.

'What about it?' inquired Bobby.

'Is the height time related?'

'Nice one,' said Bobby, clapping his hands together. 'A height of fifty-two metres to show the number of weeks in a year.'

Kassia turned this explanation into sign and Dante answered by asking her about the width of the building. 'What's the diameter?' Kassia called out on his behalf.

'Three hundred and sixty five metres,' said Bobby. 'Anyone?'

'Number of days in the year,' called out Nat.

'Sweet. That's our monument to time deciphered. Good job, team. So let's get climbing.'

Jed didn't know why these details made his heart thump or his mouth go dry, or why it was suddenly harder to swallow.

'You are OK, aren't you?' Kassia asked as they packed their things away into the lockers.

Jed rechecked the fastening on his climb suit and then fumbled with the wristband for the locker key. 'I'm totally fine. Let's do this thing.'

Nat completed the waiver forms then led them after Bobby. He'd made sure to book them in with a small group of climbers. The others were American tourists who seemed to know each other. None of them was interested in the group of teenagers, except for the large American woman, who stared intently as Dante signed, apparently completely unaware he could see her, even though he couldn't hear. She grew bored quickly though and returned to her group.

Bobby took them outside towards some stairs winding up to a platform. He gathered them round a small gate and repeated the safety information from the video. 'There are one hundred and fifty brackets on the safety line on the way up to North Camp. You need to link two fingers under your safety latch and slide it though each bracket. Don't force things. Just take it slowly.'

Jed's heart quickened again. He shook his head, trying to clear it. He was sure he remembered how to have fun. Positive this sort of adventure was just his thing. He could feel his pulse increasing, but it felt like something more than excitement. It felt like fear and he had absolutely no idea what there was to be afraid of.

Bobby positioned the group on the east side of the safety line. He walked on the west, moving up and down the blue walkway stretched towards the top of the building.

Jed wasn't prepared for the give of the path under his feet. His legs felt spongy, as if the ground was made of marshmallow. The latch was hard to slide through the brackets. It was windy and his hands were cold. He gripped tightly to the safety rail for a moment and tried to make his breathing slow. But his heart was pounding at the base of his throat.

Bobby was keen to point out all the sights and the promise of things it would be possible to spot from the top. 'You can sometimes see for fifteen miles,' he boasted. 'And a whole slap up meal of sights waits for you on the way down. Thames Barrier, Olympic Park, The Shard. You can see it all as you descend. Even Canary Wharf.'

None of these words meant much to Jed. Though they made him feel uncomfortable. One of the Americans asked about the Thames Barrier and Bobby droned on about flood defences and holding back the river. Jed felt like there was a barrier inside his head. It was straining. Choking back the memories that would make sense of all he was. The band inside his head tightened and tightened so his temples throbbed.

Each step was harder than the one before. His feet were getting heavier, his calves aching; the ground more pillow-like below his step. His fingers fumbled with his safety latch. Every bracket was an obstacle. Every movement forwards, suddenly painful. And he had absolutely no idea why this was. Maybe he was sick? Maybe it was something in the soup he'd eaten? The wind was picking up. The world felt like it was falling away either side of him. Words around him mixed and muddled. Nothing made sense. It was just him and the safety line stretching towards the summit. Jed was sure that any second, the line would snap. And he would plummet to the ground, which, he knew now, was exactly fifty-two metres below him.

Bobby the guide unclasped the wire roping strung across the access to the top platform. 'You've made it to the summit, guys. Come on through and feast your eyes on the view.'

Jed slid his latch from the safety rail and stepped on to the solid ground of the platform. He should have felt more secure but his legs were still like sponge below him.

'Make sure your latch is tucked away in the holder on your suit,' added Bobby. 'You don't want it getting caught on anything up here.'

Jed fumbled with the latch. His hands slick with sweat.

'Here. Let me help,' said Kassia.

He remembered how she'd tucked the stray strands of hair away into his baseball cap before they'd escaped from the hospital. His heart had been straining in his throat then. Like it was now. 'It's OK. I can do it.' The latch slid through his fingers again.

She moved his hand slowly out of the way and nimbly tucked the latch into the holder. 'Just to save time.'

Her words were too loud. They echoed. The word *time* repeating again and again in his head.

Just in front of them, Bobby was calling people together for a group photo. 'One for the memory banks,' he said, taking phones and laughing as he organised each shot. Jed pulled away from the group and steadied his weight on the edge of a metal information board stretched around the viewing platform. The words on the sign were swimming, each letter doubled. '*The Thames is Liquid History*', the title declared, though the rest of the information was blurred and out of focus. Jed lifted one hand and pressed it to his temple. The trace of a handprint stayed on the metal board, shrinking and drawing into itself before it disappeared altogether.

Jed tried to breathe slowly. Air thundered at the back of his mouth. He tried to swallow, but his throat was too tight.

Behind him, Bobby and the group of American tourists were laughing. There was a flash of light from a phone. The flash repeated behind Jed's eyes. Again and again so his pupils burned. He tried to look away. The burst of light came again. From the phone or from his mind he wasn't sure. He tried to look down at the river. It bulged around the base of the O2 like a noose, tightening and choking so there was less and less air.

Jed could see Kassia's hands dancing. Dante's and Nat's moving in return. He knew they were talking about him, but the words they made were like spilled water, splashing away on the ground before he could catch them. He'd no idea what they were saying.

To his left, Bobby was still talking and pointing into the distance. His voice was too loud. 'The Royal Observatory is in that direction. You can make it out just over there in the direction of the Power Station and the Gasworks. It's so much easier at night to see it because they beam a green laser from there to mark the Prime Meridian.'

Bobby's words were a laser. Jed pulled both hands up to his head and staggered against the information board. Behind him another camera phone flashed. Laughter. Too loud. The river tightened in an ever shrinking loop. Words repeated. *Time. Gasworks. Meridian.* Again and again.

He lurched out and grabbed the information board beside him; clutching at anything to keep him from falling. His palm was flat against the picture of the Gasworks. His hand twitched. His fingers flexed and a spear of pain sliced down towards his elbow. And then everything slowed down.

People were moving around him. Chatting about the view. Posing for photos. Nat and Dante's hands carving the air slowly now so he could see every flex of their fingers. Like ice, not running water now. Cold and sharp. Kassia was hurrying forwards.

And he knew they were watching and worried and he couldn't move his face to smile or reassure them. It was all about this moment and being above the river.

In his mind's eye a dragon circled. Numbers churned. 1999 and 2003. It was suddenly so cold he felt like he was trapped in ice; then so hot he felt he was on fire. The segmented body of the dragon, swirling behind his eyes, became the frame for an image dragged from another time. Jed saw an old man standing in a Gasworks. The man wasn't speaking English but that didn't matter. Jed could make out the words and they were words of warning. About a terrible danger. And a terrible plan. And across the memory a green laser scored its path, clipping against the twelve yellow pillars of the building Jed stood on.

He expected the building to crumble. To disintegrate below him and wash away in the Thames. But the building stood strong. It was only him who fell. Crumbled to the floor, his hands pressed tight to his head. The circling dragon, melted like ice in the glare of the burning sun, and the image of the Gasworks drifted up into the air like dust and was gone. His heart marked time like the second hand of the clock. So quickly he could barely breathe.

'Is your friend on any medication? Does he have asthma? Need an inhaler?' Bobby was kneeling beside Jed's crumpled body. 'I don't think he's breathing right. Has he ever done this before?' The guide's voice was frantic.

'He's scared of heights,' Kassia mumbled.

'Well, what's he doing climbing the O2! Is this just a panic attack?'

Just panicking didn't really seem like the best phrase to use about whatever had happened. Jed's skin was drained of all colour and clammy to the touch. Bubbles of sweat lined his top lip and his eyes were twitching, rolled back in his head so only the whites were visible.

Kassia was kneeling too now and clutching at Jed's

hand. 'Jed, please. Can you focus? Can you focus on me?'

The change of routine was supposed to build new memories. Not do this! What had they done? They had to get him down from here.

The other guide was steering the rest of the group towards the far side of the viewing platform. Nat was beside Jed, pulling his legs upwards. Dante was gesticulating wildly. 'We need to get him down to the bottom,' Kassia translated. 'To the ground.'

Bobby scrambled for the radio he carried. 'Code Seven up here,' he bawled. 'Kid's fainted. Apparently scared of heights!'

There was static feedback on the radio. A woman's voice, calmly asking for details, though Bobby was struggling to keep his voice in any way measured. Dante had joined them now, and was helping to ease Jed's legs higher.

'Should we be doing that?' Kassia whimpered.

'Blood to the head. Standard response to fainting,' said Nat.

Jed's eyes flickered, and for a second his irises focused, his pupils wide as if they'd dilated to take in any light they could.

'OK. He's coming round,' said Nat, lowering Jed's legs and easing his shoulders up so he was sitting, his back slumped against the sign.

'You sure this is just a panic attack?' said Bobby. 'He doesn't look good.'

Kassia didn't know how to answer and she could tell her uncle was trying to share as little information as possible. He took the water bottle Bobby held and pressed the mouthpiece gently to Jed's lips. Dante waved his hands, trying desperately to fan the air and drive away some of the heat.

Jed's eyes flickered again and Kassia was sure he saw her. 'Can you drink?' she begged him.

He turned his head from the water, batting the bottle away.

'Please, Jed. Nat wants you to drink. It'll make you feel better.'

He turned again, and this time there was no doubting his eyes locked on hers. And there was fear in them.

Nat lowered the bottle and it tipped, pooling its contents on the floor.

Bobby was taking instructions over the radio. 'We should take him down in a wheelchair. There's a rope system. It'll be safer. We just have to get the chair up here.'

Jed was shaking his head and trying to pull himself to standing.

'We need to wait for the chair,' urged Bobby, 'then we start from here on the platform. If he tries to walk and faints again halfway down, we'll be in real trouble.'

Jed grabbed for Kassia's hand. His voice was catching incoherently in his throat.

'We should let him try,' begged Nat.

'The chair is safer.'

'The chair isn't here!' blurted Kassia. 'And if I walk with him, I can stop him panicking.' She'd no idea if she could. But it was totally clear from the way her uncle looked at her that waiting for a chair wasn't an option.

After more discussion with the ground staff, Bobby helped Jed to stand. He checked for several minutes that he could take his own weight. 'I'm fine,' he said again and again. 'Please. I just need to get to the ground.'

Bobby clipped Jed's latch to the safety line. The rest of the group stayed on the platform, Bobby reassuring them the boy was OK, just a little woozy. The second guide stayed with the group as Bobby radioed once more to the control centre. 'We ready to do this?' he said, turning to Kassia. 'It's steeper on the way down. You have to keep him calm.'

Her fingers shook as she scrabbled with her own latch on the safety line. 'I will. I will.'

She glanced at Dante and Nat and then at Jed's hunched figure and she hoped with all her might she could do what she promised.

The wind whipped at them as they climbed to the bottom of the O2. The sky grew darker. The air was heavy with the threat of rain.

Jed moved slowly, his shoulders bowed. He didn't look up. The walkway was steeper than it was for the ascent. Kassia had to turn her feet sideways so they wouldn't slip. It felt like walking on wet sand. She wasn't sure if the path was strong enough to hold her weight.

The sign at the bottom of the climb announced they'd conquered the O2. But it didn't feel like a victory.

Nat persuaded the support team a trip to hospital wasn't necessary. That he was a doctor. That he would deal with it.

Kassia wasn't sure anyone could deal with the mess they'd made.

Jed was slumped in the back of the car. His heart was still racing. Kassia could see the vein throbbing in his neck. He had even less colour than before and his eyes were glazed again as if he was focusing on something far away.

Nat and Dante helped him upstairs to his room and into bed. Anna offered food and drink, but he wanted nothing. He just turned his face away to the wall. And he was silent.

They huddled round the table in the dining room. No one trusted using their voices. They'd left the door to Jed's room slightly ajar in case he called out and so they used only sign. Kassia's words were broken and stumbling as if her hands had frozen on the climb back to the ground and were taking time to thaw. 'What happened? He was OK on the ground and then—'

'We've no idea what's going on inside his head,' interrupted Nat. 'Maybe things have started to come back to him.'

'But it looked like he was drowning. He couldn't get enough air,' signed Dante.

'Well, it would be overwhelming, wouldn't it? If memories that were lost suddenly came surging back.'

'He looked so scared.' Kassia's hands were shaking.

Nat tried to smile reassuringly. 'Any memories at all have to be easier than none. We just have to hope he can cope with them as they come.'

Jed moved away from the crack in the doorway and slumped back on the bed. He pressed his hands against his ears as if this would shut out the noise roaring in his head. White noise. Loud and relentless.

They'd said any memories at all would have to be easier than none. And he'd thought that too. Until the memories had come.

The dragon again, circling inside his head. Round and round in perfect rhythm with the noise thundering in his ears. *An old man hurrying through cobbled streets. A glass flask. A liquid bubbling inside. Glass shattered. A squeal of brakes. And the hands of a clock sweeping in an arc like a knife cutting into skin.*

Jed pressed his hand hard against his eyes. He didn't want to see any more. Silence and darkness were better than this.

In Room Seven, Floor Fifty of The Shard, Victor Sinclair was reading. It seemed the science books left on the shelf weren't as bad as he'd first imagined. What he was learning about digital downloading was mind-blowing.

Suddenly there was a thumping on the door.

Victor hurried to answer it. He hadn't had many visitors since his arrival, but Martha Quinn had promised it wouldn't be too long before they sorted out his education programme, and he hated to admit that the prospect wasn't too awful. You could get kind of bored stuck in a vertical city with hardly anyone to talk to.

When he opened the door though, it wasn't Martha Quinn. Neither was it someone Victor thought he'd be that keen to chat to. The man was tall with slicked-back blond hair that fitted his head like a helmet. He was dressed completely in black, the tails of a long leather coat billowing out behind him. The man was probably only twenty, though his eyes looked older. Victor figured he was the sort of man who'd seen a lot in his lifetime, however short it might have been.

'Job for you,' said the man.

'Sorry?' Victor wasn't sorry at all but it seemed the only possible answer.

The man in the long leather coat pushed his way into the room and walked over to the window. 'Cole Carter,' he said.

'Erm. No. I'm Victor Sinclair.'

'Not you, you numpty. Me. I'm Carter. I work in Department Nine.'

Suddenly Victor was interested. 'The restricted bit?' Victor had, of course, made a tour of as much of The Shard as he could in the last three weeks. It seemed to be mainly offices and large rooms full of scientific equipment which he presumed were laboratories, although he had no idea what went on in them.

The man called Carter nodded. 'You got any chocolate?'

This seemed an odd request, but the mini-bar was stocked daily, so Victor was never short of chocolate, although it tended to be the very dark kind, which he personally thought was rather bitter. 'Sure.' He grabbed a bar from the unit and passed it over.

'So we have a job for you,' Carter repeated, through a mouthful of chocolate.

'I thought I was going to go to school here,' Victor said.

Carter laughed. 'I think you'll find they probably said they'd *educate* you, mate. Your school days are over.' He took a photograph from his inside pocket. It wasn't a posed shot. It looked to Victor like some sort of face recognition print and was incredibly blurry. There was something about the face he recognised but Carter snapped the photo away before he had a chance to be sure. 'Game's on, son. I hope you're ready for the ride.'

The Ouro[boros] ... Greek οὐϱοβόϱος ὄφις or
tail-devou... [symbol] depicting a serpent or
dragon ea...

The Ouro[boros] ... [recepti]vity or cyclicality,
especially i... ...re-creating itself.
the eternal ... ...phoenix which
operate in cy... ...nd It can also
represent the ... ...mething
existing in or p...
qualities io or p...
Ancient Egypt, the ...
mychological symbol...
alchemical illustrations...
of the alchemist's opus...
Gnosticism, and Hermeticism...

Carl Jung interpreted the Ouroboros...
significance to the human psyche.[2] The...
Erich Neumann writes of it as a representation of the pro...
"dawn state", depicting the undifferentiated infancy experience
of both mankind and the individual child.[3]

*It was first used
in ancient Egypt*

Lucas Jennis' engraving published on an alchemical
emblem-book entitled De Lapide Philisophico (1625)

*It can represent
the aternal return*

*The Ouroboros is
connected to cycles.*

It is an important
symbol across the wor

DAY 35
3rd April

In the morning, Jed took the notepad from the unit beside the bed. He'd written nothing since that day in the hospital. Now he steadied the pencil tip against the fresh white page. The symbol of the dragon came easily this time. As if he was writing something as natural as his own name.

Below it, he drew shapes and images that ran like water from a tap. More and more. Not in segments this time. Whole figures.

Then numbers. Lots of them.

1926; 1933; 1951; 1999 and 2003.

Then dates. January 14th; December 25th; August 20th.

The page was a mess of figures and lines. A mixture of languages; some he could read and some he couldn't.

None of it made any sense to him. But one

thing was very clear.

He was starting to remember.

'The shapes are from alchemy,' said Kassia. 'Like the ouroboros. Signs which mean elements like earth and water and stuff like that. I've looked them up.' She was sitting with her back against her bedroom door. Not her room any longer, but Jed's. She was outside, he was inside. He'd been inside all morning. He'd pushed the pages through the gap under the door and waited. 'And the numbers could be phone numbers. Or pin numbers for off-shore accounts where you've stashed loads of money.'

She heard him make a noise which sounded remotely like a laugh.

'And maybe one of the dates is your birthday?'

'Shouldn't you be doing school work?' His voice sounded as thin as paper.

'Probably. Don't you think you should come out now? Talk to me properly about what happened.'

'Probably.'

She heard a slight thumping noise and guessed Jed was sitting too now, his own back against the door. Their heads could have been touching, apart from the thick plank of wood between them.

'I get that you're lonely. And frustrated and I can't

imagine how scared you are. If the memories have started coming back, then don't you think you should tell us? We're here to help you.'

There was a pause. A slight movement against the door. 'You're wrong.'

Kassia turned her head to the side, her ear against the wood. 'You're not scared?'

'I'm petrified.'

'So why am I wrong?'

'I'm not lonely.' The door clicked open and she wobbled a little where she sat. When she looked up, Jed was standing over her. 'You don't have to do this, you know.'

'Do what?'

He helped her to stand. 'Put up with me. Help me look for answers. This is my mess. You have your own life to live. Things you should be doing. Things your mum wants you to be doing.'

'And what *I* want to be doing is helping you find your life. Can't you tell me anything else you remembered?'

He took a deep breath, pulled his hands up to his mouth and pressed his fingers to his lips as if he was scared the truth might escape without him knowing what was said. She was so close to him she could feel his breath on her face.

'I see this dragon. Spinning and spinning. It sounds stupid, I know.'

'Not stupid.'

'Weird then. And there're always six segments to the body. And it's eating its tail like the one I drew in the hospital. But there's always something else. Like the dragon is a frame and what I need to see is inside. And that's where the numbers and the dates come from.'

'Do you see people? Anyone you recognise?'

'Yes and no. There're people sometimes. But I don't know them. And most of the time they don't look happy. There's this one guy. He's old and he's stressed and I feel like I should know him. The others . . .' He shook his head and blew out a breath as if speaking was becoming more difficult and the words were clogging his throat.

'It's OK,' she said. 'You don't have to rush things. We've got loads of time.'

She noticed the vein, pulsing in his neck like it had done in the car journey back from the O2. Something about what she'd just said had scared him.

Anna had drawn another pink square on Kassia's schedule. It was worth two hours. She'd added an asterisk. *Fresh air and brain architecture*. Kassia read the key. It meant that she and Jed had two hours in which to take a walk. Her uncle was doing well.

They took a number 11 bus to Liverpool Street Station, then a train to Manor Park Station and finally boarded a number 101 bus travelling towards Wanstead. They didn't discuss why they took this route. Jed just seemed happy to be out of his bedroom, even if he wasn't sure where he was going.

'Have you thought about the things you wrote down?' Kassia said at last. She knew it was a silly question. He'd probably thought of nothing else. But she had to start somewhere. 'The signs like the ouroboros? Maybe it's just something you were interested in before.'

'What, alchemy? But why does that seem important to me when I've still got no idea *who* is important to me?' He hesitated for a moment. 'I mean, important from the past?'

Kassia felt her face warm a little.

The bus pulled to a halt and Kassia nodded for them to get off. They walked for a while, stopping at a newsagent's, where Kassia bought a small bunch of flowers. Once outside, Jed spoke again. 'There's something else.' His hands were deep in his pockets, though it was clear to see the fingers were balled into fists. 'Something I didn't tell you when we were back at the house.'

Her stomach rippled a little with nerves.

'I think I must have done something really bad.'

'Why?'

'It explains Reverend Cockren's weird reaction when we were at St Paul's. And it fits with how I felt on the climb.' He was obviously finding it hard to look at her.

'Go on.'

'Me doing something terrible is the only thing that makes sense of why no one's come forward.'

'But there could be all sorts of reasons. There could be . . .' Her words dried up.

'If I've got parents out there, or friends, why don't they come and claim me?'

Kassia could only think of one answer. But she couldn't be sure that saying it aloud wouldn't make things worse.

'You're thinking something. Tell me, please. Because however I try and work this through, I keep getting back to this point. I *must* be someone bad.'

Kassia tried to swallow and the air caught in her mouth making her answer just a whisper. 'Maybe it's not you. Maybe it's them.'

It was obvious he didn't understand what she meant.

'Maybe your friends and family haven't come forward, because they can't.' She wanted to claw the words back as soon as she saw them sink into his brain.

'You think my family are *dead*?'

Her shoulders sagged as if to infer yes; scared to put what she thought into actual words.

He looked down, his hands unclenched in his pockets, as if something very precious had run away between his fingers.

They walked in silence for a while, until, in front of them, was a huge gateway with three enormous arches. Kassia took the central arch and led the way past the signs, which explained they were entering the City of London Cemetery.

'I shouldn't have said anything.' She could barely speak.

'It's OK. I suppose part of me knew that could be possible.'

'Is that worse? Thinking maybe no one *can* claim you instead of that they haven't because you did something bad?'

'I'm not sure. Does it matter to you?'

She didn't know how to answer. 'We don't know anything for certain yet about what you've done. Like you said, this is all a muddle.'

She could tell it wasn't the answer he'd hoped for.

The quiet of the graveyard pressed in on them. There was only the sound of their footsteps on the gravel and it sounded like something was being ground into a million pieces. 'We should talk about something else,' Jed said eventually. 'I need a break from thinking about me. Can't we talk about you for a while?'

'OK . . .' She chose her next words cautiously. 'My dad died over ten years ago.' She knew Jed hadn't asked about her dad specifically, but she felt she needed to offer him something of hers that hurt. To balance the pain that he was wearing now like the thick winter coat he'd borrowed from her brother.

He looked at her and she was pretty sure his eyes were saying thank you and so she carried on.

'My mum and dad were separated. I hardly knew him. I don't really understand what happened. I think my mum was different then.'

'The box I found?'

'Yep. That was from before.' She hesitated for a moment. 'But we're good. Things will be OK. I'm going to be a doctor. And mum has a plan for Dante too. He's still having speech therapy. One day he'll be able to speak.'

'Does he need to? With the signing I mean?'

'Now you sound like Dad, apparently.' She looked awkwardly down at the ground. 'I don't think they agreed about what was best for Dante.'

They'd reached a junction in the pathway and Kassia took the track to the left.

'Anyway, it caused problems and Dad moved away. He was driving down a country lane in France and the police think he lost control of the car. It was in the middle of nowhere. No one found the car for hours. Mum had his body brought back over here. Said he'd want to be buried in England and that's when I think she realised she still loved him. But it was too late.'

Jed walked a while without answering. He loosened the buttons on his coat. The sun felt warmer.

They'd reached a neat section of grass punctuated by a row of fairly new graves.

'I should stay here,' Jed said quietly.

'You don't have to. I'd like you to come with me. Please.'

They walked together through the rows and rows of stones and memorials. Carved winged angels and crosses and harps.

'You OK?' Kassia said gently.

'I'm not sure.'

Kassia looked down at the closest grave. 'You want it to be like that. Just a few sentences about who you were. Brother, husband, friend. That kind of thing.'

'Would be good.' He tried to smile.

'But someone has to choose what to put there. Out of all the stuff that could be true about a person, they have to filter it down. That's not all a person is, is it?'

she said awkwardly. 'That's why they put the bits of poems and the carvings and the pictures, I guess. To add extra meaning. Like all the hidden messages about time in the O2.'

Jed seemed impressed. 'So you're telling me things aren't ever really as simple as I'd want them to be.'

'Not really. Even flowers people bring to graves can have hidden messages.'

Jed folded his arms and waited for her to explain.

'Type and colour are all part of the message. Like with roses. Red ones for love, obviously, but yellow means friendship. So if you leave orange roses, because it's the colour between yellow and red, then it's a sign you wanted more than friendship.'

Jed was looking at the tiny bunch of flowers still in Kassia's hand.

'*These* are because they're all I can afford. When Mum and I come at the weekend, we'll bring a better bunch. She's quite fussy.' She laughed. 'You know there's this story about blue roses. They're impossible to find. So if you leave purple roses at a grave, then it's a sign you're hoping for the impossible.'

'You're clever.'

'I have a good memory, that's all.'

She regretted the words as soon as she said them. But, like before, it was impossible to take them back.

Jed turned away from her and focused on the gravestone. Kassia kneeled down and rested the flowers on the marble. She touched the headstone gently. 'This is Jed, Dad,' she whispered quietly. 'He's my friend.'

She turned slightly to look up at him. And the colour had drained completely from his face.

'Jed?'

'August 20th 2003. The date your dad died?'

She couldn't form the word yes but she nodded.

'2003,' he blurted. '2003. August 20th. From my list. Not a phone number. Not a pin-code. A date.'

'You can't read too much into it,' Kassia pleaded. They'd found a bench on the outskirts of the cemetery and Jed was sitting, peering into the distance. 'That number. That date. My dad. It's all chance. You've got no idea what's memory and what's just your mind playing tricks.'

'But what if these things are connected, Kassia? The words; the dates; the people I see. I've got pieces of a puzzle and no idea what picture I'm supposed to be making.'

'So you can't second guess!' she urged. 'Not until you have all the pieces.'

'When will that be?'

She wanted to say something clever. Something

reassuring. 'I don't know. I'm sorry.'

He turned to face her. 'It's not your fault. None of this is your fault. I just don't know what to do.'

'So you carry on living. One day at a time. One hour at a time.'

'*Time* again,' he said. 'If nothing else, I know that's important.'

They sat for a while and the sound of the city pressed in on them. Clouds scudded across the sky. Birds called out to each other. Kassia could tell Jed was wrestling inside, but he sat completely still, his hands clasped together, the only sign of his struggle the whiteness of his knuckles.

Finally, he looked at his watch. 'We've only got one hour left before your mum calls in the extra homework.'

'So let's get out of here, then,' she said. 'There's something I want to show you.'

They left the graveyard and travelled back by train and bus to Fleet Street. Jed's coat was unbuttoned now, the spring sun fairly high in the sky. Kassia untied the scarf from around her neck. It was flapping loose as she walked.

'My mum worked as a journalist,' Kassia began, determined to take the conversation in a different direction. 'She wrote stuff before my dad died. But when I left school to be home taught, she kind of lost focus a bit.'

'Do you ever think about going back? To school?'

Kassia took a long time to answer. 'I did. I was off for a while. And then going back seemed too difficult. And it works being at home. I like it.'

Kassia could tell he wasn't sure if she was being entirely honest, but the answer would do for now. 'Mum was asked to write a story for a Sunday supplement. I'm not sure she's going to do it. It's about this.' They'd entered a park ringed by tall buildings and St Botolph's Church. 'Postman's Park. People who worked in the Post Office headquarters used to come here for lunch.'

Kassia watched as Jed looked round. Birds pecked at the grass surrounding some old gravestones that had been moved to rest against the far wall. Tourists sprawled on picnic blankets or relaxed on the benches, obviously enjoying the chance to take a break from the business of the city. One city worker, dressed in sports gear but still wearing his lanyard from the office, was practising some rather complicated yoga moves.

'What's that?' said Jed, pointing to a long wall with a canopy roof stretching along it.

'A memorial to everyday heroes. This guy, called George Frederic Watts, thought we didn't celebrate everyday self-sacrifice enough. There're all these memorials for people who die in war. But there isn't really the same for people who died in peace – even if they made sacrifices too. Watts wanted this place to put that right.'

Jed walked along a line of ceramic plaques that had been fixed to the wall under the protection of the shelter. Even rows of painted tiles told the story of those who'd died. There was one for Harry Sisley, who'd died at the age of ten trying to rescue his brother from drowning. Another for Alice Ayres, who'd rescued three children from a house fire before dying herself in the blaze. Jed stopped at the plaque for Mary Rogers, who'd given away her life-belt in a sinking ship. 'They all died saving other people,' Jed said quietly.

'All of them. And they were just ordinary people who did extraordinary things. Amazing stories don't you think?'

Jed stopped walking.

'We *will* find your story, Jed. I promise.'

Postman's Park was just round the corner from the Devaux's flat in Fleet Street. Kassia pulled her door key from her pocket and went to slide it into the lock. The door swung open before she had a chance, as if someone inside had been waiting for their return.

Dante was standing on the threshold. Nat, Jacob

and Anna stood behind him on the stairs.

'What's going on?' said Kassia.

Her brother opened his hands, trying to pull together the signs he needed to make sense of this moment. But the fact his hands stayed open was all the sign she needed.

'Someone's come forward?' she asked, making each word solid with her hands even though her voice shook and made all she said sound fragile.

Her brother nodded and turned to point upstairs.

Kassia observed the whole scene as if she was watching a film. The sitting room was full of people. Her mother hurried backwards and forwards with cups of tea and gluten-free, low-calorie biscuits, and every now and then she bent down to pick up crumbs from the carpet or slip an extra coaster under the visitors' cups.

Jed sat on the settee facing the fireplace and Kassia thought he looked small.

A tall man was leaning his weight on a walking stick, resting his elbow on the mantelpiece. The man was oddly dressed; a suit jacket over a T-shirt that seemed faded from over-washing; the name of the rock group 'Thin Lizzy' flaking across the chest. And jeans, frayed at the ankles. This man seemed to be in charge.

There was a woman. She was older and rather plump

and was filling the armchair as if it had been moulded around her. And there was a tall man of about twenty who refused to remove his long leather coat even though the fire was on and it felt almost tropical with so many people packed into such a small place. This man was watching Jed as if he was a wild bird and was afraid any sudden movement would scare him off.

Over by the window was a black boy with buzz cut hair who hadn't stopped eating, hardly pausing to draw breath.

'My name's Montgomery,' said the man with the stick. 'My associates are Martha Quinn and Cole Carter.' He stared directly at Jed. 'And I've brought Victor with me. To assist in my introductions.'

Kassia watched Jed look around the room. Nothing in his eyes suggested any recognition of the people who surrounded him. This did not deter the man with the stick. He leaned forwards. His voice was a whisper. 'And most importantly,' he said slowly, drawing out his words for emphasis. '*You* are William Jones.'

Kassia watched Jed's reaction. Nothing.

The man remained undeterred. 'You've been through a terrible trauma, William. But I'm delighted to say I'm here to take you home.' He smiled triumphantly, then bit off the end of the biscuit he'd been waving like a miniature flag. 'I'm sure you've got lots of questions.'

Jed glanced from Montgomery to Nat and back again. 'Well, you could say that.'

'Of course. Of course.'

'Like, are you my . . .' Jed pulled a face, '*dad* then?'

There was a flicker behind the man's eyes. 'I'm afraid, William, both your parents died a long time ago.'

Kassia felt her stomach plummet. She saw the colour wash away from Jed's face as if he'd been plunged into icy water.

Nat lurched forward, his hands wide in an attempt to stop the man saying more. 'Seriously, the boy's recovery is very fragile. I would beg you to—'

'It's OK,' mumbled Jed, but Kassia knew the last thing it could be was OK. 'I want to know everything. I've waited over a month for this.'

Nat lowered his arms.

'Go on,' Jed urged. 'I need to know.'

Montgomery wolfed down the rest of his biscuit. 'Your care was assigned to us after the death of your parents. Victor here is another candidate for our company's very generous employee protection scheme. Some companies offer free dental work and travel insurance. Our staff care is second to none.' He reached smugly for another biscuit. 'Your identity was reassigned at the point of transfer. This thing, which was done for your protection, is the reason all the searches for someone connected to you failed, I'm afraid.'

The man was making it sound like Jed was a library book that had been unfortunately misfiled in the horror section rather than the comedy.

'But *you* knew about me, right?' pushed Jed. 'And you made me wait this long until you came forward?'

'We waited for the heat of publicity to die down. It was in your best interest.'

'Is that so?' The words were forced through Jed's teeth as if he was scared he would choke on them. Kassia could see his hands were in fists, clenched so tightly, the knuckles whitening like they'd done at the cemetery. 'So why was I in the river?'

'A sleepwalking disaster, I presume. You suffer from times of extended blackout. Add that condition to the stress of nearly drowning and it makes sense of the memory loss.'

Jed shot a look at Nat. 'Does it? Does that work?'

Nat looked apologetic. 'I've explained to you, we don't understand memory fully or what causes it to fail. It *could* be a reason.'

'To forget *everything*?'

'But I'm here to help you remember, William,'

Montgomery boomed, his voice too loud for the small room they sat in. 'And you will remember. I promise you.'

Kassia looked down. Jed's knuckles were whiter still. Dante tapped her on the arm, demanding a recap and she tumbled the last few minutes into a muddle of signs. By the time she'd finished, Jed was talking again.

'What's the deal with the symbol I drew?'

'A poster from your bedroom wall. Modern art, based on a classical design. Nothing more meaningful than that, I'm afraid.'

'And St Paul's?' Montgomery was confused. Jed looked embarrassed. 'There's something about the cathedral. It felt important.'

Montgomery took a third biscuit from the plate. 'It's just a building, William. I think your stress has played tricks with your mind. I've no idea why the cathedral should feel important to you.' He snapped the biscuit in half. 'But everything is over now. All the unknowing and the drama finished with.'

'I was scared!' Jed fumed.

'So were we, William. We thought we'd lost you. We have you now, though, and everything's going to be OK.'

Dante jabbed Kassia on the arm. His signs were large and in her face.

'My brother wants to know what happens now,' she said, and Jed looked sad somehow and Kassia wished she'd asked the question for herself.

Montgomery wiped the back of his hand across his face and swallowed the last of the biscuit. 'William should return with us. I appreciate you've all been very good to him and we are exceptionally grateful for what you've done to keep him safe.'

'He can't just leave,' said Anna.

Kassia could hardly contain her surprise.

'We should have a small celebration. Between seven and eight. Some food. Here tonight. Give . . .' she hesitated, '*William*, a chance to get his head round leaving.'

Was this really her mother speaking?

'A sensible suggestion, Mrs Devaux. You see the problem with the care scheme we've set up for William is that it relies on restricted contact. It explains why we took our time to get in touch. Once William returns to us, I think it best he has no more contact with you all. For his own safety, of course. A party tonight will be an excellent chance to say goodbye.'

Kassia looked down at her hands. She was surprised to see her own knuckles were creamy white.

Jed stood by the table at the window. Anna had

excelled herself. There were bowls of houmous and celery sticks; fruit skewers with a yoghurt dip and various flatbreads with a selection of goats' cheese.

Jed ran his finger round the inside of his collar. Dante had given him a new outfit to wear for the occasion, but the neck of the shirt felt tight like a noose.

'You're going to love our home, William.' The boy Victor was helping himself to a third mango and grape kebab. Raspberry sauce dripped from the end.

'Did we live there together?' Jed asked. 'I'm sorry. None of this is coming back to me.'

'Hey, that's OK. It'll take time. That's why they asked me to come. Help you adjust and everything. But I'm new to the home anyways, so you won't remember me.'

'It's a good place, though?'

'Hey. I've lived in some hellholes I can tell you, but where you're going tonight is fantastic. Views are awesome. Facilities amazing. You're going to have a blast.'

Jed pondered this answer and his collar felt looser around his neck. 'Why are you there?'

'Same as you, I guess. My parents died and eventually these people turned up and said my old man had left some instruction in his will. As soon as I reached fifteen I was to move in with them.'

'And Carter?' Jed said, glancing over at the young man who still wore his long leather coat like a suit of protective armour. 'Do I know him?'

'Trust me. You'd *know* if you did. He's the biggest pain in the universe. Thinks he runs the place.'

Jed toyed with the end of a cheese straw but didn't eat it. 'I don't remember.' He lowered his head and Victor took this as a sign to take a newly laden plate and search for a seat. Jed stood for a moment in the sea of chattering people, but he heard nothing they said. It was blurred and distorted as if he was underwater.

He was suddenly aware of Nat standing beside him. 'You OK?' Nat asked.

'Of course.' It was the only answer he could think of. 'I'm found. I'm going home.'

'I'm sorry we didn't make the connections.'

'Hey. You've got nothing to be sorry about. It's come together now.'

'Yeah, well. I'm still sorry about all the confusion and the dead ends and the problems on the O2 climb and stuff.'

'It's fine. Honestly. We got there in the end.' He rubbed his hands together. 'Your boss is going to be happy, right?'

Nat tilted his head from side to side. 'Ermm. Not sure if this will do it, to be honest. I took a blood test today and the patient fainted. Fell to the floor and broke their nose. Didn't go down well.'

Jed laughed despite himself. 'Anna will be relieved to see me go. That's why there's the party, isn't it? Bet she can't wait to get Kassia back on track for those exams she's taking.'

'You know, my sister was coming round to having you here. It was almost like seeing the old Anna. Giving Kass two hours off schedule was a major breakthrough, I can tell you.' Nat took a deep breath. 'And the kids are really going to miss you.'

'Don't let Dante hear you call him a kid.' Then he covered his mouth in embarrassment. 'I didn't mean that. About the hearing thing.'

'Don't worry. Dante *does* hear things. But things from our hands which he hears with his eyes. It's just an expression.'

'Like the ouroboros was *just* a picture. Not a symbol of anything important after all.'

'I suppose. But anyway, the point is, they'll miss you. We all will.'

'I'll miss you all too,' Jed said. And he wondered why saying those words made him feel so strange.

'Had enough of the party?' Jed asked quietly. He was standing near the top of the ladder leading to the loft room, a small Tupperware food container in his hand.

Kassia was on the bed, her knees drawn in tight to her chest. 'It's kinda noisy. I just needed a break. But you should be in there celebrating.'

'Yeah. I guess.' He climbed the final two steps of the ladder and sat down at the end of the bed.

'Isn't this what you wanted? It's great news. You should be having a ball.'

Jed fiddled with the edge of the container.

'You *are* happy, right?'

'Of course. It's brilliant. Amazing after waiting so long. But I suppose I thought when someone came forward everything would just slot back into place in my mind. And it hasn't. I don't remember those people. They're strangers to me.'

'At the moment they are. But you've got to give it time.'

'Yeah. *Time.*' He shrugged. 'Maybe that's all it meant. That I had to give things time. I had this idea that time was running out. And it wasn't. I had this idea the ouroboros and the symbol and the dates meant something. And they didn't. And I kind of thought that when I met the people who'd take me home, they'd mean something too. More than the people I've been with. And they don't.' His voice trailed away.

'Maybe everything will seem different when you see

the place they're taking you to. Maybe when you go home, that's when everything will feel OK.'

He shuffled round on the bed so his legs were against hers.

'What's in there?' She gestured to the container he was holding.

'I made you something.' He held the box towards her. 'Careful. It's fragile.'

Kassia took it and peeled back the lid. The insides seemed to sparkle, like the box contained slithers of gold.

'It's a bird. Made of caramel. The nest is spun sugar. One wing's slightly damaged. It would've been better if I'd had longer.'

'My mum let you in the kitchen to make this? When she had guests coming round?'

'I had to disinfect every surface afterwards and rearrange the sugar packets in height order after I used them. But I think she enjoyed watching. She seemed happy.'

Kassia lifted the cardboard base from the container and held the bird up into the light. The final reaches of the setting sun streamed through the sugar, making it shine like glass. 'It's incredible.'

'Doing things like that; changing things; *that* I'm sure I remember. The heat; the solutions; it feels like I know what I'm doing. I don't remember stuff about myself. But when I came here I was too scared to even speak, and you and your family gave me words back. And more.' He took a deep breath.

Kassia put the sugar bird back in the box and set it on the unit beside the bed. 'I have something for you too,' she said. 'Something to remember us by.'

She picked up a small package wrapped with tissue paper and passed it over. The wrapping was covered in tiny blue roses. There was an orange bow. Jed looked at her for a moment and she nodded for him to unwrap it. He slipped the bow free and unfolded the paper.

Inside was what looked like a small silver locket connected to a long chain. Engraved on the casing was a small bird in flight. A swallow. Jed pressed the plunger and the casing sprung open to reveal the face of a pocket watch.

'It was my dad's,' she said quietly.

'I can't—'

'Please. I want you to have it.'

'You sure?'

She nodded.

'And the bird?'

'I don't know. It could mean lots of things. A free spirit, maybe. I think my dad was one of those. I read once that sailors had swallows as tattoos to show how far they'd sailed. Each swallow represented five thousand miles.'

'It feels like I've come a long way since I first arrived here.'

Kassia agreed silently. 'And sometimes a sailor got a swallow tattoo when he left home. Kind of like a reminder of what he was leaving. Then, when he got back from his travels, he had another swallow tattooed.'

Jed held the watch closely. 'To show he'd come home?'

Kassia nodded. 'Anyway, I thought a pocket watch might help you remember being here. If you *wanted* to remember.'

'It's perfect. Thank you. And I do.'

Kassia blushed a little and stared intently at the carpet.

'Want to remember, I mean.'

He turned the present over and over in his palm and they watched the second hand swoop across the face in a perfect arc.

Jed shut the watch and rubbed the casing with the heel of his thumb. 'I like the reason about coming home best,' he said, and he wondered why he didn't think of the people downstairs as he said that.

It was agreed that standing out in the street, or even at the window, might draw attention to their leaving. Dante's signs were too large and Anna stood next to him, looking as if she needed support to keep upright. Nat seemed unsure how best to say goodbye. He went first for the handshake and then fumbled an awkward hug.

Kassia stood still. She bit her lip. And she kept her arms clasped tight together.

Jed couldn't really hear what was being said and any words he tried to say clogged in his throat. So he pressed his fingers against his lips and then let his hand fall away in a broken movement. It was a rather amateur signing of the word thank you, but he hoped they understood.

Back out in Fleet Street it was dark.

A people-carrier with blacked-out windows collected them. They drove past St Paul's. It was glowing pink in the floodlights, the golden gallery glinting. Jed turned away. He didn't want to look.

Victor chatted the whole way there. 'You're going to love the bedrooms. If you're into reading, there's a whole load of stuff in my room you can borrow.' Carter said nothing. He watched the road.

'Nearly there,' said Montgomery, as they turned right into King William Street. Victor was babbling on about the monument to the Great Fire of London, but Jed was focused on the river as they crossed above it. In the darkness the water was black like spilled ink.

Finally, the car turned left on to St Thomas Street and pulled over to park.

Jed stepped on to the pavement nervously. They were outside The Shard. The building stretched metres above them, its jagged top straining up into the clouds. 'Seriously?' Jed said. 'I live *here*?'

'Pretty spectacular, isn't it?' said Carter, his coat tails flapping behind him. 'Europe's first vertical city. Tallest building in London. Let's get you inside.'

Jed was steered across the entrance lobby. A guest ambassador, manning the lift, nodded politely at Montgomery and waited until everyone was inside before tapping the control panel. It barely felt as if the lift was moving. Jed only knew they were ascending because his ears popped.

When the lift reached Floor Fifty, Martha Quinn and Victor got out. 'William not on our floor then?' Victor asked, holding the lift door open with his palm.

'No. We've got a different arrangement for William. For tonight, at least.'

Victor had told Jed all about what he could expect in his room. He wondered how what was in store for him could possibly be an improvement.

'See you around then, Will. Great you're back.'

Jed nodded. In his pocket he slipped his hand tightly over the silver watch case.

The doors slid shut and the lift began to rise imperceptibly again. Jed looked awkwardly to his side. It was just him, Montgomery and Carter left. He suddenly felt a little cold. As if sensing his nerves, Montgomery tapped the end of his walking stick on the floor. 'Don't worry, Jed. This is when the real fun begins.'

Jed thought it a little odd that Montgomery hadn't called him William.

'I think you've got lots to share,' Carter went on. 'And we're going to make it easy for you to tell us.'

The lift stopped moving. The doors led into a small, dimly lit corridor.

Jed followed the two men as quickly as he could. 'You said my name was William, sir. And I'm afraid I don't remember anything. That's the whole problem.'

Montgomery pushed open a door. Beyond was a sparse laboratory. In the centre of the laboratory was a cage. Carter pushed Jed hard through the open door of the cage and swung it closed behind him, expertly padlocking it shut.

'It's not a problem any more,' said Montgomery. 'As I promised you, we have ways of making you remember.'

uweken tällä tawall:
6. Armias Jumal! anna armos Auring'
7. Se armon Auring! Christus tull
Meit wapahtamaan ald' kadotuxen
minull syndiä
sydämmeen, Raskamis
Jong alla walkiasi
Sanas olisi, Kuin
4. Se sama
minull tuotta
Kuin piinas
katuwat,
Niill' armon
NON VI S
département
niveau
floor 50
POLAROID

DE MONOCEROTE.

NOAH

Spire
Levels 75-87

The View from The Shard
Levels 68-72

Residences
Levels 53-65

Shangri-La Hotel and Spa
Levels 34-52

DAY 37

5th April

Three days after Jed left, Kassia moved back downstairs from the attic room. It hadn't seemed appropriate at first. It had taken that long to believe Jed had really gone.

She put the sugar bird on the unit inside the door. Here it caught the sun on its crystal feathers. She didn't mind that one wing hung unevenly, almost heavily, as if it was broken. In fact, it made her love the sugar bird more.

She saw her mum and her brother sharing knowing looks. She didn't join in their conversation.

That morning there was a story in the newspaper.

The picture of Jed fresh from the water of the Thames was used again and Kassia hardly recognised him. His hair was long and bright, but his eyes looked empty and scared. He'd begun to look different when he'd lived with them.

'Do you think he's happy?' she asked.

'Of course,' said Anna. 'He's found out who he is. He's where he's supposed to be.'

The news story was sketchy to say the least. Short on details, but long on closure. River Boy's guardians had been found. There was no mystery any more. Kassia was pretty sure it would be the last time she saw the story in the paper and so she cut out the photo, even though the likeness to the Jed she'd known was slight. She folded it up and slid it underneath the cardboard base of the sugar bird.

When she came back into the kitchen, Dante's hands fell by his side. Anna pretended to count packets in the cupboard as if suddenly the number of containers of mung beans and chickpeas was of world-changing importance. 'We need to make the most of the time we've gained,' she said. 'The dates for your GCSEs have come and I was thinking we should increase your work on maths. I've ordered some extra books for you.'

Kassia didn't think she could feel more depressed. 'No more fresh air then?' she said wistfully.

Her mother looked across at her brother. Dante waited a moment and then he took Kassia's hands and steered her round to face him. 'I wondered if you'd like me to come with you to Dad's grave today?' he said with his hands.

Kassia hugged him. Because she knew there was nowhere he'd like to go less, and there was nothing he could do that would show her he loved her more.

The three of them went together. Dante stood by the path. Kassia carried the flowers. And for once Anna left the scissors in her bag.

Jed was only allowed to leave the cage to use the bathroom. They cuffed his hands together and led him down the corridor at the start and the end of the day. They allowed him five minutes. He stood under the shower and the black dye from his hair ran away; the red re-emerging in ragged clumps.

Then they took him back to the cage.

Panic soaked him like icy rain. His throat was frozen like a water pipe in winter, so hardly any breath reached his lungs. His chest fought to pull in air and his ribs strained like the bars of his cage.

On the first evening, he shouted and called until his voice rasped. No one came.

On the second day, when his voice was as rough as sandpaper, Carter stood by the door and watched him. 'Why am I here?' Jed pleaded. Carter said nothing.

On the third day, when Jed felt so weak and tired

he could barely stand, Montgomery came. He pulled a high-backed stool from behind the laboratory bench and he sat and he stared. Behind him, the key to the cage hung on the wall. Jed could hardly focus. His eyes burned in their sockets; sleepless lids scratching with every blink. Exhaustion made the key look as if it was swinging, like a pendulum marking out each agonising minute. Jed's stomach cramped with hunger, his fingers raw from scratching at the bars. 'Please. Please,' he begged. 'Why am I here?'

Montgomery sat back on the stool. 'It's my turn to ask the questions,' he growled.

Jed sat slumped on the floor, his back against the metal bars, his knees drawn up to his chest, his arms linked round them, trying to hold himself together. 'I don't know!' was all he could say. 'I don't remember!'

On the afternoon of the third day, Montgomery leaned forward and in the light it looked as if even the irises of his eyes were black. 'I'm getting tired of this, Jed.'

'You said my name was William Jones!'

'We said a lot of things to get you to come with us.'

'So my name's not William?'

Montgomery shook his head.

'What then? Tell me and I might remember answers.'

'There's only one answer we need. Only one that really matters. How you did it. That's all we really need to know.'

Jed rocked his head back against the bars. 'I keep telling you! I don't know what you mean. Did what? Why am I here?'

'No one understands why you're here, Jed. That's the puzzle we need to solve.'

Montgomery reached for his walking stick and levered himself up from the stool. He began to pace. It was possible to make a complete circuit of the cage. Jed stared at the ground as he walked. Who was this man? Why the cage? What were they going to do to him?

'We're getting nowhere, Jed, so let me try another tack. Tell me what you know about death.'

Acid from his stomach burned in his chest. He was sure he was going to be sick. Death! What had death got to do with any of this? With him?

'It's the great leveller, isn't it, don't you think?' Montgomery went on. 'The thing that comes to all of us, no matter how clever, no matter how rich, no matter how brave. Some of us can fight it off for longer than others, but eventually it comes to us all. Death has a way of making us equal in the end. So, imagine if death could be controlled. If the hands of time could be stopped, or even reversed. If death could be defeated. Suddenly, we'd have inequality in a way never been seen before. The ultimate apartheid. A separation between those who would die and those who would live.' He stopped walking and, with the tip of his stick, he traced a circle on the floor. 'To have control over death would be the ultimate power. The ultimate wealth. The ultimate prize. Surely you see that?'

Jed struggled to his feet. The room was spinning and the image of the dragon swirled in front of his eyes, each of the six segments of its body sharp and bold. In the centre of the frame the dragon body formed, a fire burned and raged until everything he saw was black. 'Why are you telling me this? Why do you keep going on about death? Why won't you let me go?'

Montgomery moved his face close to the bars. His eyes level with Jed's. 'Because we've been tracking you for nearly a hundred years. And the time has come for you to give us answers.'

'A hundred years! What are you talking about? You're crazy!'

Montgomery pressed his stick to the floor and steadied himself. Then he began to walk again. 'My life's work,' he said, pointing at the pictures and maps and cuttings pinned to the walls. 'Everything NOAH has been about. You've had people across the world looking for you for decades. Their work, just to understand yours. And after all this time, after all the false leads, you're here. Isn't it easier, now the running and the hiding is over, just to tell us?'

'Tell you what!'

'How you cheated Time!'

Jed clutched at the bars. His palms were wet with perspiration. He could feel Montgomery's breath hot on his face. The man was obviously determined not to be the first to look away and when he spoke his voice was taut with anger. 'Maybe leaving you again will give you the time you need to come up with the information we're waiting for.'

Jed held fast to the bars. 'No wait, please.' He knew what would happen when the man left the room. He couldn't be alone. Couldn't be in the dark again!

'*Have* you got answers for me?'

'I'm telling you the truth!' Jed yelled. 'I don't know what you expect me to know.'

'The solution to the Great Work itself!'

'Please. Don't leave me here.' He tried to shake the bars. 'Please!'

'The time for pleading has run out, Fulcanelli.'

His words throbbed in Jed's head. He stumbled

and slid to the ground. And the memory of the dragon swirled and consumed itself as the final word echoed round the cage.

Montgomery walked out of the laboratory and flicked the switch. The cage was plunged into darkness. Jed rested his aching forehead against the bars. He wrapped his palm round the silver-cased watch in his pocket, but even that couldn't stop the panic thundering in his chest. For the second time in as many months, he was sure he'd drown.

While Victor had been growing up, looked after by the social services, he'd been pretty sure no one could know less about what their parents did as a job than he did. That was until he'd met a kid with no memory. Kind of lucky that their parents had both worked for the same organisation. It certainly had an impressive after-care system for your children if you died. Odd though. Two teenage boys being signed over to the care of their dead fathers' work place. It was either a very big company with a lot of employees, or a very unlucky place to work.

Victor had hoped Martha Quinn would finally explain something about his dad's job to him. It had to be interesting if it took place in The Shard. He'd worked out, from the signage about the place, that his father's company was called NOAH. He'd been spending much of his time reading the books left in his room, which all suggested NOAH was some sort of science set-up. But the weird book about unicorns didn't seem to fit with anything. He wanted details. No one had been near for days. And Victor had a gnawing suspicion he knew why.

William.

Victor had given the problem lots of thought. If part of the deal of taking on kids of dead employees was that some of them would go on to work for the company, then William had to be more valuable. Maybe he showed more potential. And that was annoying. Because the only good thing living in Etkin House had taught Victor was that you had to fight to be noticed. And so Victor was determined no one would forget he was here too.

He knew most of the working floors of NOAH were below Floor Sixty. His and Carter's bedrooms were on Floor Fifty. Not that he'd seen inside Carter's bedroom, but he knew where it was now. The guy had returned to his room at the crack of dawn for the last three days, and he was hardly quiet about it. Martha Quinn's office was on this floor too, so she could keep an eye on them, he guessed. All this led Victor to surmise that William must have been taken to a room

188

between Floor Fifty-one and the skyscape on Floor Seventy-three. He also surmised that if he found William, he'd find answers about what was going on.

Victor figured his best hope was talking round a guest ambassador. The fancy-named lift attendants doubled as security staff, and with access to all floors, he could be sure there was little they didn't know.

He knew enough to realise the ambassadors were sworn to secrecy, though. NOAH seemed big on that. But Victor had a cupboard full of complimentary chocolate – and a plan.

He rode the lift a couple of times every hour before the ambassador changed to one he felt he'd have most luck with. This one made eye contact. There was a glimmer of a smile. Victor got out his bar of chocolate, unwrapped the end and broke off a square. Without saying anything he held the bar out in offering. The ambassador mumbled a polite, 'No thank you.'

Victor chewed the chocolate quickly. 'You sure?' he said, holding the bar out again. 'It's really good.'

The ambassador looked embarrassed. Victor broke off a line of squares. 'Here. I can't eat it all. I'm supposed to be meeting with the kid we brought in three days ago. Think we're having a meal. Don't want to spoil it.'

'Oh, he's finally started talking, has he?' said the

ambassador, taking the squares almost too keenly. 'That'll be a relief for Mr Montgomery.'

Victor tried to look relaxed. 'The trouble is, I've forgotten what floor I'm supposed to go to.'

The ambassador pressed the button and the lift door slid shut. 'Oh, that's not my place to tell you. Best to report to Ms Quinn. Don't want to talk out of line.'

Victor pulled a face and dug around his pockets. 'I had it written down. The room I was supposed to go to. I guess getting the money out for the chocolate I must have pulled her message from my pocket.' He made a conspiratorial face in an attempt to suggest that anyone eating the chocolate must be implicit in the crime. And the ambassador looked duly embarrassed as he swallowed the final square. 'Well, as you had it written down, I guess I wouldn't be hurting anyone by confirming what you were supposed to know.'

'Exactly,' said Victor, blowing out an elaborate breath as a sign of relief.

The ambassador pressed some buttons on the control panel and the lift began to glide upwards.

When the lift shut behind him, Victor stood alone in the hallway. This was the restricted floor, he knew it. This was perfect. Find out what was going on with

William and learn more about Department Nine at the same time. Result all round.

Floor Fifty-five was certainly more sparse than his own floor, and there seemed to be only one door at the very end. If it was this easy, he was annoyed he'd waited three days before tracking the new guy down.

He marched towards the door and knocked. No answer. The boy was probably at some important meeting even now. Still, it would be good to see what sort of palatial accommodation they'd given the prodigal son. Victor turned the handle and opened the door. The lights flicked on immediately.

He'd expected a panoramic view of the city. Floor to ceiling windows. Plush furnishings.

He hadn't expected a cage.

The bolt of new light burned in Jed's eyes. He scrambled for the bars, trying to pull himself to stand, but there was no strength left in his legs and he crashed to his knees.

'Hello?'

It was the boy! The one from the party. 'Victor?'

Victor stood in the doorway, his forehead wrinkled in confusion as he tried to take in the scene. 'William? What the . . .'

Jed hauled himself again up the bars. This boy

could help him! Get him out! 'Victor! Please!'

'What you doing in a cage, man?'

'I don't know!' Jed's voice was rasping in his throat, his vision swimming. 'You have to get me out!'

'What have you done?'

'Nothing! These people are crazy!' He was finding it hard to breathe. The bars were slipping between his hands. He was going to fall again. He blew out a breath and bit the inside of his lip. 'There's a key. Look! On the wall!' He was pointing wildly through the bars, jabbing his hand.

'But you must have done something bad, mate! Why would they put you in a cage?'

'They think I'm someone else!' Jed's hand was straining so far through the bars his shoulder ground against the metal. 'The key, Victor! On the wall.'

'They think you're William Jones. Aren't you?'

'No! There *is* no William Jones!'

'What? You're making no sense!'

Jed lurched forward. His shoulder pummelled the metal again. His fingers clawed the air. 'The key, Victor!' He had to make the boy listen. Had to make him see before Montgomery came back. The clock on the wall was marking each second, the ticking booming in his ears. The boy was his only chance!

But Victor was standing awkwardly in the doorway,

his hands plunged deep into his pockets. 'I don't know, mate. These people have been good to me.'

'They've locked *me* in a cage!' Jed pulled his arm back. He thumped his hands hard on the bars and something like a growl rumbled in his throat. 'You *have* to let me out!'

He could see the boy thinking, glancing up at the key.

'Victor! Please!'

He was weakening. The key was swinging on the wall in the draught from the door. 'But they must have their reasons, mate.'

'How can there be a reason for this? Look at me! Look at what they've done!' Jed flung his arms outstretched from his side. 'Have they told you why I'm here?'

'No.'

'So you've no clue what this place is all about, then?' If the boy couldn't understand the wrongness of the cage, maybe there was another way to break him.

'They're going to tell me!' Victor was spitting his words.

Jed slid down and slumped with his back against the cage. His hands were shaking, his shoulder bruised. The key rocked backwards and forwards on the wall. 'OK, Victor. You're right. They're going to tell you everything. I suppose they wanted to tell me about what our dads did first before they got round to telling you.'

'They've told you! About your dad?'

'And yours. Mind blowing stuff, mate. But they're wrong about me. I didn't need to know. He wasn't my dad. They've got it wrong. I'm not who they think I am. But you! You have a right to know.' Jed's stomach was knotting. His head was pounding. This was risky. He'd no idea if the boy would fall for the trap. He had to try, though! And he had to do it now! Jed swallowed his desperation. To make his words clear. 'Just let me out so we can talk. Please!'

'You're really not William Jones?'

'No!'

'But you know about my dad?'

'Yes!'

Victor took a deep breath. 'OK. Just so we can talk. Where's this key?'

Jed jabbed his arm through the bars again and pointed wildly. He wanted to hurry him. Needed him to move faster but he was terrified to speak unless one wrong word made him change his mind.

Victor took the key.

Jed's heart raced. His breathing spluttered. Sweat pooled in the palm that still circled the bars.

Victor slid the key into the lock. He opened the padlock and swung the door tentatively. 'Slowly, OK? I'm only letting you out so you can tell me about my dad. And then we can go together and explain about you not being who they think you are.'

Jed staggered out of the cage. His feet faltered and he fell against the laboratory benching. Then he pulled himself up tall. 'I'm so sorry!' he yelled.

The stool skidded across the floor and thudded into Victor's stomach folding him forwards. 'What?'

'I'm really sorry,' Jed called again. He charged forward as Victor fought to steady himself. Adrenaline surged through Jed's veins. His heart beat so hard, he was sure it would rip through his chest. The dragon image circled in front of his eyes. *A laboratory. Older than this one. Shattered glass. A fallen friend.* Jed stumbled and the dragon's mouth opened wide and devoured the image so all Jed saw was the open door. 'I'm so sorry!' he yelled again, and he wasn't sure if his sorrow was for Victor or the friend in the memory.

But Victor had realised what was happening. He tugged Jed back by the shoulder, landing a punch squarely on the side of his face. Jed collided with the door. His top lip burst open and blood splattered on the wood. Victor tried to hurdle the fallen stool. He grabbed at Jed's shoulder again, digging his nails hard into the bare skin.

Jed ripped free. And ran.

And as Victor followed, he fell across the fallen stool and crashed to the floor, his head thumping hard against the base of the laboratory benching, knocking him out cold.

Jed careered down the corridor.

He saw the lift. That was surely too risky. It had been manned by some guy in a uniform last time. He couldn't chance being seen.

There was a fire exit door on the right. He could only guess how high up he was, and how many flights he'd have to cover to reach the ground, but it was his only choice.

He thundered down the stairs, his bare feet catching as he ran, lurching from floor to floor. His heart was banging in the back of his mouth and he was sure he was going to pass out. He doubled over the handrail and clutched at his stomach. He had to do this! Had to keep going! To get away!

He'd no idea how long it took him to reach a door marked 'street exit'. He hurled himself forward and the door ricocheted open. The blast of night air was overpowering. It choked any breath he had.

His eyes strained in the dark and the sound of traffic clogged his ears.

He tried to make sense of where he was and stumbled towards the main street to his right. He'd no plan about where to go. But he knew he had to keep moving.

He heard the rumble of trains. The air whipped against his chest and he pulled his arms around himself to cover his lack of shirt. Turning right at the end of the road, he saw a street vendor packing up for the evening. Scarves 'Two for a Fiver' ringed the display of T-shirts emblazoned with versions of the 'Keep Calm and Carry On' logo. He watched as the vendor took a rail of scarves and tipped them into a cardboard box. Jed tugged a grey T-shirt from the hanger, pulling it on as he ran.

'Oi! What you doing?' The vendor dropped the scarves and charged after him, but the cold air had fired Jed's muscles. He pushed through the crowd and charged forward.

Turning right, he could make out a break in the skyline. It had to mean he was near the river. He raced on, shouting apologies at the sightseers and tourists he bumped against as he moved. The street vendor's cries were drowned in the swell of voices all around him.

Traffic streamed across the bridge. Tail lights a red

ribbon spiking above the water.

He couldn't do this. Couldn't cross the river. Something about the water. About the Thames surging below him. But freedom was on the other side.

The terror squeezed his heart like a fist, tightening and tightening. He couldn't look at the water. He had to keep moving.

Once over the bridge, he ran straight on, crossing Upper Thames Street.

The road dead-ended in front of him. He clutched his side, hesitating for just a second, before turning left into King William Street. Was this where the car had driven three nights ago? When everything had been different? He wasn't sure. Nothing looked familiar. How could he trust what he saw anyway? How could anything make sense again?

Both the most terrible things he'd imagined had to be true. There really was nobody who could claim him. And he was bad. So bad he needed bars to hold him.

His feet could barely keep moving and he pumped his hands in fists to help carry himself onward.

There was another junction. He turned left again.

He could hear bells ringing. Church bells. He pushed towards them. Maybe it was St Paul's! His side was stitching, pain tugged through his empty belly, bile bubbling in the back of his throat. He doubled over and his vision twisted and swelled.

A dragon framed image. *Another chase, this time through cobbled streets. A car behind him. A driver hunched at the wheel, a medallion swinging from his neck.* The dragon frame of the memory reared up. The jaws of the snake widened then clamped shut swallowing the image they'd circled. Pain seared through Jed's temple.

He stumbled from the pavement into the road. A car crossed the 'Give Way' sign. The driver floored the brakes and the tyres squealed. Jed thumped his hands on the bonnet and the driver's face was so close to the windscreen, Jed could see the whites of his eyes. The driver's lips were moving. Shouting angrily but the sound was trapped inside the car. Like the screaming trapped inside his own head.

The flecks of the memory lifted and swirled on the night air and Jed had no idea what was happening now and what was in the past. He fell into the gutter and above him the stars pricked the sky like needles on thick black cloth. Any strength he'd had seemed to wash away like water spilled on to bare and dusty ground.

'How can you have been so stupid?' Montgomery stood with his hands latched tight to the bars of the open cage. His walking stick was discarded on the floor. 'We had him here! After all this time. How could you have let him out?'

'How was I supposed to know?' Victor shouted indignantly.

'He was in a cage!'

'But he's just a boy.'

Montgomery swung round to face him, hands still keeping him steady, gripped tight to the bars. 'That's the point. That's exactly what he isn't!'

Martha Quinn picked up the walking stick, passed it to Montgomery and steered him towards the laboratory stool she'd just up-righted. 'Let's try and calm down.'

'Calm down! Decades of tracking and hoping, and this idiot blows everything.'

Victor stepped forward. 'I'm not an idiot!'

'Your actions say otherwise.'

'Now hold on—'

'Enough!' Martha was standing with her hands raised. She stood between him and Victor, her tubby frame belying the power of her stare. 'That's quite enough! Let's try and work out what happened and what exactly we all do from here. The horse, as they say, has bolted, so it's no good now moaning about the stable door.'

Montgomery muttered something under his breath about how the door had been firmly shut, but Martha was guiding Carter towards a seat in the corner and therefore chose not to respond. Victor stood by the benching, his arms folded tightly across his chest. He refused all offers of a seat. The empty cage stared back at them, its door swinging open like a tongue lolling from a mouth.

'I'm afraid, Victor,' Martha began, 'that you made a serious error of judgement and what you have done has cost us dearly.'

'You've told me nothing. You turn up out of nowhere and tell me you're going to care for me, but you tell me nothing! I'm supposed to help you bring this boy back to his loving surrogate family and you tell me nothing! And then I find him in a *cage*! Why would you do that? What aren't you telling me?'

'I'm afraid there's a lot we have yet to tell you!'

'So get talking!'

Martha looked first from Montgomery to Carter and then back again.

'There's no point keeping anything from him now, is there!' groaned Montgomery.

Martha pressed her fingers up to her temples as if she was drilling for information and seeking for the best way to share it. Then she began to explain.

201

'NOAH. It's a National Organisation searching for Advanced Health. Our eight major departments research ways to hold back the advancing years and threat of bodily decay. To still aging in its progress. Cryonics, gene manipulation, vitamin onslaught, digital download – all ways to beat Time. But Department Nine,' she hesitated, 'Montgomery's department, the one your father worked for, and the one Carter works for, is different. Its focus is the Unicorn Protocol. Here, in Department Nine, our job is to look for unicorns.'

Victor opened his mouth to speak, but Martha ploughed on regardless.

'There's a museum of medicine in Rome called the Museo Storico dell'Arte Sanitaria. Inside, there's a dark laboratory. And in the laboratory, in an embossed leather case, there's the horn of a unicorn. People believe it's capable of curing ills and restoring health.'

'He said you were crazy! When he was in that cage, he said you were all mad!' exclaimed Victor. 'Unicorns don't exist!'

'No, probably not. And yes, absolutely.'

OK, everyone here was insane. At least that was obvious now.

'I doubt very much there are silver-white horses running around with long pointed horns,' said Martha.

'I wouldn't stake my life on it, though. But I'm pretty sure those animals are lost for ever. But myths and legends can make sense of the nonsensical. Stories, you see, can help us grasp truths.'

'What are you on about?'

'That boy wasn't just a boy.'

'He told me he wasn't William Jones!'

'No. He wasn't. He was *the answer*. To why your mum died and why your sister died. Even to why your father died. He was the answer to all those questions eating you up for years.' She flung her arms apart. 'And *you* let him go.'

Victor felt his inners twist. Anger at himself and at them and at the boy he'd freed, churned inside him.

'We had the answer to it all, Victor. Locked in that cage. And you opened the door and let the answer disappear.'

Kassia wasn't really sure why she went to Postman's Park. Her mum had marked a section on her schedule with yellow highlighter. She'd never used that colour before. It was for 'free time'. Kassia could hardly believe it, but her mum had folded her arms, as if fighting the impulse to take the schedule and adapt the plans. 'Just an hour,' she said, chewing the words like vegetables she knew were good for her but she was having trouble swallowing. 'I'm sure that won't hurt.'

Kassia needed to be outside. But she wanted to be quiet. The park was nearly deserted. Sunday sightseers long gone.

She made her way to the wall of remembrance and, because they'd done it together, she read her way through the commemorative plaques. Everyday heroes, now lost.

Suddenly, she was aware she wasn't alone. Huddled in the far corner of the canopied area of the wall was a crouched figure. He was wearing a grey T-shirt that was far too big, and he was rocking backwards and forwards, shaking uncontrollably.

Kassia was scared. An addict maybe. Someone in trouble. She knew she shouldn't speak to strangers. Knew she was out of her depth and should leave. But the figure appeared to be sobbing. 'Hello?' she said softly. 'Can I get you some help?'

The figure lifted his head and looked at her.

'Jed?' She could hardly breathe. 'William? Is that you?' She hurried forward and kneeled beside him. In the fading light she could see his face was bruised and puffy, one eyelid closed and swollen. Blood streaked from a gash on his lip.

'Jed,' he mumbled. 'Not William. It's Jed.'

She'd no time to work out what he meant by this.

'What happened to you? Who did this?' She was tilting his head gently to the side, dabbing hopelessly at his lip with a tissue pulled from her pocket.

'They did.'

'Who's they?' Her fingers were wet with his blood.

'I can't go back there. You mustn't let them take me back.'

'The people who claimed you did this?' Is that what he meant? She rocked on to her heels. His face looked even more battered from this angle. She bit her own lip to stop it trembling. 'We need to get you home.'

'No. That's where they'll look for me. We can't go there.'

'The hospital then? To have you patched up.'

'Not there either. Nowhere connected to Nat. They'll check and I can't be found!'

'OK.' She tried to concentrate. To come up with a plan. 'Jacob's,' she said. 'It's in Old Mitre Court. It's not far from our flat. Not far from here either. I'll get Nat to come and clean you up and we can work out what to do and—' She gulped. Tears were burning in the back of her throat. 'I don't understand what happened.'

He clutched at her hand. 'Neither do I.'

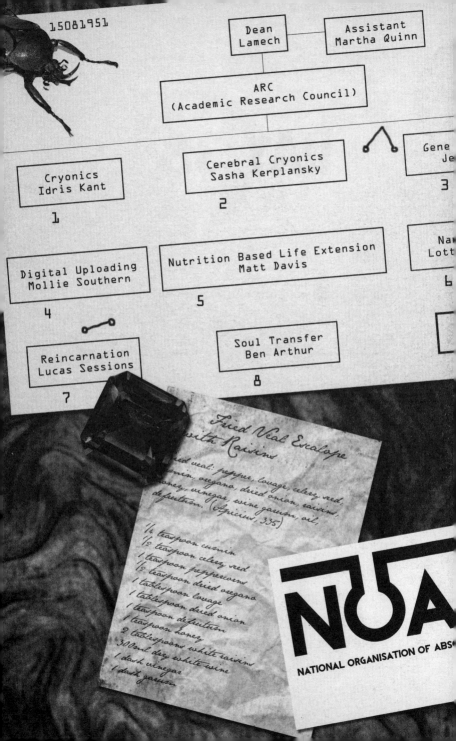

DAY 38

6th April

Nat arrived with Anna and Dante. 'Where is he?'

Jacob guided them through to the sitting room. Kassia had already started cleaning Jed's face. The T-shirt lay on the edge of the couch. Jed could feel blood oozing from the deep scratches in his shoulder.

'What on earth happened?' said Nat, dumping his bag down and rummaging inside.

'He escaped,' said Kassia. 'There was a fight. That Victor guy from the party.'

'Woah, hold on there.'

Kassia stepped back to let her uncle get to work. 'They had him in a cage,' she seethed.

Nat faltered for a second. 'Those people? The ones we returned you to?'

Jed nodded, and pain seared through his head.

'But their story added up. We checked them out.

Everything made sense.'

'Everything was a lie,' said Kassia. 'A trick, to get Jed away from us.'

'Jed? Not William?' said Nat, reaching for more gauze and splashing it with saline. 'So who are you? And why did they do this?'

Jed tried to move his mouth to answer. His lips were swollen, his eye so puffy now it was hard to see.

'We should give him time,' said Anna, putting on gloves from Nat's bag and collecting up the gauze he'd used with almost frantic speed.

But Jed was desperate to explain. 'They were crazy people!' Every word hurt him, but he was determined to plough on. 'And they wanted to know how I'd done it.'

'Done what?'

'I don't know!'

Dante stepped forward and moved his mum out of the way. His hands were moving furiously and Kassia turned his words into sound. 'Jed, we need to call the police. Tell them what happened.'

Jed leaped up from the couch, his hand pulled free of Kassia's. The saline solution toppled off the table and splashed on to the floor, streaking the carpet with tears. 'No police. Those people are capable of anything! They'll come after us!'

'OK,' said Jacob calmly. 'No police. For the

moment. But you have to tell us anything you remember. We have to work out who these people are and what they want from you.'

'They used the name NOAH.'

Jacob opened the laptop. Kassia grabbed it from him and waited for the Google search page to load. 'NOAH.' She typed in the search bar. 'National Organisation for Advanced Health. It's a research organisation looking into prolonging life. Do you think that's them?'

Jed looked across at the logo. A crucible waiting, as if over a fire. His mind jerked. The thick black segmented shape of a dragon filled the space behind his eyes. *A glass container smashed on the floor.* He recoiled as if the shards of broken glass were raining down on him.

Kassia eased him back on to the couch. 'Just take it slowly. Let's work this out together. Was there anything they said that made sense?'

'No! It was all about death and answers!'

'But you're sure you're not William Jones?'

'Positive!'

'So did they call you anything else? Apart from Jed?'

Jed pressed his hands to his head. 'Erm. There was this word. I don't know if it was a name.'

'Go on!'

Jed took his hands away. 'Fulcan something. Fulcanelli.'

'Well that's a start,' said Jacob. 'Fulcanelli. Maybe that's your surname.'

'Your parents, then. Look in the online phone book,' urged Anna. 'See if there are any Fulcanellis in London we can contact.'

Jed could feel his stomach tightening. Maybe there was family after all. Maybe this was all it would need!

Kassia clicked on 'Find Person' and typed in the name. She added London as the location and pressed 'Search'. The screen flashed. Jed held his breath.

'There's more than one possible location for the search, look. London Airport. London Bridge. London.'

'So try them all,' Nat urged.

Kassia clicked the first choice. The answer flashed up. *This person could not be found.*

'Try another.'

The same answer filled the screen.

Jed watched as Kassia worked through the list. Always the same answer. *This person could not be found.*

'I'm so sorry, Jed.'

He wanted to tell her it was OK. But it wasn't. The hope of family there for a moment and then snatched away again.

Kassia held the laptop despondently and glanced

across the room, looking for help from anyone who would offer it.

'Google the name,' signed Dante, his fingers lurching through the spelling. 'Try that.'

Kassia typed Fulcanelli into the search engine. Her eyes widened. 'OK. This is good!' She scanned through the first answer.

'Well?' Jed knew his voice was frantic.

'Says he was an alchemist. Part of a group called the Brothers of Heliopolis. Lived in Paris in the 1920s.'

'Maybe you're related to this Fulcanelli, then?' said Nat. 'Connects with the symbol you drew.'

'But why did they put me in a cage?'

'Because of what alchemists do?' suggested Kassia.

'Turn lead into gold?' said Jacob.

'So maybe this guy Fulcanelli could make gold.'

'And they put me in a cage for that?'

'If they thought you knew how to make gold too, then yes.'

Jed's mind was whirring. 'What would they want with gold?'

'What does anyone want with gold?' said Nat. 'It's the means to ultimate power. Can you imagine? If this organisation had access to unlimited funds, then they could do all the research they wanted.'

Jed felt his stomach fold. 'That's it,' he mumbled.

'Those people put me in a cage because they thought I knew a family secret that could make them richer than they'd ever imagined.

'The thing is, how can I know a family secret when I have no family . . . ?'

Kassia was the first to hear the sirens.

The road outside thrummed with the noise. Fire engines and police cars fighting through the early morning traffic.

Jacob flung the door open and peered up Old Mitre Court to where it bent round into Fleet Street. The sky was thick with black smoke. It was billowing like a huge cloak caught in the wind.

Anna hurried after her brother and the two of them stood at the junction beside Jacob. She covered her mouth, perhaps to keep back the fumes but more likely to stifle a scream.

'Mum?'

'You need to go back. Keep inside. It's not safe.'

'Mum?' Kassia pushed out into the street beside her mother. Fire engines had clogged the road. People were running in all directions. Shouting at each other. Police were trying to herd everyone away. The smoke was getting thicker. Jed could feel it burning his eyes and his nose.

Nat began to run towards the crowd, Anna racing after him.

'Mum, wait!' Kassia pushed her way out into the cacophony of noise and confusion.

Jed struggled beside her, moving with the crowd to where the fire engines had gated across the road.

'Mum!'

Jed could see their home. There were flames at the window of the room he'd slept in, churning now with the smoke. A crazy orange and black cocktail of light and dark, spilling into the street. The glass had been blown out by the blaze. Broken fragments made the pavement glitter like it had snowed.

Jed reached for Kassia's arm. 'It's not safe. You need to—'

'It's my home!' she wailed.

'Kass!' He tried to pull her back. But she struggled free, and in the scuffle she spun round to face him.

'Is this to do with them? Is this because of you?'

Something snapped inside him. A tie holding things together, burned through by the fire. Anger surged, unrestrained, like the backdraught caused by fiercely fanned flames. 'This isn't my fault!' he yelled at her, pressing his fingers tight around her wrist.

'Let go of me!' Her eyes were wide. Her body recoiling as if his words had burned her.

214

His fingers slid free. 'I'm sorry. I'm sorry.'

But Kassia didn't hear him over the sounds of the shouting and the squeal of the sirens.

She lurched towards her mum.

Jed stood on the broken glass. Dante stood beside him. 'Please,' said Jed and he used no signs.

Dante's face was a mask of confusion.

Jed screwed his hand into a fist and thumped it hard against his own chest, rubbing in circles. 'I'm sorry! I'm so sorry!'

Behind him, he was aware of the sound of a thickening crowd. Cameras and mobile phones held high like battle flags to record the scene. He needed to leave. He needed to stay.

Kassia was totally still.

She stood in front of her home with her back to him.

Jed looked away and began to run.

Upstairs in a burning bedroom, a bird made of sugar melted in the flames.

And round the corner, hiding from the crowd, Carter wiped ash from his fingers. The tail of his coat floated behind him like thick black wings as he strode down Fleet Street and back towards the river.

There was nowhere to go but the cathedral.

St Paul's stood tall, as smoke formed a ring around

the spire. The golden gallery looked like the head of a match, sparking with flame.

Jed lurched up the steps and through the only door that had been opened. Reverend Cockren had hurried out to see what was happening. Jed slipped in behind him.

In the silence of the empty cathedral, Jed made his way to the crypt.

He needed to hide.

The crypt was long and cavernous. The walls were whitewashed; the ceiling lifted in peaked domes. Jed stumbled to the furthest corner. He slumped down against the pillar, pulled his knees into his chest and lowered his head. He held the silver pocket watch and the ticking marked the seconds as they passed.

He'd sat like this in Postman's Park. Then he'd hoped Kassia would find him. Now he prayed she wouldn't. Even with his eyes closed, he could see her. And the anger blazing in her eyes as her home had burned behind her. 'This is your fault,' they'd said. '*This* is because of *you*.'

He lifted his head and leaned back against the pillar and he tried to wipe away these things from his memory. Why, when his memory had failed him before, did it work so well now? And why had the look she'd given him, hurt so much he could hardly breathe?

* *

The fire had burned itself out and Fleet Street had
been re-opened to traffic for a couple of hours by the
time Reverend Solomon Cockren led Nat into the
crypt of the cathedral. 'I don't know what time he got
here,' the chaplain whispered. 'He's in a bad way. I got
your number from the hospital helpline. I was afraid
to move him, he looked so scared. I've closed the crypt.
You won't be disturbed here.'

Nat nodded. 'You did the right thing. Thank you.'

Reverend Cockren hesitated for a moment.
'This is awkward, but I need to ask that you get him
out of here as soon as possible. It's not good for
visitors, I mean.'

Nat's repetition of the word thank you made it
clear the doctor understood.

The chaplain turned to leave, relief obvious in his
expression. 'I'll be in the transept, if you need me.'

Nat nodded again. Then he walked to the end of
the crypt.

Jed looked up. His eyes were ringed with bruising,
though the shadowing had lessened. The swelling
around his lip was beginning to go down too. But his
skin looked grey and clammy.

'Can I?' said Nat, gesturing to the ground.

Jed shrugged his shoulders. Nat took this as a

positive sign and sat down beside him.

'I know how you feel,' said Nat.

'No you don't.'

'But I can imagine.'

'I thought knowing nothing was bad. I had no idea that things could be worse.'

Nat blew out a breath, considering how to go on, but before he could, Jed started to speak again.

'Is everyone safe? Dante? Anna? Jacob? Kassia?' The final name caught in the boy's throat.

'They're all safe.'

'But the house?'

'Destroyed. The building was old. Lots of brittle wood and beams and the flames caught hold quickly.'

'I'm so sorry.'

'Why? You didn't light the fire.'

Jed made a noise that sounded almost like a laugh. 'I didn't light the match. But you know, and I know, I'm the reason it happened. Kassia saw that.'

'We're not in the blame game, Jed. You can't be responsible for what other people have done.'

'Can't I?'

'Of course not. We're dealing with madmen. People who thought it was all right to keep you in a cage.'

'Perhaps that's the best place for me. Hand myself in to them, whoever they are, and then all this is over.'

Nat grabbed the boy's arm. 'I took an oath, Jed. A Hippocratic Oath. To do no harm and to protect those in my care. Granted, the broken nose after fainting last week was an issue. But I never mean to do harm.' He tried to lighten the mood with a smile. 'You're in my care and it's my job to keep you safe.'

'How exactly?'

'We have a plan. And it involves Spain.'

Things were moving quickly and Jed was struggling to keep up. His eyes hurt, his lip throbbed, and Nat's words echoed in the crypt and bounced around his head. But he finally understood the gist of the plan.

It was totally clear NOAH was after him. But proving this to the police, and that NOAH had been responsible for the fire, would take time. Jed didn't have time. They couldn't risk him being taken again. So Jacob had suggested the witness protection programme. It was used in times of crisis for people who needed to be out of harm's way. And in this case, out of harm's way meant Spain.

Anna's family owned a farmhouse there. They'd stayed on occasional summers, but the house had been empty since Kassia's dad had died. Jed would go to the farmhouse. It would be a perfect place to hide until things in London had settled down. With Jed out of the picture, Kassia and her Mum *had* to be safer.

Dante would travel with Jed. He'd be able to get him to the family farmhouse; would know his way around the village, and Dante being there wouldn't raise suspicions with the locals. They'd know he was part of the family who owned the property, even though years had passed since it had last been used – talking with your hands had a way of making you memorable. Jacob would come too. He'd help with travel plans, and he'd also been able to fix the problem of Jed's lack of paperwork or passport. Jacob had dealt with witness protection cases before. Kids who needed to take on new identities and make a rapid exit from their lives to somewhere new. He was working now to get everything in place. They could fly out of London early next morning.

Nat would stay to look after Anna and sort out the chaos caused by the fire. She'd move into Jacob's flat while he was away and until she had somewhere more permanent to move to.

So everything was arranged. Everyone was sorted. It just left Kassia.

'I need to speak to her,' begged Jed. 'I can't just leave and not say goodbye. Not be sure she knows I'm sorry.'

Nat shuffled awkwardly.

'She won't see me, will she?'

'It's not that. We need to get you out of London. They'll be watching for you. We can't give them a chance to find out where you are.'

'I have to try and make her see I never meant any of this to happen.'

'We don't have time.'

Jed tightened his grasp on the silver pocket watch and the seconds beat in rhythm with his pulse. 'Please. I'll do anything. Go anywhere. But you have to let me see her first.'

Nat looked around. Jed's voice was getting louder. Although the crypt was empty, he was worried someone might walk in and overhear them.

'Please.'

'OK. OK.' Nat looked down at his own watch. 'We need to have you on the road out of London by midnight. The flight leaves at seven. Jacob and Dante are meeting you at the airport. My job is to get you there.' He looked again at his watch. 'I'll text Anna. Get her to bring Kassia to Postman's Park at ten. You can have an hour. A chance to say goodbye. That's all.'

Jed stood beside the plaque commemorating Sarah Smith. She'd died in a fire, trying to save a friend. His pocket watch said it was now after ten, and his mind flipped between two types of worry. First, that his friend wouldn't come. Second, that she wasn't his friend any more.

Suddenly, Jed heard movement by the gate. A lone figure walking through the darkness. He practised again and again in his head what he'd say. How he was sorry. How he never meant to bring any of this chaos into her life. How he'd do anything he could to make it up to her.

He said none of these things. He tried to smile but his mouth wouldn't work and his lips wouldn't do as he wanted them to. So for a moment they just stared at each other.

Kassia looked small. Her shoulders hunched a little and her arms were folded. 'You're leaving,' she said at last.

'I don't want to.'

'It's best though.'

For her, of course it was best. He was the reason her home had been destroyed. Whether it was best for him was more complicated. He'd be safer in Spain, perhaps. He could work out what to do next, perhaps. But she would be here and he would be there and that didn't feel like it was best at all.

'Come with me,' he implored.

'What?'

'I want you to come with me.'

'I can't leave here.'

'Dante's coming.'

'Dante's different.'

'But your home's gone.'

'Whose fault is that?'

His face burned like she'd slapped him.

She tightened the fold of her arms. 'I didn't mean that.'

'No. You're right. It's my fault, and if I could go back in time and . . .' His words dried up. 'Please come with me,' he said again.

She just shook her head.

'I don't know how to deal with this,' he mumbled quietly. 'I still have no idea who I am. We're made of memories, aren't we? And I have none. Except ones with you in.'

'I have to stay here. I don't leave London. I've got things to do. Exams to take.'

'That's what you want?'

'Yes.' Her arms were so tightly folded that it looked to Jed as if she might crush her own ribs. 'I don't even go to school, Jed. How can I come with you to Spain?'

In his head there were answers. And they danced on the edge of his tongue. 'Kassia?'

'Yeah?'

'Thank you for coming to say goodbye.'

New York Times.

IS IT POSSIBLE THE PHILOSOHER'S STONE COULD BE REAL?

THE WEATHER

Fair today and Thursday; fresh north and northeast winds.

ONE CENT

Text of Austria-Hungary's Declaration of War.

JULES BOUCHER & GASTON SAUVAGE FAIL TO COMMENT

VIENNA, July 28.—Austria-Hungary's declaration of war against Serbia was gazetted here late this afternoon. The text is as follows:

"The Royal Government of Servia not having replied in a satisfactory manner to the note remitted to it by the Austro-Hungarian Minister in Belgrade on July 23, 1914, the Imperial and Royal Government finds itself compelled to proceed itself to safeguard its rights and interests and to have recourse for this purpose to force of arms.

—Austria-Hungary considers itself, therefore, from this moment in a state of war with Servia.

(Signed) "COUNT BERCHTOLD,

"Minister of Foreign Affairs of Austria-Hu—

---

of Fulcanelli as a cultural phenomenon is due partly to the mystery of various anecdotes pertaining to his life retells, in particular, how his most devote... a successful transmutation of 100 grams of lead into gold in a laboratory... georgi company with the use of a small quantity of the "Projection Powder" giv... ence of Julien Champagne and Gaston Sauvage.

Contents [hide]

1 Life
  1.1 Fulcanelli's Master
  1.2 Conclusion
2 Meeting in Paris with Jacques Bergier
3 Rendezvous in Spain
4 The Phonetic Cabala
5 Works
6 References in popular culture
7 References
8 External links

Life [edit]

Fulcanelli was undoubtedly a Frenchman, educated profoundly, and learned in the ways architecture, art, science, and languages. Fulcanelli wrote two books that were publishe... during 1926, having left his magnum opus with his only student, Eugène Canseliet. Le M... edition consisted of 300 copies and was published by Jean Schmit at 52 Rue Laffitte, P...

Theories about F... ...e that he was one or another famous French occultist... ...(he Valois), or another member of the Frères d'Helio... ...f Fulcanelli which included Eugène Canseliet, Jean-Ju... ...student of Canseliet's, believes that Fulcanelli's true ide... ...996 book, samples of writing by Jean-Julien Hubert Cha... ...and show considerable similarity.[5] In any event, by 1... ...from only sixteen, as his first student. During 1921, he accep... ...student] during 1922, two more students, Jules Boucher and... ...rue Rochechouart where he allegedly was successf...

...tion of the international bestseller The Morning of the Magicia... ...the Master Alchemist.[7]

Vulcan - Roman God of Fi...
It - sacred fire

DAY 39

7th April

The bruising on Jed's face had gone. The swelling of his lip, subsided. But his heart still felt like pulped watermelon.

'You've just got to focus on getting away,' Nat said.

'She was scared of me.'

'She was scared of the situation. And the fire. And the fact her home's been destroyed.'

'She was scared of *me*.'

'Did she say that?'

'No.'

Nat pulled the car into the outside lane to overtake a rather slow moving lorry. It was obvious he was hoping to use his concentration on the road as the excuse for the deepening silence.

How could Jed blame her?

He was scared himself.

The lights on the motorway flashed past. The car lagged behind the wake of hypnotising red tail lights. And eventually Nat put the radio on to try and drown out the discomfort. It wasn't long, though, before the newsreader made reference to the fire in Fleet Street, so he snapped off the radio and they drove on in awkward silence.

Jed's eyelids were growing heavy and his head was slipping now and then against the window when Nat pulled the car into the short-term car park of the airport. He grabbed a bag from the back seat and steered Jed into Departures. 'Head down. Don't make eye contact with anyone,' he whispered. Jed pulled up his hood and stared hard at his shoes.

Jacob and Dante were waiting to the left of the 'Information on London Transit' desk. Jacob passed Jed a passport and a printed e-ticket. 'Your name's Jack Albany,' he said. 'Best I could do at such short notice.' Jed flicked to the picture page. 'We used computer generated software to regress your image from the shot the newspapers used. It gives a sense of how you'd have looked a few years ago so the image shouldn't ring any alarm bells.'

Jed felt his pulped heart trying to beat a little faster.

He barely recognised the boy in the photo.

'We have to presume that if NOAH can firebomb a home, then they can muster up people to track you down,' explained Jacob. 'So there are three hurdles to a quick getaway. Check-in, Security and Boarding. I'm thinking you let me do the talking. If you need to communicate, then do it with Dante in sign.'

'Talking with your hands,' signed Dante, 'will make people less confident about speaking to you. They'll presume you can't hear and they won't want to embarrass you.'

Jed nodded and then moved his hand to make the sign for 'yes'.

'You're all set?' said Nat, passing Jed the bag he'd taken from the car. 'It's not much. Clothes, notebooks.' He unzipped it and let Jed rummage through. 'You packed it yourself, right?'

Jed looked confused, but before Nat could go on to explain more details about airport etiquette, Jacob pointed to his watch. Nat took Jed's hand and shook it vigorously. 'We'll find a way to make this come good. I promise.'

Jed wished he could believe him.

The first hurdle was easy. The girl at the check-in desk

seemed relieved to deal with them. The family in front had packed far too much luggage and had sworn at her about excess baggage costs. By the time Jacob reached the desk she was looking rattled and it was clear she wanted to get through things as quickly as possible.

Jacob put the three passports and e-tickets on the counter. He loaded the bags on to the belt. Jed hung back a little. He stared at his shoes and lifted his eyes only occasionally when Dante made tiny signs with his hands. Jed wasn't entirely sure how a heart turned to mush could still thunder so loudly inside him.

There were so many questions. Jed tried not to look up.

The conveyor belt moved the bags into the distance. 'Gate opens in fifteen minutes,' said the check-in girl as she flapped three tickets on the counter, indicating where she'd circled the gate number on each. 'Allow ten minutes for the walk there, and have a great flight.'

It was at the second hurdle that things got more difficult.

Jed followed Nat's lead, and when he reached Security he took off his shoes and put them into the clear plastic tub and pushed it through the screening device. Now there was nothing to stare at

229

except his socks.

Dante seemed convinced there wasn't enough metal in his hearing aids to set off the metal detector. He was right. This didn't stop the security guard wanting to see them, though.

Jed was sure his cheeks were reddening. He was sure, too, that the vein on his neck was popping. If the guard looked back down the line, he was sure to see how nervous Jed was.

Dante removed the aids from his ears and held them out for the guard to see. Jed saw Dante's palm was slick with sweat. He also saw how vulnerable Dante looked. The guard was muttering, fumbling with the hearing aids and Dante was trying hard to keep eye contact with the guy, fronting it out. He inspected the hearing aids, then passed them back, curling his lips as if slightly disgusted. Dante scooped them up and slid them back into his ears. The guard nodded for Dante to leave and for Jed to walk on. He was pretty sure his breathing was returning to normal – until the alarm sounded.

Jed looked at Jacob in panic as he was steered to the left of the security line and asked to spread his arms. A man wearing latex gloves began to pat at Jed's shoulders and torso, then slid his hands across his hips. His hand lingered over the pocket, and he reached inside. He pulled the pocket watch out and let it hang from the chain. It swung like a pendulum. 'All metal items should have been removed, sir,' the guard huffed, tossing the watch into an empty plastic tub. Jed nodded, but a hard slap of his shins made it clear the search wasn't over.

By the time the guard had finished, Jed was shaking. It took him several minutes to re-tie the laces on his shoes and he nearly dropped the watch when it finally appeared at the end of the conveyor belt.

Jacob's expression was easy to read now. He was begging Jed to hold it together and not lose his nerve. Jed wasn't sure he could.

By the time they reached the Departure Gates, all the seats in the waiting room were taken. The three of them leaned against the wall. 'Hang in there, mate,' Dante signed encouragingly. But Jed was tired and his heart felt as if it had fallen out of his chest.

They called the passengers in blocks of seats to the gate. 'Nearly there,' whispered Jacob, as the group in front made their way towards the covered ramp leading to the plane. Jed was the first to move forward as their seat numbers were called. He cursed himself for reacting to the vocal call and not waiting for Jacob to take the lead. Any chances of him being seen as deaf would be blown because of his reaction to the tannoy address. It meant anyone who spoke to him would expect a spoken answer. He funnelled into the line, his ticket and passport quivering in his hand.

'Enjoy your trip,' said the girl at the barrier. She tore his ticket and kept a section for herself. Jed allowed himself to breathe. 'Ooh, and sir.' She grabbed his shoulder and scooped something from the ground. 'Is this yours?' She thrust a crumpled newspaper at him. The front page was filled with a picture of Fleet Street on fire. Jed wobbled a little and the paper fell to the floor. 'Are you OK, sir?' she said nervously. 'Do you want me to get anyone?'

No! That's exactly what he didn't want.

Jacob pushed forwards. 'My friend's a little nervous of flying,' he offered. 'And no. It's not his paper.'

It's my story, though, Jed thought, as Jacob steadied him and the three of them made their way towards the entrance to the plane. And he wasn't really sure that, however far they ran, they'd really get away from it.

* *

It was getting dark by the time the rented car pulled up the gravel drive in front of the farmhouse. Jacob unloaded their bags and Dante searched for the key in his pocket. Jed staggered a little as he clambered from the car. The lack of sleep and stress in the airport was taking its toll.

The house hadn't been used for years but Dante explained that an agency managed things, checking on the place now and then to make sure nothing was broken.

He swung open the front door, which led into a large tiled hallway. Doors peeled off to the left and a slatted staircase wound to the right. Cloths draped over the furniture and dust mites danced in the skirt of the light.

Dante began pulling the furniture covers off to reveal seats and tables, a battered piano and a sideboard groaning under the weight of family photos. When the cloth caught on the edge of one frame and knocked it forward, he did nothing to stop it falling. The photo of his mum stayed face down.

Jacob found his way to the kitchen. He flicked switches to reinstate the electricity and turned on the taps until they stopped spluttering and gurgling and the water ran clear. Jed carried the box of food they'd bought at the service station and packed it away in the cupboards. Then he cooked them all an omelette in a huge iron pan, and they sat in the dimly lit dining room. Jed watched the other two eat, but he barely touched the food himself. Darkness closed in around the farmhouse.

Jacob was keen they got as much sleep as possible. Dante showed them the bedrooms upstairs. There were three of them. Dante's room was in the eaves. Jacob took the main bedroom, which had an office attached that was apparently where Anna worked when the house had first been used as a family home. That left Kassia's room for Jed.

He stood for a moment in the silence.

There had to have been a mistake. He understood she hadn't been here for years, but it looked so different from Kassia's room back in Fleet Street.

It was cluttered. Crammed with soft toys and patterned cushions and throws. There were fairy lights around the headboard. A dream catcher hung at the window. And the walls were papered, not with timetables and schedules, but photos and paintings; tickets to shows and theme parks. There was a sketch of a beach displayed in a crooked frame and some seashells iced with dust arranged in a spiral on a shelf. Just beside the window, the end of its shaft tucked behind the frame, was a long peacock's feather. Jed looked at the pattern of the eye. It stared back at him.

That night Jed slept downstairs in the chair by the window.

And this time, instead of trying to remember, he fought to forget.

365ft

CALENDAR, 1926

©LONGITUDIN

SECTION

Figúra XXXVIII.

V. ESSENTIA EXALTATA

Figúra XXXVII.

EXALTATIO V. ESSENTIÆ

48.8530°N   2.3498°E

DAY 45

13th April

Kassia heard the front door click open. The sound startled her, but it was only Nat. Jacob had given them all a key to make coming and going easier.

Her uncle stood in the doorway. He had a small cardboard box in his hand.

'What's that?'

He looked embarrassed as if searching for a good way to explain.

'Uncle Nat. What is it?'

'The police gave it to me,' he said. 'It's what's left from the fire.'

Kassia could see her mother choking back tears. Anna took the box and laid the things one by one on the table. 'That's all there is?'

Nat put his hand on top of hers. 'It's official stuff they thought you might need. All they'd let me bring until the investigation's complete. Which isn't going well, by the way. They think it was an electrical fault.'

'What! That's ridiculous!' snapped Kassia. 'You've told them. About NOAH!'

'It's an international organisation, Kass. If the police can pin the fire on faulty hair straighteners, then they will.'

Anna turned over the folders and files from the box. She stacked her passport on top of Kassia's. 'How did Dante—?'

'His passport was in the safe at work,' explained Nat. 'He'd needed it for some DBS check.'

Kassia came and stood beside her mother. She picked up her passport from the table. It smelled of smoke. A piece of paper caught on the cover fluttered to the floor. It was the photograph of Jed. Its edges had been chewed by the fire, but his eyes still stared forward, as if begging for someone to help him work out who he was. Anna picked up the picture from the floor, placed it on the table and then brushed her hands together, her nose curling as a tiny tear of soot smeared on her hand. Nat handed her a cloth and she wiped her fingers vigorously. If they'd been made of silver they would have shone. 'We've got to get you back on track with your revision now,' she said, turning towards her daughter. 'It will be awkward without your notes and books but we can't let things slip, particularly now.'

The way her mother looked at her forced Kassia to bite her lip.

'I've drawn up a new schedule and I think the sooner we get back on target, the better. Show the universe nothing can defeat us. Agreed?' She reached out to tap her daughter's hand.

They'd lost everything and her mum still wanted her to work. To be tested. Wasn't this test enough?

'You have the whole world open to you,' her mum continued. 'You'll make a brilliant doctor. But the work starts now.'

Kassia had no idea what to say, so she said nothing.

Nat took a deep breath and slumped down in a chair. 'When I was at the police station they also gave me this. It's a note from Reverend Cockren.'

'Him! The guy who was so freaked out by Jed.'

'Yeah, well. Maybe he feels guilty.' Nat went on. 'He knows your home's been destroyed. The note says if you need somewhere to study, some place to work that isn't here, you could make use of the Library at St Paul's. Kind of a nice invitation, I reckon.'

'*You* asked him, Mum, didn't you?' Kassia could hear the tightness in her own voice.

'The man offered us help. And this is practical. It's a way forward.'

Kassia wasn't sure she wanted to go forward.

'I want you to do this for *you*!' Anna pleaded. 'Put all this behind us and focus on the future. Where we should have been focusing in the first place. This is a chance for you, Kassia, to make something of your life. And I don't want you to waste it.'

Kassia grabbed her reading book. Her eyes were stinging. So she looked away.

'That's the date Dante and Kassia's dad died.' Jacob looked over Jed's shoulder as he wrote.

The pen jogged across the page and Jed jerked back in the chair. 'Wow, you scared me! How long you been there?'

Jacob crunched on the triangle of toast he was eating. 'Just got here, mate. You OK? You look like you've seen a ghost.'

Jed put the pen down awkwardly and shut the notebook. 'I was just thinking, that's all.'

'Thinking and writing, obviously. So what's with August 20th 2003?'

Jed rubbed his face with his hands. 'I don't know. When I went with Kassia to the graveyard, I saw that's when her dad had died. But I seemed to know that date before. Like it was important to me as well as her.' He took a deep breath. 'Did you know their dad?'

Jacob took another bite of toast. 'Sure. He was a great guy. You'd have liked him. He did a lot for Dante. With the signing and stuff. Anna was keener for oral communication. You know, lots of speech therapy to get Dante to speak. Tristan pressed for him to use sign. Caused problems, I think, but it was my job just to deal with what was.'

Jed didn't really understand the complications, but he nodded anyway.

'Anyhow, perhaps the date's your birthday?'

'Maybe,' said Jed nervously. 'But I remember others too. Four more.' He opened the notebook again and showed Jacob the list, ranging from 1927 up to 2003. 'If I'm related to this Fulcanelli guy, then all the alchemy stuff I've drawn makes sense. But the dates? I don't get them.'

Jacob pulled out a chair and sat down at the table. 'OK. Well, let's see.' He pulled the notebook closer to him. 'You know there was a heatwave in 2003. August 20th was when it was at its peak. Lots of people in France died.'

'Kassia's dad was in France, wasn't he?'

'Yep. Police reckoned the heat might have contributed to the crash. Anyhow let's look at these other dates. Wow. Some of them are a long time ago, mate. None of these can have been your birthday.'

'I know.'

Jacob looked thoughtful for a moment. 'You know, Anna used to write newspaper articles. I saw this book in the room I'm using. *The Century Through News.* Give me a mo.'

He hurried from the table and returned with a huge red book. Inside, arranged chronologically, were newspaper headlines and front pages from every date in the twentieth century.

Jed flicked to the first date on his list. June 29th 1927. The main news item was about a solar eclipse. This was mildly interesting but didn't mean anything to Jed.

The headline from December 23rd 1933 was more upsetting. A train crash just outside Paris. Jed didn't know what to say so hurried on to the next date.

15th August 1951. Another item about France. This time a story about lots of people dying in a town called Pont-Saint-Esprit. Poison apparently. 'That's awful,' said Jacob. 'Things aren't going well for France in this search.'

'Fulcanelli was French, wasn't he?' said Jed. 'So maybe these are dates from my family history?'

'Maybe?' Jacob turned to the next date. 'December

26th 1999. Well if you're right, your relatives were caught up in a terrible storm on this date. This isn't a happy list, mate.'

No it wasn't. 'Could be coincidence, though, right? Five dates I think are important when actually they mean nothing?'

'Of course,' said Jacob quietly. 'Could just be a random list of dates you think you remember and actually mean nothing at all.' He closed the book firmly. 'I wouldn't worry about it. We're safe here now and we just have to concentrate on keeping away from those nutters at NOAH. Give yourself some slack and try and rest.'

Jed nodded. And he made a promise that he would, but the words tasted like sawdust on his tongue.

DAY 46

14th April

'I'm so sorry for your loss.' Reverend Solomon Cockren made it sound as if someone had died. 'Losing a home with all those memories and important things stored away,' he explained. 'I certainly understand the importance of a physical building.' He stretched his arms out and lifted his eyes to take in the Cornhill paintings on the inner dome above him.

Kassia mumbled her thanks and looked down at the floor.

'I take it from your mother that you are home-schooled,' the chaplain went on. 'So your little ruse about a school project had many holes in it,' he chuckled.

'I do have to do projects,' said Kassia, almost snappily. 'My mum has to fill in forms about the work I do. She makes me study quite hard.'

'Of course.' He paused, and Kassia wondered if he was allowing time for her to apologise for misleading him the last time she was at St Paul's. She said nothing. She didn't want to remember that time.

'Still, a home-schooler without a home is in need of a school and so if you follow me I'll show you the Wren Library. I think you'll find it a satisfactory place to do your studies.' He twisted his hands together for a moment, as if he'd lost the next sentence he wanted to say. Then, as if finding it tucked inside his palm, he spread his hands and blurted it out. 'The boy's gone, has he?'

Kassia nodded.

'I don't want to know where, but I do need to be sure . . . for security reasons you understand . . . that he is – how shall I put this? – out of the picture.'

Again Kassia nodded.

'So you never did find out exactly who he was, then? Shame. Great shame.'

'He's gone,' Kassia said.

She was sure she saw a smile twitch across the chaplain's lips but he said no more, and led her instead through the cathedral and up a winding staircase. 'We're in the process of planning renovation,' he said eventually, as they climbed. 'There's no access to the public, so apart from the occasional historian coming in to take books to re-catalogue, you should be undisturbed.'

He opened the door and led her into a huge vaulted space lined with books. There were two levels. The upper floor was a balcony running all around the room. Huge stone pillars, with sculpted pictures of open books stretched between the dark wooden shelving. The lower floor was a confusion of tables and display cabinets. There was a huge oil painting of a man, who was looking very serious, hung above a vast fireplace, and in front of that, a long oak desk with intricately carved edging and thick bulbous legs. To the left of the desk sat an enormous book with a thick leather cover and metal clasps keeping it shut.

'Wow, where do all these books come from?' said Kassia. The hundreds of soft brown and red spines circling the room made the space feel warm, and it was almost as if the room was glowing.

'People donate them when they die. We're lucky to have copies of some of the rarest books in the world here.'

'And what are they all about?' said Kassia, walking along the line of numbered shelving, her shoes clipping on the wooden floor.

'All sorts really. Religion, of course, but we have lots here you might find unusual. Ancient books covering all sorts of areas, like superstition and herbal remedies. In the past there was little separation between the physical world and the spiritual.'

'Do you have alchemy books here?'

'None,' said Reverend Cockren sharply. 'Not things a church tends to keep copies of. When Sir Isaac Newton died, his books on alchemy were all nailed shut to the shelves by well-meaning monks who'd decided the books were an abomination.' He took a deep breath. 'Anyway, you'll be wanting more modern modes of study, I'm sure. Your mother tells me you're preparing for GCSEs. There's a socket to plug in your laptop just here.'

Kassia put Nat's laptop on the table next to the enormous book with the huge metal clasps.

'Make yourself at home,' said Reverend Cockren. 'Ooh, and here's the password for the Wi-Fi.' He scribbled a series of letters and numbers down on the edge of a blank page in Kassia's notebook.

'St Paul's has Wi-Fi?'

'St Paul's has a staff cappuccino machine and a Facebook page, my dear. We're not in the Middle Ages any longer.'

His words rippled like lake water pushed out by a stone as he shut the door behind him, and as Kassia sat down at the huge wooden desk in front of the fireplace, she felt as though she'd slipped back in time. The room was quiet, but the air hummed slightly, as if the books were breathing.

She entered the password Reverend Cockren had given her and waited for the wireless to activate. It seemed strange to be using something so modern in a space so filled with history; the old and the new so close together. As the connection icon whirred round and round, she ran her hand across the huge leather book on the edge of the table. The thought of more online past papers practice filled her with dread, and she wasn't sorry at all that the Wi-Fi was taking a long time to connect. The leather under her fingers felt good. The smell of the books as enticing as newly cut grass. The icon continued to whir. Like a dragon eating its tail.

She shook her head. She must concentrate. She'd come here to work. To keep her mother happy. And thinking about Jed wouldn't do that. Still the icon spun.

She pushed back from the screen. She had to think about something else.

She unlatched the clasps of the huge leather book next to her and heaved it open. She couldn't make out a word. The text was in Latin maybe. Or Greek. The words on the thin yellowed pages were a jumble of shapes and figures, almost like a code. She eased the book shut and a soft cloud of dust lifted on the air and then scattered. It was as if the book was whispering its secrets, but Kassia had no idea what it was saying.

She wondered if that was how it felt for Jed. His life a story he couldn't read.

And there she was again.

No matter how hard she tried to block him from her thinking, Jed was there. Always there.

The Wi-Fi had finally connected. She clicked angrily on the keyboard and pulled up the Google search page. Her finger hovered over the letter M. She seriously couldn't face another past paper yet, and if Jed was going to nag away at her, despite being miles away, then she could use just a tiny bit of time to check things out. Her mother wouldn't know how long it had taken Reverend Cockren to sort things for her. Ten minutes wouldn't hurt. Surely?

She enjoyed the logic of the timing. It was a relief to allow herself to think about him. To use ten minutes to check the only meaningful clue they'd discovered. *Fulcanelli.* Maybe there weren't Fulcanellis living in London any more. But maybe there were clues about the Fulcanelli name from history that might lead somewhere.

There were lots of pages to view.

The first page talked about how the name might have been a play on words. Vulcan, the ancient Roman god of fire, plus El, the Canaanite name for God, and therefore meaning sacred fire. Kassia didn't like all these fire references.

She clicked on another page. This one said Fulcanelli the alchemist they'd read about was French. They hadn't dwelled on that bit back at Jacob's. Maybe that's why there were no Fulcanellis in London. Maybe all Jed needed to do was to track down his family in France. Why hadn't they thought of that? Her thinking brought her back to the fire. It had been such a rush. Such a nightmare. No time to really think through the information they'd found.

She clicked on another page.

Fulcanelli certainly had lots of mentions. This new page went on about the alchemy. The Brothers of Heliopolis were pointed out too. Seemed like there was a group of four of them. Eugene Canseliet, Jean-Julien Champagnes and Jules Boucher, along with Fulcanelli. And yes, here were the references to making the philosopher's stone. And the fact they'd made gold. So that really *was* the reason NOAH was after Jed. With all the funding in the world, science could lead them anywhere they wanted. No wonder they wanted him to share the family secret.

Kassia scrolled through the page. Fulcanelli had written books apparently. And there was stuff about a gasworks and . . .

Kassia narrowed her eyes. She re-read the sentence. She zoomed in on the page.

And then she lifted her hands from the keyboard and clamped them tight over her mouth.

No. No. No. This couldn't be right. That couldn't be true.

She stifled her breath in her hand and closed her eyes, blotting out the words that had burned into her brain.

It wasn't about gold.

It was about something worth much, much more than that.

And now the reason NOAH were really after Jed made complete and utter sense.

DAY 50

18th April

They'd been in Spain for over a week. They hadn't really got a plan. And every time Jed tried to sleep, he had nightmares about a car driving fast, its headlights blazing. He'd jerk awake, his forehead beaded with perspiration.

He thought it was just a dream this time too – until the room exploded with light. He jumped up from the chair and stumbled to the window, clutching the edge of the curtain hard. Wheels spun on the drive, crunching on the gravel. An engine droned.

Then silence. Then darkness.

It had taken them eight days, but NOAH had found him. Jed had two choices. Fight or flight.

These people had already kept him in a cage and burned a house to the ground. Jed knew he should run.

Jacob and Dante were upstairs. Shouting up to

them wouldn't be enough. He had to be sure Dante knew. He charged the stairs two at a time, crashed open Dante's door and shook him awake. Jed's signs were scrambled, but not incoherent. Dante had no doubt they were in danger. They raced together to Jacob's room. Jed could hear voices. Outside the house in the courtyard, but in Jacob's room too.

Jed thundered his fists at Jacob's door. 'We have to leave!'

Jacob stood with his arms raised, a mobile phone clutched in his left hand. 'It's OK. It's OK!'

'They've found us. We've got to go.' Jed lurched towards the window, assessing the fall into the back garden. Jacob tugged Jed back. Jed could hear the front door opening. Voices on the stairs.

'Jed. Wait!'

Jacob tugged at his shoulder. Dante too, pulled at his arm as if he'd read the situation differently. Were they scared of the drop to the garden? Did they think they should stay and front this out?

Another voice, this time in the hallway.

'Jed. Wait.'

Jed turned from the window.

Kassia.

She stood in the doorway. Her hands were stretched. A mobile phone in her hand. 'It's me.'

Jed looked across at Jacob. He nodded and put down the phone he held.

Jed had no words. No signs. Nothing.

'I'm so sorry.' She was walking towards him. 'I didn't mean to scare you.'

'You came!'

She nodded. 'I came.'

'But . . .'

She held her finger up to her lips. 'It's going to be OK,' she said.

'But how? Why?'

'Nat arranged the flight. I got a taxi from the airport. Mum wasn't happy about it, but hey. I'm here now.'

He waited for the other part of her answer.

'I realised we were in this together,' she said, 'and I couldn't let you face it alone.'

Jacob nodded over at Dante. 'We'll go and make drinks . . . or something else useful,' he said, winking.

The corners of Kassia's mouth curled up slightly.

Dante closed the door as he and Jacob left the room.

'You came,' Jed said again.

Kassia nodded. 'I'm sorry I took so long.'

Jed was one hundred per cent sure he could forgive her.

in parti-colored robes of yellow and white, which were distinguished from each other only by the nature of the stuff; the first was of gold and silver brocade; the second, of silk; the third, of wool; the fourth, of linen. The first of these personages carried in his right hand a sword; the second, two golden keys; the third, a pair of scales; the fourth, a spade: and, in order to aid sluggish minds which would not have seen clearly through the transparency of these attributes, there was to be read, in large, black letters, on the hem of the robe of brocade, MY NAME IS NOBILITY; on the hem of the silken robe, MY NAME IS CLERGY; on the hem of the woolen robe, MY NAME IS MERCHANDISE; on the hem of the linen robe, MY NAME IS LABOR. The sex of the two male characters was briefly indicated to every judicious spectator, by their shorter robes, and by the cap which they wore on their heads; while the two female characters, less briefly clad, were covered with hoods.

Much ill-will would also have been required, not to comprehend, through the medium of the poetry of the prologue, that Labor was wedded to Merchandise, and Clergy to Nobility, and that the two happy couples possessed in common a magnificent golden dolphin, which they desired to adjudge to the fairest only. So they were roaming about the world seeking and searching for this beauty, and, after having successively rejected the Queen of Golconda, the Princess of Trebizonde, the daughter of the Grand Khan of Tartary, etc., Labor and Clergy, Nobility and Merchandise, had come to rest upon the marble table of the Palais de Justice, and to utter, in the presence of the honest audience, as many sentences and maxims as could then be dispensed at the Faculty of Arts, at examinations, sophisms, determinances, figures, and acts, where the masters took their degrees.

All this was, in fact, very fine.

Nevertheless, in that throng, upon which the four allegories vied with each other in pouring out floods of metaphors, there was no ear more attentive, no heart that palpitated more, not an eye was more haggard, no neck more outstretched, than the eye, the ear, the neck, and the heart of the author, of the poet, of that brave Pierre Gringoire, who had not been able to resist, a moment before, the joy of telling his name to two pretty girls. He had retreated a few paces from them, behind his pillar, and there he listened, looked, enjoyed. The amiable applause which had greeted the beginning of his prologue was still echoing in his bosom, and he was completely absorbed in that species of ecstatic contemplation with which an author beholds his ideas fall, one by one, from the mouth of the actor into the vast silence of the audience. Worthy Pierre Gringoire!

It pains us to say it, but this first ecstasy was speedily disturbed. Hardly had Gringoire raised this intoxicating cup of joy and triumph to his lips, when a drop of bitterness was mingled with it.

A tattered mendicant, who could not collect any coins, lost as he was in the midst of the crowd, and who had not probably found sufficient indemnity in the pockets of his neighbors, had hit upon the idea of perching himself upon some conspicuous point, in order to attract looks and alms. He had, accordingly, hoisted himself, during the first verses of the prologue, with the aid of the pillars of the reserve gallery, to the cornice which ran round the balustrade at its lower edge; and there he had seated himself, soliciting the attention and the pity of the multitude, with his rags and a hideous sore which covered his right arm. However, he uttered not a word.

The silence which he preserved allowed the prologue to proceed without hindrance, and no perceptible disorder would have ensued, if ill-luck had not willed that the scholar Joannes should catch sight, from the heights of his pillar, of the mendicant and his grimaces. A wild fit of laughter took possession of the young scamp, who, without caring that he was interrupting the spectacle, and disturbing the universal composure, shouted boldly,—

"Look! see that sickly creature asking alms!"

29061927

OSS X-2 C
Branch su

Bremen
Kassel
Heidelber
Nuremberg
Hamburg CLAS
Munich
Innsbruck
Klagenfur
Linz

Walter Lang reports that Fulcanelli
communicated with ▓▓▓▓▓ergier to
warn French atomic physicist André
▓▓▓▓▓▓▓ of man's impending use of
nuclear weapons. According to
Fulcanelli, nuclear weapons had been
used before, by and against humanity
Prof. Helbronner and ▓▓▓▓▓▓▓▓▓▓▓ among
others were assassinated by the Gestapo
towards the end of ▓▓▓▓▓▓

The meeting between Jacques Bergier and
Fulcanelli occurred during June 1937 in
a laboratory of the Gas Board in Paris.
The meeting was arranged so that
Fulcanelli could warn Bergier about
man's impending use of nuclear weapons.
According to Neil Powell, the
following is a translation of the
original verbatim transcript of the
rendezvous. Fulcanelli told Bergier:

"You're on the brink of success, as
indeed are several other of our
scientists today. Please, allow me, be
very very careful. I warn you... The
liberation of ▓▓▓▓▓▓▓▓▓▓ is easier
than you think and the ▓▓▓▓▓▓▓▓▓▓
artificially produced can poison the
atmosphere of our planet in a very
short time, a few years. Moreover,
atomic explosives can be produced from
a few grains of metal powerful enough
to destroy whole cities. I'm telling
you this for a fact: the alchemists
    known it for a very long time

The secret of alchemy is this: there is a way of manipulating
matter and energy so as to produce what modern scientists
call 'a field of force'. The field acts on the observer and puts
him in a privileged position vis-à-vis the Universe. From this
position he has access to the realities which are ordinarily
hidden from us by time and space, matter and energy. This
is what we call the Great Work."

When Bergier asked Fulcanelli about the Philosopher's
Stone, the alchemist answered: "...the vital thing is not the
transmutation of metals but that of the experimenter
himself. It is an ancient secret that a few people rediscover
each century. Unfortunately, only a handful are successful..."

DAY 51
19th April

The sun was just rising.

Kassia and Jed sat in the kitchen. Light danced on the table. Kassia's hands were gripped tightly round a mug of coffee. She was watching the patterns ebb and flow across the wooden surface. She didn't look at Jed.

'I still can't believe you came. I thought when I said goodbye to you in London—'

'I found something out.'

Jed put his own mug down on the table. 'OK. That's good. It *is* good, right?'

Kassia kept looking down. 'I'm not sure.'

'Hey. You can tell me anything, you know. I've literally got nothing to lose.'

She knew he was trying to laugh, but his voice sounded as thin as paper.

She took a deep breath, put the mug on the

table and looked up. 'What do you remember about alchemists?'

Jed shrugged. 'Oh, OK. The family link thing. Erm, they made gold, or tried to anyway. That's what NOAH wants, isn't it? Gold to fund their research. They thought I was their way in.'

'What else did alchemists try and make? Besides gold.'

'Well, the philosopher's stone was the key, wasn't it? The thing they all hoped they'd find. And if they made that, then they'd be able to turn lead into gold.' He fidgeted nervously. 'That's it, isn't it? It seems so long ago when we were looking into all that alchemy stuff to do with the symbol. It feels like another lifetime.'

Kassia folded her arms in front of her and bit the edge of her lip. She couldn't do this. She couldn't move him on from the place of not knowing to the place she'd found. Once she'd said the words, nothing could take them back.

'Kass. You're scaring me.'

Back at Fleet Street she'd been scared of him. That was because of the destruction. Now he scared her again. But the reason was reversed.

'They didn't just hope to make gold,' she said.

'So what else then?'

'After gold there was one thing left to make. One thing which was even more precious.' She looked across the table. Nothing in his face showed he knew where she was going with this. But in a second he'd know everything she did. There'd be no going back. The phrase made her blanch. Going back. Could she really tell him?

Jed got up from the table and walked so that he was standing beside her. He took her hands and turned her round in the chair, then he kneeled on the floor so his face was close to hers. 'What are you trying to tell me?'

'They wanted to make the elixir of life. A way of living for ever. That was the alchemists' ultimate aim. Not gold.'

His eyes seemed smaller. Tightened in concentration. 'So you reckon NOAH think I've got the family recipe for making everlasting life?' he laughed. 'That really would be a recipe worth having, and I suppose it makes sense of all that stuff they said about death. Fulcanelli knew how to make the elixir and they think I know the secret. Shame I never met the guy then, isn't it?'

Something was happening to her breathing. The air wasn't reaching down into her lungs any more.

'But you've found out about this Fulcanelli, have you?'

She nodded.

'And did you find out where he wrote down this recipe?'

She shook her head.

'OK. So we know what NOAH wanted now. But we don't know where it is. Right?'

'Jed . . .'

'Come on, Kass. You've travelled all this way and you said we're in this together. And I can't tell you how good that makes me—'

'You're Fulcanelli, Jed.'

'Well, it's my name. We got that bit back in London.' His face was lined now, the eyes so small they were straining for light.

'I mean THE Fulcanelli.'

He sank back on to his heels. He angled his head to the side. She watched him. And she knew the line she was about to cross was as sharp as wire.

'Fulcanelli lived in the 1920s. In Paris. And he *did* make the elixir of life. And it reprogrammed his lifespan.'

His hands were tight around hers. So tight she feared the circulation would stop. But this was no time for stopping. She'd come this far. There were only a few more steps to take before the fall from the precipice was complete.

'The websites say Fulcanelli left the Brothers of Heliopolis after he'd made the elixir. When his friends saw him again, he hadn't aged. In fact, he looked younger than before.'

She was sure her fingers would break.

'Fulcanelli had managed to make his body age backwards in time. That's why NOAH want you. It makes sense of everything. You're Fulcanelli. You've taken the elixir for eternal life.'

Jed clambered to his feet, reeling as if he'd been struck hard across the side of the head.

'Jed, please!' Kassia pushed the chair away and it clattered to the floor.

He lurched against the table, his back towards her, his hands pushed down hard to keep him standing. 'You shouldn't—'

'What, Jed? I shouldn't have come? Or I shouldn't have told you?'

He tried to focus on her but in front of his eyes a huge dragon swirled and turned, boring a hole deep into his memory. *A train careered off the tracks; the sun blazed red and then dissolved into darkness; winds tore trees from the ground; fallen bodies lined the streets. And a river rising higher and higher choking all the air from the sky.*

'It makes sense of everything!' she cried. 'Why no one knows you. Why you don't remember. The symbol you drew. The alchemy shapes. All of it.'

'No! You're wrong! You have to be wrong!' He could feel his voice coming in spurts, as if she'd gashed open a wound and blood was pumping from it.

'We can work this out.'

'How? You're telling me I'm some guy from a hundred years ago!' The dragon in front of his eyes twisted and circled, faster and faster. Jed heard again the words he'd heard in the cage. *We've been tracking you for over a hundred years.* 'You're wrong! You have to be wrong!'

She was clutching her hands together; the fingers linked as if she was praying. 'There're sites all over the internet. Theories about how he did it. But they say the same thing. That Fulcanelli stopped time. He reversed it. Realignment. Transdifferentiation. There're all these words. But they mean the same!'

'That I'm a freak!'

'No. That you're clever and wise and you've done something incredible!'

'You're wrong!'

'Please listen. Let me explain.' Her hands were open now, reaching towards him, but he pulled away.

'You're telling me I've messed around with life and

death. That I'm old. That this . . .' he pummelled his hand against his chest, 'that all this is messed up! How can you be right?'

'The gasworks.'

'What!'

'From the top of the O2. When you panicked. Fulcanelli went to a gasworks in the forties.'

'So?'

'It fits, Jed. It *all* fits.'

The dragon swirled again, its jaws opening wide, its massive fangs ready to pierce their prey. And centred by the six segments of its body, Jed saw a memory he'd seen before. *An old man breathing words of warning.*

'Please, Jed. We can work this out!'

'My god, Kassia. What am I?'

'You're YOU. That hasn't changed. You're still the person I met nearly two months ago. The person who walked with me in Postman's Park, who made a bird out of sugar. None of this changes that.'

'It changes *everything*!' He thumped his hand against the table, desperate to feel something, anything, that wasn't this.

'Please, Jed. You're scaring me!'

'I'm scaring *you*? You come here and you tell me that I'm . . . what? An immortal? That I'm going to live for ever?' He ran his fingers through his hair.

Then, as if dug from somewhere deep inside his mind, he knew what he should say. 'Prove it!'

'What? It makes sense. Everything fits. It's why NOAH are after you!'

'Prove it!' He was shouting now.

'How? What d'you want me to do? Test whether you'll live or die? Strangle you? Drown you? To see if you survive. Is that what you want?'

The dragon in front of Jed's eyes opened its jaws wide. *Water bubbled in its mouth, dripping like blood from its fangs. Raging, roaring water that peaked upwards then surged towards an open sea.* The jaws of the snake clamped shut and Jed felt the jolt through every single muscle in his body. He staggered against the table. He reached out his hand and the mug tumbled to the floor and smashed into a hundred pieces.

In his memory he was back in the River Thames.

And he remembered why.

'I couldn't stop him. He was so scared.' Kassia was sobbing and her signs were broken.

Jacob watched from the doorway as Dante put his arms around his sister and hugged her tight. He didn't use signs to talk to her. He didn't need to. She knew he was telling her that he would find Jed.

'Where d'you think he'd go?' she asked, hiccoughing through her tears.

'Where do you go, when things overwhelm you?'

'I should come too.'

Dante took a deep breath. 'Let me try to bring him home first.'

The white city of Olvera sat in the shadow of a castle and at the foot of the castle was a cemetery. It wasn't like the cemetery in London. Here, coffins had been slid into small niches in the wall, the bodies of the dead lined up like books on a shelf. Jed sat with his back against the cold marble stone. He pulled his knees into his chest, his body as near to the dead as it could be. He closed his eyes. But even in the darkness he could still see Kassia's face. And the words she'd said, replayed over and over in his head.

He'd run, like he'd done in London. Then, it had been to escape. When there had still been hope that if he ran hard enough and for long enough, he would be free. He knew now that if he kept running for ever he wouldn't get away from the truth she'd told him.

And it was the thought of 'for ever' that scared him most.

Is that what this meant? If he really was Fulcanelli and he'd made the elixir of life, would he live for ever, his life stretching on for eternity; all that he was, trapped inside his re-aged body. He'd swapped one cage for another and this time he couldn't see the key.

Footsteps on the cobbles made him look up.

Dante stood in front of him, the sun forming a halo behind him.

Jed couldn't sign. His hands sat limp in his lap. He wasn't sure he could speak either. He felt like he had when he'd first woken up in the hospital, his mind a mess of noise and fear – every word he'd ever known drowned out. Had he known then, what he knew now? Is that why the words had failed him and his mind had suffocated all memory?

Dante sank down to sit beside him. He leaned his back against the marble too. And he took a notepad and pen from his pocket. He waited for a moment, looking around at the rows and rows of memorials and the plastic flowers arranged in vases in front of them. Then he wrote across the paper and put the notepad down on the ground.

Jed looked to the side and read the note. 'Do you want to talk?' Jed shrugged. What was there to say? He was a freak. Conversation over.

Dante took the paper and pen and added more. 'I thought perhaps words on the page would be easier.

Not sure your sign language is up to a conversation like this yet.'

Jed took the paper and scribbled an answer underneath. 'She told you, then?'

Dante nodded.

'And you're weirded out?'

Again Dante nodded.

'So there's nothing left to say!'

Dante searched for the right words, then pressed the pen against the paper. 'Except: Welcome to the World of Being Different.'

Jed was angry. 'You think being deaf and being Fulcanelli are the same!'

'No. You have no idea how hard it is to cope with being deaf!'

Jed laughed in spite of himself.

Dante doodled on the edge of the notepad. He was drawing an ouroboros.

Jed grabbed the paper and crossed it out.

It was Dante's turn to laugh. 'You think I don't wish I wasn't deaf?' he wrote.

'This is bigger than that!'

'What, because it's *you*?'

'No!' he wrote in capitals. 'Because this is about life and death.'

'OK,' scrawled Dante. 'But it's still about being

different and I've had to cope with that every day of my life.'

'Great for you! So you've had time to get used to it.'

'I think you'll find you have all the time in the world to get used to what you are.'

Jed took a deep breath. He let the pad rest on his knees. 'I'm scared,' he wrote eventually.

Dante wrote the next words with care. 'I know. Me too.'

Jed wasn't sure if Dante was scared for him or whether he meant that not being able to hear scared him. He guessed it could mean both things at once. He screwed up the used piece of paper and balled it together in his fist.

Dante sat still too for a moment. Then he moved his hands as if he was going to reach for the notepad, but instead he shaped his fingers into words. 'What do you want to do now?'

Jed sighed and shook his head.

'Come back to the house with me,' signed Dante. 'Kassia needs you to come back. And together we'll find a way of working out what this means.'

والشفا وانه سان النفس في الجوهر
دعلى نفسط العمر وان نقان الفت
والم الجرء والعقود نيل على طول ا
والله اعلم حساب المريض وهو
تعدوا اليوم الذي انت فيه وتضيف ال
تعددي الذي انت فيه زين تجعله لو
خل الجمع ۳۰ ، ۵ والذي يبقط
خل باقى الجدول لقى احدها الوج
الجياة فالحياه وان دنت مان لوح
لوح الحياة

'Fulcanelli, like most of the Adepts of old,
in casting off the worn husk of his former
self left nothing on the road but the
phantom trace of his signature ~ a signature,
whose aristocratic nature is amply shown by
his visiting card.'

'under the divine flame, the man he used to
be is entirely consumed. Name, family,
country, all illusions, all mistakes, all
trivialities crumble into dust. And from
these ashes, like a phoenix of the poets, a new
personality is born.'

335. PARIS — La Rue Rochec...

DES ALCHIMISTES

DANS SON LABORATOIRE, PRÈS

Un vieil homme poursuit o
la "Quête du Grand C

par Bernard LESUEUR

...miste devant son fourneau : l' « Athanor », demeure du feu
secret qui provoque toutes les métamorphoses...

...HIMISTES, Frères de la
...se-Croix, Templiers, ces
...ures légendaires d'un
...ublié ont-elles vraiment
...de notre monde » alo-
...?

...rypte poussiéreuse. Sur-
...i et là de la pénombre :
...ues effilées, des vais-
...verre et d'étain, des
...ntrues, de lourds mor-
...bronze, des pinces, des
...Au milieu de ce fatras,
...omme, dos voûté, visage
...rides, méditait, éclairé
...flammes d'un antique

...A cette image tradi-
...e l'alchimiste du Moyen
...arons celle d'un autre
... », l'an de grâce...

...ues kilomètres de Pa-
...p petit village de l'Oise.
...de 65 ans, Eugène
...ls d'un maçon sculp-
...nagé son officine à
...d'une petite maison
...a mi-picarde. Depuis
...s, ce disciple de Ni-
..., Basile Valentin et
...celse, poursuit obsti-
...quête du grand œu-

...vre, de la fabuleuse pierre phi-
losophale.

Un visage affable de bon grand-
père, le front haut, coupé de
rides, le cheveu rare, le nez
chaussé de lunettes rondes, ce
petit homme fait irrésistiblement
penser à Pierre Larquey. Le type
du modeste retraité. Mais dès
qu'il parle « laboratoire » et
« oratoire » — l'un et l'autre
sont inséparables dans l'esprit du
chercheur — ses yeux brillent,
sa parole se précipite. Aucune
ostentation toutefois. Pour lui,
rien que de très naturel.

Si anachroniques que puissent
paraître ses travaux, ce moderne
« fils d'Hermès » ne se sent pas
seul dans sa thébaïde. Des dizai-
nes de lettres lui arrivent chaque
semaine. Héritier spirituel du très
mystérieux Fulcanelli, cet autre
alchimiste du XXe siècle, mort
en 1923 — mort « officiellement
car pour les Adeptes, Fulcanelli,
ayant accompli le grand œuvre,
continue de vivre à nos côtés
mais dans un univers « paral-
lèle » — Eugène Canseliet vient
de préfacer la réédition, chez
Jean-Jacques Pauvert, des traités
hermétiques de son maître.

DAY 52
20th April

Victor heard the knocking on his bedroom door. He untangled himself from the bedclothes and stumbled across the room.

Carter stood in the hallway.

'Seriously?' mumbled Victor, looking back at his alarm clock, his eyes squinting in the brightness of the light from the hallway. 'It's four o'clock in the morning.'

'There's been a development.'

Victor tried to wipe the sleep from his eyes. 'What sort of development?'

Carter's face was arranged in a sneer, as if explaining himself was something he felt was totally unnecessary. 'Since the day after the fire, Department Nine has been tracking Doctor Farnell and the family. We thought they were all based at another home just off

Fleet Street, but we've been vehicle watching. Seems the doctor has just returned from a trip to the airport.'

'And?'

'We've picked up use of a passport.'

'Whose?'

'The girl's.'

Again Victor rubbed at his eyes. This was getting interesting. 'Where was she flying to?'

'Spain.'

'Why there?'

Carter looked annoyed. 'Come on, you should know this.'

'*I* should know this?' groaned Victor. 'At four o'clock in the morning?'

'It was in the research you were shown after your total mess up with the cage,' snapped Carter. 'The family has a holiday home in Spain, remember?'

Victor did remember. For someone who had no real home at all, the idea of having two had certainly stood out.

'And there's been email activity, picked up by our Department Nine team who are on high alert in Paris. It's from an untraceable account somewhere in Europe, to Anna's account in London. It all suggests that maybe River Boy was already in Spain and the girl has flown out to see him. So you need to hurry.'

'Hurry to do what?'

'Get yourself sorted and get a bag packed.'

'Why?'

'Because we're going after them. There's a team of us going to Spain.'

Dante led Jed back to the house. They stood in the doorway for a moment then pulled out chairs at the kitchen table. Kassia made a pot of tea and Jacob took the only food they had left, some bread that was about to turn stale, and warmed it through in the oven. But no one was really in the mood for eating or drinking.

'It could be a mistake,' said Jacob. 'We could be jumping to conclusions. The Fulcanelli idea fits with all the clues we have. The ouroboros; no one remembering you; the other alchemy things you drew; the list of dates; even the cooking. And it makes sense of why NOAH was after you. But we could be wrong. Making connections when there aren't any.'

Jed rubbed his face with his hands. He took a deep breath. 'Can you sign this, Kassia? I don't think my mind can—'

'It's OK. I'll do it,' she said.

Jed nodded. 'It's not a mistake.'

'So you remember, then?'

'Not everything. Patches and pieces. Very little is clear. But there's one thing now that makes sense and it never had before. The river.' He rubbed his face again. 'I think I was testing.'

'Testing what?'

He looked around the room and he thought he could feel a little of the fear Kassia must have felt when she told him what she'd found out. He knew that once he'd said what he was going to say, there would be no going back. It would change things. 'Whether I would die. And I didn't. So I guess we have our answer.'

Kassia's hands stopped moving.

'You said you'd sign, Kassia!'

Instead she was holding her fingers to her lips. Dante thumped the table with the palm of his hand.

'Tell him,' Jed urged.

'What? That you tried to kill yourself!'

'No. It wasn't like that! I was trying to be sure.'

She pursed her lips and made clumsy movements with her hands. Dante sat back in the chair. His eyes were wild and when he replied, each word bounced off the next, as if trying to make itself the most important.

Jed looked to Kassia for a translation. His eyes couldn't cope with the size or the speed of the signs.

'He's cross with you!' she retorted.

'What did he say, Kassia?'

'He said you must never try and test things again! That you must never do anything to put yourself in danger and that he'll be furious if you do anything so stupid for a second time.'

'He said all that?'

'I'm adding. But that was the gist of it.'

'Seriously, Jed,' cut in Jacob. 'We have to know you won't try anything crazy.'

'I drank an elixir that made me immortal. I don't think I can promise not to do anything that might be a bit far out.'

'So what do we do then?' said Kassia.

'We could just wait here,' signed Dante, and this time Jed was sure Kassia's translation was word for word. 'Nothing wrong with spending time in Spain for a while.'

'Could do,' said Jacob. 'What if NOAH tracks us down? They had the power to keep you in a cage. How long before they work out where we are and try and take you again?'

'So we find somewhere else to hide,' said Kassia. 'We keep moving. Like outlaws in films. Always one step ahead.'

'This isn't a film, Kass. We're talking about a huge organisation that's after Jed. They will find us. Eventually. And I'm not sure we can rely on witness protection any more unless we want to explain the whole living for ever thing. Everything's changed now.'

'And this can't be just about hiding any more,' said Jed slowly. 'I've done enough hiding for a while. I think it's time I did some seeking.'

'For what?'

Jed blew out a breath. 'Answers. I need to know what this means. I need to know about the technicalities. Will I stay like this for ever? Will I go back in age? What exactly did the elixir do?'

'OK. We can look for those answers.'

'We?'

Kassia looked confused.

'Listen, Jacob has just said NOAH are after *me*. I have to do this alone. There's no way you lot can come with me.'

'Great,' snarled Kassia. 'We tell you that you're immortal and already the hero complex is kicking in!'

'What are you talking about?' Jed said indignantly.

'The "I have to do this alone" rubbish. You don't have to do anything alone. And anyway, do you have a single clue where to *start* looking for answers?'

Jed tapped his hands on the table. 'Erm. Paris maybe. If that's where Fulcanelli was from. The dates make me think France is important. I can track down where he lived and worked. See if there're answers there.'

'Oh, really smart move!' groaned Kassia. 'Because there's no way NOAH will have people stationed in Paris just waiting for you to turn up there!'

'OK. Maybe not then.'

'So where?'

He strained his brain for an answer. 'I don't know yet!'

Kassia laughed. 'You're totally prepared to do this on your own then, aren't you?'

'Well, have you got any great ideas?'

She took her bag and tipped the contents on to the table. Leaflets, print-outs and pages from the internet sprawled across the surface. 'Heidelberg,' she said. 'I think if we want to find answers about Fulcanelli and the elixir, then we start there.'

* *

'It began with the OSS,' said Kassia, rummaging through the pile of notes she'd tipped on to the table.

'Who are they?' asked Jacob, switching on the laptop and waiting for the search page to load.

'There's all sorts of stuff online about people looking for Fulcanelli,' Kassia continued. 'And I thought at first it was just weirdos. Then I read about the OSS.'

'Got 'em,' said Jacob, turning round the screen to show an internet page. 'The OSS is The Office of Strategic Services.' There was a logo to the right of a spearhead next to a raft of information and dates. Jacob scanned the page. 'Oh, OK. I get you. The OSS came before the CIA.'

'What, the spying guys in America?' signed Dante.

'Central Intelligence Agency, yes. Place in America that collects information about people. But the CIA took over from the OSS, it says here.' Jacob looked across at Kassia. 'So why are they relevant?'

'The OSS was around in the Second World War,' said Kassia. 'And they had people looking for Fulcanelli.'

'So we're talking about a serious, important national organisation who thought Fulcanelli had really found the elixir,' said Jacob. 'Not just a bunch of crazies making stuff up, or scientists who want his secret.'

'Exactly. So while I was in London, I tried to track down where the offices of the OSS were,' said Kassia. 'Thought if I could find out where the people who were looking for him were based, we might find stuff about him there.'

'Bit of a long shot, isn't it?' said Jed. 'If this organisation was around as far back as the Second World War?'

'I know. But people are careful about preserving stuff from the war. Important history and that.'

'Fair point,' cut in Jacob, though it was clear he wasn't totally convinced. 'But I also know that during the War, loads of stuff was kept secret. Classified information and all that. OSS probably didn't go around making their search for Fulcanelli common knowledge.'

Kassia was getting exasperated. 'Will you let me finish explaining, please?'

Jacob looked subdued. He folded his arms and the laptop hummed slightly. 'Sure. What's your next point?'

'OK, so I found a list of OSS offices in Europe,' Kassia went on. 'You can search for them if you like.'

Jacob tapped the request into the search bar.

'Lots of names here, Kass.' He read from the list. '*Hamburg, Munich, Bremen.* Heidelberg's on here but why d'you think we need to go there out of all the places mentioned?'

'The OSS were looking for Fulcanelli, right? They were working out of offices in that town and others. But look at what's in Heidelberg.'

She took a print-out from the centre of the table and passed it to Jed.

'There's a castle there. And in the past, the castle was called the centre of alchemy.'

Jed nodded. He put the paper down. 'It's good. Connecting the OSS and alchemy. But is it enough?'

'Not on its own,' said Kassia. 'But with this it is . . .'

She took another sheet of paper from the table. A photograph this time, of the inside of the castle. It showed a laboratory, filled with bottles and glass flasks and containers. And painted on the wall, so huge it dominated the picture, was a symbol. A dragon eating its tail. The ouroboros.

'You OK?' It was nearly dark in the kitchen, a single light bulb failing to spill enough light to fill the room. Jed turned from the sink. Kassia was standing in the doorway in her pyjamas, her hair tussled and uncombed. 'Couldn't you sleep?'

He didn't tell her he hadn't slept properly for days; not since the cage. 'I'm fine,' he said. His hands were still plunged deep into the soapy water, though it had long since run cold.

'Need some help?'

That was what he needed most. Help to make sense of this mess he'd made and had no memory of starting. He knew it wasn't what she meant. 'Sure.'

She took a tea towel and waited as he soaped a glass and passed it to her. She rubbed it clean then put the glass on the counter and ran the fingers of one hand through her hair. They left a glittering of soap. 'You're scared?'

'Terrified.' He laughed. 'I'm scared NOAH will find us. I'm scared I won't find out what being Fulcanelli means. And then most of all, I'm scared I will.'

'We don't have to go to Heidelberg. We could just keep moving. Go for the "outlaws on the run" thing.'

'Sounds tempting.'

'But you need to know, don't you? What you've done. What it means. All of that.'

The water in the sink was so cold now his arms were getting numb. 'I think so.' He rested his hand against the counter where she'd put the final glass. 'You said

282

you were scared before.'

'I still am. But not of you. I'm just scared.' She paused for a moment. 'I read a story about Heidelberg, when I was looking things up. Do you want to hear it?'

'Sure.'

'The guy building the castle had his twin sons visit him every day. But there was a terrible accident. Both boys fell from the scaffolding and were killed.'

'Is this story supposed to be cheering me up?' groaned Jed.

'The builder was devastated. He couldn't go on building the castle. Instead, he made a new wreath of white roses every single day and took it to his sons' grave.'

'Seriously? Your story could do with a few laughs.'

'Anyway, one night, the builder had a dream and he saw his two sons like angels. In the morning some spare white roses he'd got for the wreath that he'd left withering in his room had turned into beautiful red blossoms. And so the next day, the builder carried on his job. And the castle was finished. On the keystone above the door there's a sculpture of two young boy angels holding a wreath of red roses.'

Jed took a deep breath. 'OK. The story got better. Just.'

'What I'm trying to say,' said Kassia gently, 'is that finishing things is hard. But you were right when we were together trying to work out what to do. You need to know all the answers. Hiding isn't enough any more.'

'When did you get to be so clever?' he said.

'Ah well. All those hours of home schooling had to pay off in the end.' She hit him on the arm playfully with the tea towel and then slipped it over the rail by the sink. 'You should try and sleep, Jed. We've got a long drive tomorrow.'

He nodded as she walked out of the door.

And then suddenly there was a snapping inside of him. The same feeling he'd had as they stood and watched Kassia's home in Fleet Street being engulfed in flames. His hand spasmed. His fingers locked and the glass toppled from the counter. It shattered on the tiled floor, shards scattered like a flock of birds disturbed by gun shot. He stumbled forward to reach down to pick up the pieces, and his vision sloshed around inside his head like the soapy water in the sink. There was no swirling dragon this time. This wasn't memory. This was now.

'Jed?' Kassia's voice sounded far away. 'Jed?

Are you OK?'

From his knees on the tiled floor, surrounded by broken glass, he told her that he was. But for the second time since she'd come into the kitchen, his answer to her question was a lie.

The Immortal Jellyfish

Man has been searching and experimenting with different types of tissues to find out the clue for immortality. But nature has already perfected this by millions of years of 'Turritopsis nutricula' aka the immortal jellyfish has the ability to live forever by transforming to its primordial birth-stage after maturity. It is the only species in the whole world to be capable of transforming through the cell transdifferentiation.

In the early stages the matured cells transforms into new polyps forming a new colony of immatured cells and all other matured cells die.

STAGES OF TRANSFORMATION

1. The jellyfish is absorbed in a new colony of immature cells. First goes the umbrella (the outer-part of the jellyfish) followed by the tentacles and last goes the mesoglea (the inner-part of the jellyfish.)

2. Then all other supporting cells are formed, completing the transformation.

After these stages the adult jellyfish is transformed into a baby jellyfish and continues its life cycle once again. This process cycles to infinity.

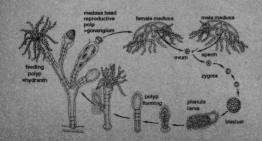

DAY 53

21st April

It took about an hour and a half to get to Olvera from Malaga.

Carter drove, Montgomery navigated and Victor sat in the back. He felt decidedly sick.

They parked the car about two hundred metres from the farmhouse.

'Element of surprise,' said Montgomery.

The plan was simple. Victor would take the front door. The other two would ring around the outside, cutting off the side and back exits. They knew Fulcanelli wouldn't be alone. But *he* was their target. The others were small fry. Could be awkward maybe, though not a real threat if Victor was quick and if he used some of the skills he'd picked up from the playgrounds of the seven secondary schools he'd attended.

They walked without talking. There was no need now. They'd been planning this since the plane had taxied down the runway in London.

The approach to the farmhouse was gravelled. Victor lifted his feet as if they had glue on their soles. There were no lights on. But this wasn't surprising. It was nearly midday.

They'd talked about a night-time visit. That wasn't their style. They weren't doing anything underhand, just collecting what was rightfully theirs, and so the daytime approach seemed more appropriate.

It would also make tracking him easier if he got away.

Victor reached the door. This had been thought through too. Breaking in was the fallback plan. Knocking first would be unexpected.

Victor rapped hard against the wood.

There was no sound from inside.

No running. No sound of hiding. Nothing.

He rapped again.

Still nothing.

Fall-back plan it was then.

There were no glass panels, so no entry this way. The door was solid wood. But the jamb was old. It reeked of holiday home neglect.

Victor took the crowbar they'd bought in the first hardware shop in Malaga and jimmied it between the door and the support. The frame creaked under the pressure and the wood splintered. The door shuddered and then swung open.

He was inside.

Victor looked left and right. The hall was wide and unfurnished. He moved quickly through to the main room. Cloths and covers swaddled the furniture. One cabinet remained uncovered. A photograph was resting facedown on the surface.

He spun around, watching his back.

Nothing. No one. No sounds at all.

He moved through the room to the dining room, a table front and centre swathed in cloth. Finally, the kitchen. No food out. No pots on the stove. Everything away.

Victor looked down at the floor. It seemed to be sparkling. He kneeled and pressed his hand against the tiles. When he lifted his fingers, one bled from the cut of broken glass.

He licked the blood away and then took his mobile from his pocket. The text he typed was smeared with blood. 'We're too late. They've moved on.'

* *

The driving directions said it would take twenty hours. They'd been on the road for about ten and Kassia was desperately hungry. Jed sat beside her, his body pressed against the side of the car, his head lolling against the window. He'd been sleeping fitfully, mumbling in French. His face looked grey and waxy.

Kassia was in charge of the money needed for the tolls. She was impressed Jacob had thought ahead. And she was impressed with Dante's navigating skills. He had the map and the computer print-out of the driving directions spread across his knees.

They'd shown their passports at the border, and they were waved through without question. They had stopped a couple of times to buy bread and crisps and cans of drinks, but somehow their destination didn't seem to be getting closer.

Dante tapped the dashboard to get Kassia's attention. He signed into the rear view mirror so she could see. 'We should stop. Stay somewhere overnight. He doesn't look good.'

Kassia had hoped it was just the light in the car playing tricks on her. She hoped she'd been the only one to notice how bad Jed seemed.

'His head must be messed up,' Dante signed. 'We need to be careful, now we haven't got Nat with us.'

Kassia made her hand into the sign for 'yes'. She'd been trying not to think about the fact that Nat wasn't with them. Or her mum.

Just for a second, she wondered what her mum would think about this. There'd been no time for real explanations. When Kassia had come back from St Paul's in a state about what she'd discovered, her mum and Nat presumed she was reacting again to the stress of the fire.

It made sense for them to believe she didn't want to be in London because she was scared. It hadn't taken much to make them work out she wanted to be in the safe house far away with Dante. They'd seen the signs of her distress and they'd read a different story . . . sending her away to safety with her brother had made sense. Somewhere calm to work. A place to revise.

Now Kassia wished she'd told them the truth. But she hadn't. And they'd stayed. To sort insurance claims and deal with fire investigations while she'd flown across the Channel and everything had changed.

So things were as they were, and this was what they had to deal with. Four of them, in a foreign country, trying to get to another one.

Suddenly the task seemed huge and overwhelming.

Jacob could tell there was silent chatting going on in the back. 'You want to stop?' he said over his shoulder. 'The night here, then on to Germany tomorrow?'

It seemed the most sensible option.

It took them about thirty minutes to find a small guesthouse. Jacob passed over cash for three rooms. Dante and Jed took the room downstairs, Kassia the one next door and Jacob was on his own in the loft.

Kassia tossed and turned in the bed and tried to settle. She heard running water next door, then pacing across the room, and she wondered if it was Jed or her brother who was still awake.

She climbed out of bed, draped a blanket round her shoulders and opened her window. She squeezed through the opening and stood tentatively on the tiny balcony. It ran along the front of the guesthouse, railings sectioning it into segments in front of each room. The sky was cloudless. The moon a slice of light. The stars so bright they looked in reach.

'Can't sleep either?' came a voice from the next-door section of balcony.

Kassia gripped tight to the hand rail. 'Jed?'

'Amazing, aren't they?' Jed said in answer, looking

up towards the stars too. 'But don't you think it's odd that some of them aren't really there?'

She didn't know much about stars. They weren't on her revision list.

He shuffled towards the edge of his balcony so his arm brushed against hers. 'Some have exploded. We still see stars because the light's coming from so far away.'

She was struggling to understand.

'It's *present time*, and it's *past time* and the two are muddled.'

She understood him now.

'You are still Jed,' she said quietly.

'But I'm also Fulcanelli. And I think there's more I'm starting to remember.'

She sat down on the balcony and the bars of the railing were cold against her skin. He sat too, a barrier between them.

'I told you about the dragon. It swirls round and round inside my head and it's as if its body is a frame made of six segments.'

'Six. A perfect number,' said Kassia.

Jed looked confused now. 'It's an all right number. I wouldn't say it was perfect.'

'No,' she laughed. 'It's a maths term.' This *was* on her revision list. 'You take all the numbers that *divide* into six and when you add them up they *make* six.'

Jed still looked confused.

'It doesn't matter. You were saying, about the frame.'

'Yes. So the dragon's body makes this frame and inside are pictures. I don't know if they're memories. Sometimes there're people; sometimes things and lately there've been dates.'

'Like the date on my dad's grave?'

He nodded. 'Jacob and I checked out four other dates. Bad things happened on all of them.'

'Five bad days? If you've been around for as long as we think you have, then five bad days isn't really *that* bad.'

He pressed his arm tighter against hers. 'I keep trying to make things settle in my head but the thoughts are exploding and I can't catch them.' He looked back at the sky. 'You'd die if you got too close to a star. But from a distance they look harmless. What if I'm like that? What if what you see now seems OK, but the me that's in the past is full of fire?'

'You were just a man, Jed.'

'A man who played with time and death.' He looked down, away from the stars. 'What if we find out I was dangerous? That they were right to put me in a cage?'

'I chose to come here. What we find, we find together.'

'All of us?'

'Both of us,' she said softly.

They didn't say any more.

They looked at the stars and then under blankets spread between the bars and shared between them, they slept, and the night rolled away into morning and it was time to leave.

Jacob checked them out of the guesthouse and they headed back to the main route to Germany.

They stopped twice for food. Kassia wasn't sure how much more bread she could eat squashed in the back of the car.

On the final stop, Jacob bought them all coffee and they sat at the side of the road and drank. 'That was the last of the cash,' he said awkwardly.

'What do we do now?' asked Dante.

'Debit card,' said Jacob, tossing his empty cup towards the bin. 'Then credit card. We can't use the social services funds any more as we've sort of broken free of witness protection now. But there's always my overdraft. We'll be good for weeks yet.'

Dante looked relieved, but Kassia noticed Jed

was shaking a little.

She helped him towards the car and they followed the final road signs to Heidelberg.

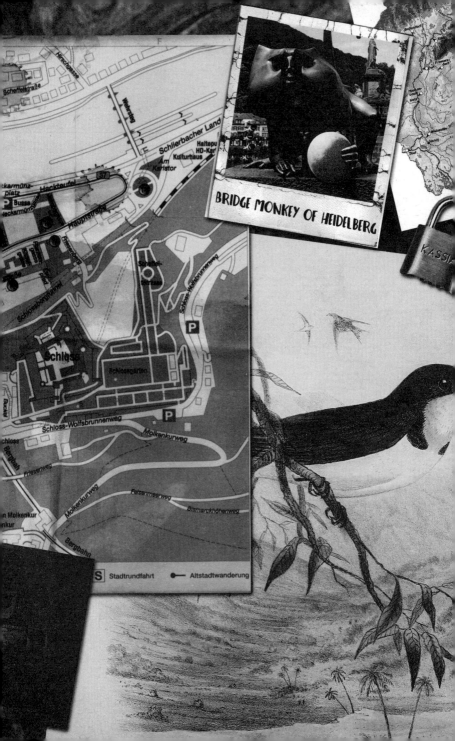

BRIDGE MONKEY OF HEIDELBERG

Schloss

Stadtrundfahrt • Altstadtwanderung

DAY 55

23rd April

Victor's phone was ringing. He pressed answer and Martha Quinn's face filled the screen.

'You all OK?' Martha said, her picture pixellating a little.

'What, apart from being bored and hungry and fed up?' said Victor. 'Yep, we're fabulous!'

Martha adjusted her glasses on the bridge of her nose. 'Well, things are about to get interesting.'

'How?'

'We've picked up some unusual activity on Jacob Zane's bank account.'

'Who's Jacob Zane?'

'The social worker assigned to the family!'

'Why do we need to know that the social worker felt the need to do a little shopping?' asked Victor.

'It's *where* exactly he's doing his shopping that's important.'

'So tell us.'

'Heidelberg,' said Martha. 'The card has been used to pay for food in a service station in Germany.'

'We have to get some weird mountain train up there.' Jacob had been into town early to get cash and a guidebook. 'Castle's open till six.'

Kassia finished her orange juice and pushed her empty plate across the table. 'Shame we can't walk there. I need to burn off that breakfast.' She blew out her cheeks making Dante laugh.

'Maybe you can run after the train,' he signed.

'You won't be saying that when you see how high up the castle is,' said Jacob.

They'd arrived late the previous evening and had been too tired to look round. But the steepness of the Heidelberg hill was obvious when they stepped outside their guesthouse and into the early morning sunshine.

The castle kept watch over the town. Jed had presumed it would be one building, but this looked like a mixture of old and new. Ornate red walls grafted on to sandy stone ruins. Once out of the train, the jumble of styles was even more obvious. They walked across the courtyard and Jed peered up at the brickwork straining towards to the sky. Some walls were covered with statues; some were bare stone; some housed elaborate rooms behind and some held up empty windows like cruel tricks because beyond them the ground fell away and no rooms existed. Some walls lay fallen, as if they were giant beasts and were simply resting. Stairs curled round to nowhere. Creeping plants crawled through damaged doorways. Birds flew through the shadows of long vanished ceilings. The castle was beautiful and odd; complete but broken. And above a door, two angels holding a wreath of flowers looked down at them.

'Ready for this?' said Kassia.

Jed didn't answer.

The map showed them the way to the Apothecary Museum. They avoided the queue that waited to enter the hall of mirrors. Jed had no interest in seeing reflections of his modern self. It was his past he wanted to see.

It took a while to reach the laboratory. The ceiling was domed and painted white. Set into recesses along the walls were cupboards and shelves groaning with glassware and all sorts of silver implements for measuring and mixing. There was a pair of gold coloured scales. They reminded Jed of the scales of justice on top of the Old Bailey Law Courts back in

London, and he couldn't help wondering how the world would weigh what he'd done. There was a statue of a man holding out the branch of a tree. A snake wrapped around the branch, its mouth wide open, fangs on view.

Jed ran his finger along the inside of his collar. A bead of sweat ran down his back.

And then as Jed turned, he saw the ouroboros. Not in his mind this time, swirling and circling, but large and still, marked indelibly on the wall above him.

This was one of the places, then, where alchemists had worked. Trying to find the secret of eternal life.

Jacob hadn't come up with a strategy or a plan for the visit. The aim was just to find anything that could be a starting place. Something they could fit together with the list of symbols and dates Jed had recorded.

The place was full of tourists. All of them jostling for a better look. Jacob and Dante moved deep into the room to look at an exhibition on the use of herbs. Jed and Kassia stood awkwardly inside the door, not sure what to look at first.

The guide in the corner of the room moved over to stand with them. *'Kann ich euch etwas erklären?'*

'Erm, English?' said Kassia, smiling awkwardly.

'Ah, very good,' said the guide. 'I was asking if you needed anything explained?'

Jed almost laughed. 'We're interested in alchemy. Old style stuff really.'

'Well, yes. This museum tries to show work from the sixteenth to the nineteenth century. How alchemy fought with science to be taken seriously and to find answers. About how to live better. About how to live longer.'

Kassia pointed to some of the labels on the jars and bottles. There were a few words, but most labels had only pictures on them. 'How do you know what could have been in all these?' she asked.

'Sometimes we don't,' confessed the guide. 'We make educated guesses. Medicine in the past was shrouded in mystery. Of course there are books we can refer to. But groups of apothecaries and alchemists tended to record their secrets in other ways. In signs and symbols. We call this the golden chain of knowledge. It's how information was passed from teacher to student; from one group member to another.'

'So how do you find out what the symbols mean?' pressed Kassia.

The guide considered his answer. 'By making connections.' He pointed to a painting on the wall. Two men stood in front of a huge glass container. A fire burned and in the sky was a huge scorpion. 'Odd, isn't it?' he said. 'A scorpion hanging in the sky? But of course it's symbolic. It shows the time the fire should be lit under the glass container. Early November. Because the star sign Scorpio is dominant then.'

Kassia looked more closely at the picture.

'Time is one of the many things important to the alchemist,' explained the guide. 'And they could leave clues hidden anywhere; in buildings, in pictures, in statues. As we try and understand how they lived and worked and what they used, we have to learn to read the signs around us.' He paused. 'Like your friend reads the hands of his friend,' he added. 'A language shared only by a few.'

Kassia nodded and moved over to join Dante and Jacob, who were looking at a row of painted drawers that ran below a workbench.

'We're particularly interested in the elixir of life,' said Jed quietly.

'Who isn't?' said the guide, turning back again to face him. 'There's no doubt alchemists here in the castle tried to make it.'

'And do you think they succeeded?'

The guide led Jed to the furthest corner of the room. He pointed to a shelf set apart from the others. On it were six bottles. A label marked with an ouroboros curled around each one. The bottles were empty.

'You'll see that where we can, we've filled the other

305

bottles in this room with modern representations of what was used in the past. But what could we fill these bottles with? If we had the secret to making the elixir to eternal life, it would be madness to display it here.'

Jed stared at the six empty bottles. Light bounced around inside the bevelled glass, and for a second it looked like molten gold.

'Why are there six?' he asked.

'Ah. Good question,' said the guide, in a whisper which only Jed could hear. 'Everything here is symbolic. Six bottles to show the power and the limits of the elixir.'

'Huh?'

'The six doses,' continued the guide. 'According to the golden chain of knowledge, taking the elixir just once wouldn't be enough. Aging would be reversed. Halved in fact. Each dose would reduce age incrementally. By a quarter, then a third and so on.' The guide reached out and ran his finger around the neck of the sixth bottle. 'But to make the effects of the elixir permanent; to fix the effects and to really live for ever; the elixir had to be taken a final sixth time.'

'Interesting stuff,' said Jacob. 'Did you see the great big furnace in the corner?'

Jed's feet were so heavy he could hardly move them.

Every step was an effort.

'Where shall we go next?' asked Dante. 'The gift shop might have some books on alchemy.'

Jed could hardly breathe. Hadn't they seen what he'd seen?

'Or maybe we should try and find out where the offices of the OSS were?' suggested Kassia.

Kassia too? Didn't she know? Hadn't she heard?

'Jed. Are you OK?' Kassia suddenly seemed aware he was having difficulty walking. 'Apparently the clock here's another monument to time. Fifty-two metres tall. Do you want to check it out?'

Jed's stomach folded as if he'd been punched. The circling dragon swirled in front of his eyes, the six segments of his body, sharp and clear. *A sun blotted out by the moon, then burning so brightly the sky sparked with fire; bodies heaped dead in the street; a train careering out of control; winds uprooting trees and tossing branches like splintered matchsticks across the path.*

Jed?' Kassia's voice sounded as if she was calling him from far away. 'Jed? Can you hear me?'

The dragon circled again, so tight against his eyes he was sure his brain would burst. *A golden spire; a grey dome speared with yellow spikes; a clock in a tower striking midnight again and again and again.*

'Jacob, help me! There's something wrong!'

A river surging; rising higher and higher. Hands slipping, falling. Hold on! Hold on! Silence. Darkness. Death. The dragon stilled. It turned its face. It opened its jaws and its fangs dripped with blood. Jed covered his eyes with his hands. But it was too late.

'We should get him back to the guesthouse,' Kassia was standing over him, her eyes creased with concern. Perhaps she'd even been crying.

Dante's hands were moving in sign but Jed's head hurt too much to translate them. He tried to orientate himself. He was slumped on the ground. He must have fallen. A small crowd had gathered round them but Jacob was dispersing them urgently. 'Show's over,' he said calmly, waving his arms. 'All's good. Absolutely nothing to see.'

Jed lifted his hands to his eyes. He wasn't sure he could trust what he saw any more. He recoiled backwards. His hands were covered in blood. He wiped them together frantically. Not blood. Dust from the ground. The dirt drifted down in a cloud. Dust to dust.

'Let's get you up,' said Kassia, attempting to link her arm around him.

He pulled away again. 'It's OK. I can do it.'

Her face fell. His words had hurt her.

308

'Thank you, though,' he said, standing awkwardly.

'You're overtired,' she said. 'The journey. The news.'

'The hundred years,' he said.

'You need to rest,' she said, clearly finding it difficult to speak.

That was the last thing he could afford to do. 'I'm fine. I think I need to take a walk.'

'Sure. We can take a walk by the river and—'

'No,' he blurted. Anywhere but the river. Never by the river again. 'I think I need to be alone.'

'Oh.'

It was all she said. And he said nothing to give her more to say. He didn't have the words.

The Philosopher's Walk was a path running like a scar around the town. A walkway beaten down over years. People stretching back through time had strolled here to make sense of the biggest questions life had to ask.

Jed followed in their footsteps and every stride hurt him. But he walked on. Alone. Until the sun had set and the darkness had come.

Victor stood with Carter and Montgomery in the market place of Heidelberg. The town was throbbing with people. Some hurried down from the castle, others dashed into gift shops for last minute presents, emerging with folded German flags and cheap plastic beer tankards. The people were flowing like the river, backwards and forwards.

And yet through lamplight and the bustle of the crowd, Victor noticed one figure who was perfectly still.

She was sitting by the fountain. Her back was to the water; her hair rippled behind her. She'd sat like this for a while. He and Carter and Montgomery had watched. And as they'd watched, they'd planned.

'You think it will really work?' said Victor, crushing the can of Coke he'd been drinking and tossing it into the trash.

'We used fire to drive him out and it failed,' said Carter. 'This makes sense.'

'Using her?' said Victor.

'Oh, yes,' beamed Montgomery. 'She's the key to the whole plan.'

'So we think we've found where the OSS offices were,' said Jacob, stretching his arm across the open doorway to his bedroom. 'We can check it out tomorrow, if you like.' He looked past Jed into the corridor. 'What else did you and Kassia uncover at the castle?'

Jed's stomach tightened. How could he tell Jacob what he thought he'd found? But as he was trying to untangle what to say, his mind jarred in his head. Kassia. Jacob had asked what he and Kassia had uncovered. 'Kassia's not with me,' he said. 'She came back here.'

'No, she didn't, mate. Last we saw, was you two leaving the lab. Dante and I stayed to see if we could get any useful info from that guide. By the time he'd finished going on about pelican flasks and herbs picked at sunset, you were both gone.'

Jed was trying to choke back the sense of panic pushing against the base of his throat. 'She was with you!'

'She wasn't, mate.'

Dante pushed his way between them. 'Where's Kass?'

'I thought she was with you!'

'OK, so let's not panic,' Jacob said in words and signs which indicated that panicking was exactly what he was doing.

'What do you mean, "don't panic"? You telling me my sister's alone in a strange city when we know there're nutters around who want to harm us?'

'NOAH are not in Heidelberg!' said Jacob, in a voice dressed with signs that Jed guessed he was trying to make look and sound confident. He was failing miserably.

'Call her mobile,' sputtered Jed.

Jacob took the phone from his pocket and slid the icons on the screen. The screen made it clear it had gone straight to voicemail. He left a garbled message.

'We need to get out there and find her!' said Dante, and his signs were shouting.

Jed was about to make for the stairs when the owner of the guesthouse rounded the corner and grinned at them broadly. 'Package,' he said bouncily. 'Delivery boy said I was to pass it over personally.'

Jacob made a grab for the parcel. 'Which delivery boy?'

'Tall black guy,' said the owner, turning to face Jed. 'Very short hair. About your age.'

Any muscles in Jed's stomach not tightened already, clenched fast.

The owner continued to beam brightly. 'Six flights of stairs,' he said. 'I didn't take the lift. Thought the exercise would do me good.' He patted his stomach.

Jacob dug around in his pocket and pulled out a bank note and pressed it in the man's hands.

The owner obviously couldn't believe his luck and was still mumbling about the generosity of the British as he ambled his way back towards the lift.

'What is it?' urged Jed, following Jacob into his room as he unwrapped the parcel.

Jacob let the tissue paper fall free. But he clearly had no idea how to answer.

Inside the wrapping was a small hand mirror. Written across the shiny surface, in red marker pen, was a time. Eight p.m. Attached to the edge of the mirror was a padlock. Kassia's name had been scrawled in the same red marker across the metal.

'Where do we have to go?' signed Dante, his hands flailing wildly. 'If anything has happened to her. Anything at all.'

They had no time to think about that. They had to unscramble the clues.

Jed clicked open his pocket watch. Seven o'clock. They had one hour to find her. 'You said NOAH weren't in Heidelberg!' he barked at Jacob through gritted teeth.

Jacob shook his head as if he knew any answer he offered would be meaningless.

'We should call the police,' signed Dante.

'How can we trust them? At the beginning, we thought NOAH were the good guys! We can't be sure about anyone now.' Jed was turning the mirror over and over in his hand. 'We have to solve this ourselves. Go to wherever this crazy clue is sending us.'

'Hall of Mirrors!' signed Dante. 'We saw the

queues. Up at the castle.'

'Excellent!' yelped Jed. 'I'll go up to the castle. Jacob, if you hurry you might catch this delivery boy. Dante, stay here in case another message comes.'

Jed was pretty sure Jacob was saying something else in answer. But he had no idea what. He was already on his way out of the door and towards the train that would take him up the hill.

Jed thumped the bars of the castle gate with his hands. This couldn't be right. It couldn't be locked.

A security guard strode purposefully down to the gate. He did not look happy.

'*Wir haben geschlossen, mein Herr.*'

'You don't understand! I have to get in to the Hall of Mirrors.'

The guard registered Jed's use of English and pulled a disgruntled face. 'We are closed, sir. Come back tomorrow.' He paused for a second, looked at his watch and then took a deep breath. 'Student prison has late opening tonight. If you're that desperate to sightsee.'

Student prison? What was the man going on about? He had to let him in to the hall of mirrors.

If only he'd brought the package, he could show him and explain. If Jed could let this guard see the mirror and the padlock then . . . Locks. Prison. Maybe the Hall of Mirrors was wrong. Maybe the guard was right.

'Where's the prison?' Jed growled through the bars.

The guide looked amused. It obviously wasn't common for a tourist to be so keen to see the sights. He pulled a map from his pocket and began to point in the half-light of the security lamps.

Jed strained to see. Then he jabbed his hands through the bars and grabbed the map. 'Thank you,' he yelled, careering towards the path which led back into town.

He pulled the pocket watch from his jacket and flicked open the case. Just over half an hour. He pressed the case closed and let his thumb linger for a second on the image of the swallow.

The student prison was back down towards the centre of town. The air was cold and the sky pressed tight. A storm was drawing in. What would they be doing to her? These people were capable of cages and fire. If they hurt her … If they did anything to her at all…

Blood pounded in his ears. He could hear the clock ticking as he ran. He had half an hour.

The map flapped in his hand as his feet thumped on the path. He turned left, pumping his arms as he followed the fall of the hill onwards. Then he turned left again into a narrow cobbled street.

The lock. A prison. It had to be here. But why the mirror? What did that mean?

The entrance was unassuming. It looked like the door to a house. A small gaggle of tourists huddled together. Jed joined the group and tried to look as if he belonged. The tour guide was tired. It was the last visit of the day and she was obviously keen to get home. Her explanation in German was fast and monotone. Her group were tired too and shuffling past the small prison rooms in silence, cameras clicking occasionally at the graffiti pictures covering the walls and ceilings. Writing. Images. Pictures of people in profile, drawn in thick black pen. Did these images connect with the mirror reference? Is that what the message meant? Jed pushed through each room. The writing on the walls was overwhelming. Political statements in German sprawled across every whitewashed gap. No space was left uncovered. The walls were screaming to be heard. But Jed had no idea what they said. And no idea where NOAH had taken Kassia.

He pressed his hands against the tiny barred windows which looked out into the street. Where was she? How would he find her?

'Sir, are you OK?' A member of the tour group

tapped Jed gently on the arm. 'English, yes?'

Jed nearly laughed. Or French, he wanted to say. Or sign language. Any words that make sense and will tell me where Kassia is. 'I was looking for a mirror,' he blurted.

The tourist looked perturbed. 'This is a prison, sir. It was used by students from the university. I'm not sure there are mirrors.'

Jed felt sweat prickling on his forehead.

'Maybe you'd like to see the Old Bridge statue, which holds a mirror,' she said quietly. 'It's only five minutes from here.'

'Statue?'

'Of a monkey. It's a little odd.' She was smiling encouragingly. 'But it holds a mirror. Being outside in the fresh air might do you good. You're looking a little unwell.'

Jed spun round. 'Old Bridge?'

The tourist backed away slightly. 'Turn first right and then first left and continue on to *Neckarstaden*. You can't miss it. Oh, but sir,' she added nervously, 'the bridge itself is closed from eight o'clock tonight. Preparation for a parade later in the week.'

'What?'

'The bridge will be locked down at eight. So you'll have to hurry.'

317

Jed wanted to hug her. A mirror and a lock. He was nearly there.

Jed pushed on, even though his muscles were screaming for him to stop running. He could see the buildings thinning. He had to be close to the river. Had to be getting closer to Kassia.

He pulled the watch from his pocket again. The case sprung open. It was seven fifty. He had ten minutes.

He rounded the corner and the gatehouse for the old bridge came into view. Two huge white towers like pepper pots extended towards the sky; their red tops lit by floodlights pierced the night clouds, which rumbled and began to spill rain like giant tears. A portcullis gate bit down on the ground like the angry teeth of a monster clenched shut.

And to the left, perched on a wall, was a bronze statue of a monkey. His arm was outstretched. He held a mirror.

Jed span round. Where was she? Why couldn't he see her? The mirror. The lock. Both here. But where was Kassia?

He stumbled towards the entrance to the bridge. Tape hung across the opening, barring the way. A notice in German, no doubt explaining about the bridge being closed.

There was no sign of Kassia. No sign at all.

He leaned forwards in an attempt to pull air into his lungs. And as he looked at the ground, he saw a clump of padlocks chained to the edge of the bridge, sparking in the rain. Pairs of names had been scrawled on the padlocks. He'd no idea why they were there. No idea what they meant. But the line of locks led on to the bridge, spanning out across the waters of the River Neckar.

Jed's heart thundered inside him. Not on the bridge. She couldn't be on the bridge. He could hear the water surging. Could feel the rain washing his face. He couldn't walk on the bridge. Not now. He couldn't be that close to the river.

And then suddenly, out of the darkness, he saw the dragon. Spinning and spinning in front of his eyes. The six segments of its body arcing and twisting and in the centre of the frame a river lifted and swelled. The water rose and rose and then it crested like a tidal wave and overwhelmed him.

Jed was shaking.

His heart was racing.

He was soaked by the rain.

But he knew now where Kassia was. And he knew there was only one way to reach her.

He climbed over the tape and began to walk across the old bridge, above the heaving river, towards its centre.

Three figures stood in the middle of the bridge.

Jed felt sick.

Montgomery and Carter were there. And the boy, Victor, too.

Set back a little from these three, was Kassia. She was on a chair. At first it looked as if she was resting; simply taking a moment to enjoy the view of the river raging below them. But her hands were behind her back and Jed could tell at once that they were tied with thick rope. In front of her was a small metal table. And on the table, glinting in the rain, were two glass goblets; one red, one black.

To a casual observer it might have looked as though Kassia was a guest at an exclusive tea party. Until you looked at her face and saw she was terrified.

'Kassia, I—' Jed lurched forward, but Carter put out his arm to hold him back.

'Not so fast, Fulcanelli.'

Jed was trembling and he could see Kassia was shaking too.

'It's good of you to return to us,' Montgomery said snidely. 'I have to admit that after Victor's mishap, we were a little concerned we might have lost you. We had a feeling, though, the girl would draw you in.'

Kassia mouthed the word 'sorry'.

'Let her go!' Jed bawled.

Montgomery laughed. 'Oh, we will. She's our trade. Her life for yours. I agree her life isn't as valuable as yours. It has a *best before* date. But I think we have an understanding now, of what motivates you, Fulcanelli. And if we've read you correctly then we know you'll make the trade. There's just a little something we need you to do for us. And then she can go.'

Jed's insides were twisted like the ropes holding Kassia's hands. Bile was bubbling in his throat.

'We all make mistakes,' went on Montgomery. 'Victor here's a fine example of that. And I suppose, *our* greatest mistake was not testing to be sure about you back in London. We thought we had all the time in the world, you see. Then you got away. And I suppose now, before we move on, we want to be sure, really sure, that we're not mistaken. So our request is simple.'

Montgomery nodded to Carter and he moved towards the table, his black leather coat shining slick in the rain. 'Two goblets,' said Carter elaborately. 'One filled with water, no more dangerous than the rain. And one,' he waited a moment, for maximum effect, 'holds poison. It will take three minutes to kill anyone who drinks it. It will burn. From the inside out. There will be no quenching of the fire. An agonising way to die. But quick.'

Jed looked across at Montgomery. What was the matter with these people? What did they want?

Montgomery snapped his answer as if he'd read Jed's mind. 'We want to see if you truly are *the* Fulcanelli. And so, the choice is absolutely yours.' He sighed and let the end of his stick tap against the cobbles. 'The black goblet holds water. The red holds poison. There's no trick. No catch. Choose a goblet for your friend to drink from. Drink from the other yourself. And when both goblets are empty, we will let your friend go.'

'What is this?'

'A test.'

And Jed knew exactly what they were testing. If he gave Kassia the water to drink, she would be safe. But it would leave him the poison. And they would know. His secret would be confirmed. Not just for them. For him, too. He'd be really sure and so would they. If the poison didn't kill him, then all his protests about not being Fulcanelli would be in vain. But what was his alternative? Give Kassia the poison and watch her die in front of him?

Let his friend live and reveal his secret. Protect who he was and watch his friend die.

'Are you ready?' said Carter, handing Jed the black goblet. 'The water first. Which of you is going to drink in safety?'

Jed lifted the goblet to his lips. He rocked back his head. And he drank.

Then he let the glass goblet tumble from his fingers.

The red glass shattered on the ground in front of him. Shards of red merging with the fragments of black from the goblet he'd held against Kassia's lips only moments before. Both goblets empty. Both liquids drunk.

Jed wiped his mouth with the back of his hand. There was no burning. No clogging of his throat. The poison ran into his stomach without leaving a trace of its danger.

Montgomery watched him. They waited. The minutes ticked by. Montgomery's eyes widened with glee. 'It's true. It's true,' he said, pumping the air with his fist. 'You *are* the Fulcanelli.'

Kassia's eyes sparked with tears.

'Let her go,' Jed said. 'You promised you'd let her go.'

Carter untied Kassia's hands from the chair but

kept the rope bound tight around her wrists.

'Yeah. About that,' Montgomery said. 'We lied.'

Jed pushed forwards but Victor grabbed his arms and pulled him close to Kassia. Carter took the end of the rope which bound her and tugged it hard around Jed's wrists too. 'Things are different now. We know for sure about you. We can't have her out in the world sharing your secret.'

'You said you'd let her go!' Jed yelled, his hands pressed tight against Kassia's, the rope biting his skin.

'And you said you were just a boy from the river!' bellowed Montgomery, his eyes flashing wildly.

Jed could barely breathe. How could this have happened? How could he have walked into their trap? He wanted to hold Kassia's hands. Reassure her it would be OK. That there'd be a way to solve this. But her fingers were jabbing against his palm. Sharply, almost, as if she wanted him to focus.

Suddenly, she took her index finger and ran it down his palm. What was she doing? She scored down to the base of his hand and then scooped her finger along in a loop shape at the bottom. He tried to flex his hand to hold hers but again she prodded him sharply. This time her finger was jabbing at the tip of the fourth finger on his left hand, the rope straining at their wrists.

'The world will be ours, Fulcanelli,' said Montgomery. 'You have the answer to the quest for eternal life. Can you imagine how much power that will give us? How much power it will give me!'

Jed felt a surge of air in his throat. Kassia's hands banged once more against his. This time, against the strain of the rope around her wrists, the three fingers of her right hand were beating on the palm of his left.

Jed felt his stomach heave. She was signing! Spelling out letters on his hand. She was trying to tell him something.

But what was she saying? He saw the movement of her fingers again in his head. A sweep down the middle finger and a curl at the end. J. The tip of the fourth finger. U. Three fingers against the palm. M.

'I have waited all my life for this moment,' said Montgomery. 'We will not let you slip through our fingers again.'

Kassia's thumb and finger on her right hand were forming a loop on the end of the index finger on Jed's left palm. The letter P.

Jed understood.

JUMP.

There was no way out in front of them, but behind them was the thundering River Neckar. It was metres below. She couldn't mean it. It would be madness.

Jed had risked everything for her. But the river! How could he face the river?

Kassia tapped his palm. Jed knew she was asking if he understood.

His heart folded inside of him as the river soared. He linked his hand round hers. Then they lurched backwards together as fast as a round fired from a gun.

The three men on the bridge staggered in surprise.

But Jed had read the signs. He clambered on to the wall beside his friend and together they jumped into the water.

And the surface of the River Neckar closed across them like a shroud.

'You idiot!' Montgomery wielded his stick like a weapon and shouted at Victor as he moved towards the wall. 'How could you have let them jump?'

'How could anyone have known they'd do that?' argued Victor. '*Why* would anyone do that?'

'To get away, you fool!' He struck the metal table with the walking stick and it rang like a bell.

'Her hands are tied. She'll drown!'

'But *he* won't, will he! Not the boy who'll live for ever. We must catch him before he gets away.'

Victor couldn't believe what he was hearing. Montgomery seemed to show no concern at all for the girl who'd plunged to certain death in front of them. He looked across at Carter. Did no one care that the girl would drown?

Montgomery grabbed him by the lapels and pulled him close. He'd never seen him look so uncomposed. 'Victor! You have to focus!'

'But the girl will die!'

'We're all dying, Victor! That's the great concept behind Department Nine. What your dad gave his life for.'

Victor shook himself. He peered over the wall. There was no sign of bodies in the river. No break in the waves. Just a surging mass of water battling against the rain.

The river sliced Jed's skin like knives. His body twisted and turned; his hands unable to steady himself as the water pummelled and pounded him. He knew one thing. A life moved with his. His life. Kassia's. All he'd known and all he could remember was connected to her. And he knew he could not lose her.

The water surged round him; whipped by his fall. His eyes stung with silt and mud. He wrenched the rope that snaked across his wrist. The knot was unfinished and he tugged his hands free. The cord slipped away slowly in the heaving water. He kicked with his feet and ploughed forwards. He had to find her.

There was no air in his lungs. His throat was tight; gripped by a claw. The Thames had nothing on the Neckar. This was a proper fight.

Jed kicked and scraped but would not push for the surface. He had to find her before the current pulled her to the bottom out of reach.

And then, somehow lit with a light from beyond the surface, he saw her.

Arms still tied behind her; hair like a halo framing her face.

He kicked towards her, reached out, clutched at her arm. Her body bounced against his. He looped his arm behind hers and grabbed the rope, tugging hard. One arm slipped free, the second trailing the rope like a snake biting hard to her wrist. She rocked in the water, her hair waving out again like tendrils on a jellyfish. Jed's lungs were going to tear. Water bit at his nostrils. He tugged again and strained for the surface. She was so heavy, the momentum pulling her down. Pulling *them* down.

He tugged again and clutched her body to his; linked his arm around her waist and grabbed at her belt for purchase. Soundlessly he screamed at her to hang on.

His head broke the surface. Water rushed into his mouth, burning his throat. He pulled her upwards, shoulders dipping under the strain. Her head bobbed like a cork through the water, but there was no gasp, no spluttering or gulping of air.

'Kassia, please,' His words were still in his head. Her mouth still closed. She was totally motionless.

Jed kicked his feet again, battling to keep her head above the water. He towed her to the shore, her chin resting on his hand, steering her in the direction of the bank. He scrabbled at the mud and pulled himself forwards, his arm still linked round her. Her head lolled to the side.

'Kassia, please!' Now the words were spoken, cried through the rain. He dragged her on to the riverbank, her T-shirt rising up from her jeans, her belly exposed. He kneeled beside her and ran his fingers down her chest to find the sternum, then linked his hands and pressed hard. Again and again. Nothing. Her head was back, her hair splayed on the muddy ground, her lips were blue. Again and again he pressed, straightening his arms each time, his fingers linked together desperately trying to drive life into her. 'Kassia! Please!'

A passer-by struggled towards them in the rain, dropping his umbrella to crouch next to them. 'Ambulance!' Jed gasped as the man rummaged in his pocket for a phone. 'Ring an ambulance.'

By the time the call had been made, a tiny group of people ringed Kassia's body.

Still Jed drove down and down on her chest. 'You have to breathe, Kassia!'

Finally, he moved her hair from her face and pressed his lips on hers. If it was the kiss of life, there was no response.

Kassia did not breathe.

And the rain kept falling.

Victor ran across the bridge, leaned over the wall and looked down into the water. There was no sign of them. Was Fulcanelli still down there, searching for the girl? Was her body at the bottom of the river, her hands still tied? Victor scanned the bank. Had anyone noticed them jump?

'There!' yelled Carter, pointing. 'See that group of people!'

Victor stared at the gaggle of onlookers, protected by a ring of umbrellas. It was impossible to see what they were crowded round. But along the road behind them an ambulance was racing forwards, its sirens blaring.

Carter grabbed Victor's arm. 'It has to be them. He's got her out of the water. We have to get to the hospital when they do!'

'How?'

Carter didn't answer. Instead he ran ahead towards the end of the bridge. A young couple were stepping out of a restaurant. The woman wore the man's jacket as a canopy above her head. His shirt was soaked through with rain. He moved round to the passenger side of a small and very battered Citroën car and swung open the door for her. The woman smiled dreamily and went to step inside.

Carter grabbed hold of the door and blocked the woman's way. 'Emergency! *Dies ist ein Notfall! Wir brauchen Ihr Auto! Wir bezahlen auch!*'

The woman tried to hustle forwards. Carter took a wad of bank notes from his pocket and waved it in front of the man, whose eyes widened. Victor doubted he'd ever seen more money in one place. The man shrugged at his girlfriend, grabbed the notes and threw Carter the keys.

Carter ran round to the driver's side. 'Come on,' he yelled, gesticulating wildly at the open door. 'Get in!'

Victor bundled into the back, and Montgomery, who'd only just caught up with them, clambered awkwardly into the passenger seat, his stick propped upright like the internal pillar of a stock car.

The Citroën certainly felt like a stock car. The

window by Victor's head was held in position with heavy duty duct tape, the brakes were spongy and the steering obviously out of alignment. The car spluttered and behind them the couple outside the restaurant began to shout at each other. Victor's last sight of them involved the woman tossing the man's jacket into a puddle and striding down the street in the opposite direction.

Carter was trying hard to drive. The road surface was cobbled and there was a network of one ways and no entries. At one point, Victor covered his eyes.

'We have to hurry!' bellowed Montgomery.

'Thank you so much for reminding me!' squawked back Carter, flinging the car round a very tight corner. 'Without you to tell me, I might have forgotten to be quick!'

'He cannot get away!' screamed Montgomery, and Victor could see a vein throbbing on his forehead. 'We've got to do all we can to catch that ambulance! Whatever happens, we can't have anyone asking questions!'

They lay Kassia on the stretcher and wheeled it into the ambulance. Two paramedics worked on her. *'Sie müssen zur Seite gehen, mein Herr,'* one said to Jed as he clambered into the ambulance behind them.

'English?' Jed begged. 'Do you speak English?'

'Totally,' said the paramedic. 'I'm on exchange from Chicago.'

Before Jed could mumble his thanks, the paramedic spoke again. 'I said, you have to stand clear, sir,'

'*You* have to save her!' Jed begged.

The paramedic pressed the paddles on Kassia's chest. The monitor screens recorded the pulse. Nothing.

'Please, sir! Stand back.'

This time Jed had no words.

Again the line on the screen was unresponsive.

A look passed between the paramedics.

'No!' Jed slumped down to his knees. 'Again!'

Kassia's skin was the colour of candle wax. Her hair splayed behind her like waterweed. Her eyes closed.

'You have to try again!'

The second paramedic looked across at the first. It was clear that even if he didn't understand English like his friend, Jed's pleading needed no translation. The paramedic from Chicago lowered the paddles.

'Please, Kassia! Please!'

Her body jolted with the surge of power. Her shoulders lifted for a moment. The flat line on the screen stretched into oblivion.

Silence.

And then a tiny blip and spike in the line.

The Citroën careered through the streets of Heidelberg. Carter thumped the horn and startled pedestrians flung themselves out of her way, their umbrellas wheeling like storm clouds.

'Where was the ambulance?' Montgomery shouted.

'On this road,' shouted Carter. 'That's why I'm here!'

'We must get to the hospital when he does. We can't let them take him in. You understand.' His vein was bulging again, his skin wet with sweat and rain. 'Put your foot down.'

Victor was pretty sure Carter's foot was as close to the ground as it would go. He could smell burning rubber. Thick plumes of smoke were billowing behind them.

The road narrowed. The river was beside them. And metres away a crowd was blocking the street. The air was shattered by the sound of a siren. Lights flashed.

And an ambulance pulled out of the crowd and began to head up the hill in front of them.

Jed held tight to Kassia's hand. 'You're OK. You're OK.' She was strapped to monitors; the ropes that bound her arms, released now, abandoned like a coiled dragon on the floor of the ambulance.

'You mustn't rush her, sir.' The paramedic was watching the monitors and recording numbers on a clipboard.

'But she'll be OK, right? She's going to be OK?'

'We'll know more when we have her at the hospital. She's been through a major trauma. For now we need to focus on keeping her calm.' He wrote something down and clicked buttons on the screen. 'And you, sir. We need to be sure you don't overexert yourself. You've suffered a trauma too.'

Jed tightened his hold on Kassia's hand. 'She will be OK?' It wasn't so much a question as a demand.

The paramedic said something in German to the driver of the ambulance and then turned to look at Jed. 'She should be OK, sir.'

Jed lowered his head and rested it on the edge of her stretcher. He didn't have the energy to cry. Nor the energy to wonder if those psychos from NOAH had seen them clamber out of the water.

'Jed?' The voice was barely a whisper.

Jed jolted upright and squeezed her hand even tighter. 'Kassia! Oh, Kassia. You were so brave.'

Her fingers twitched.

'I thought I'd lost you.'

Her mouth twitched too, into something resembling a smile. And then she pulled him in closer. She smelled of the river. Dark shadows of silt ringed her eyes. He could feel her ragged breath on his face. 'Jed.' He could tell every breath was hurting but her grip was tightening. Her fingernails dug into the skin on the back of his hand. 'Jed. They will come after you. They won't give up until they've caught you.'

He smoothed her hair. 'So we keep running.'

A tear leaked from her eye. And she shook her head slowly. 'It's not enough,' she said.

'But we will find a way to escape,' he said. 'Like we did on the bridge.'

Her breath was shallow now, catching in her throat. Jed was aware the paramedic was growing concerned.

'Sir. I think she's getting distressed now. I must insist you move back.'

But Kassia would not let go. She pulled Jed in even tighter and her staccato breath punched against his face.

'We need to die, Jed. Both of us. It's the only way.'

Jed recoiled. What was she talking about? He thought the jump from the bridge had been to get away. He thought it had been an act of bravery to win them both their freedom. But perhaps that wasn't what Kassia had meant at all! Had she really wanted to stop living! And how could he die? She'd seen him drink the poison. Knew he was Fulcanelli. She knew what that meant.

His horror must have been written all over his face but Kassia pulled him to her again and this time her grip was hard and forceful.

'Death is our only way out of this,' she said.

The Citroën followed the ambulance all the way to the hospital. The sirens cleared the path and the lights were a spinning beacon.

Suddenly the ambulance slowed. The lights stilled and the sirens stopped.

'Why have they done that?' yelled Carter. 'Why aren't they racing there any more?'

Victor tried to work it out. A knot began to form in his stomach.

'Why are they going so slowly?' Carter said again.

Victor knew there could only be one reason. The knot in his stomach grew.

The ambulance slowed completely on the approach to the hospital.

'What do I do now?' asked Carter.

'Keep close enough to see,' urged Montgomery.

Carter pulled the car to a halt a few metres back from the accident and emergency entrance. Two nurses hurried out of the hospital. The paramedic who'd been driving stepped out of the front of the ambulance. He talked to the nurses and they nodded.

'We need to be close enough to hear,' said Carter, as the paramedic went round to the back of the ambulance and swung open the doors.

Victor strained to see. Everyone was quiet.

And the nurse and the paramedic lowered the first wheeled stretcher out of the ambulance.

Victor covered his mouth and retched. It was as he feared. The body on the stretcher was completely covered, head to toe, in a blanket. No part of her was visible. The blanket was a shroud. The girl hadn't made it.

'We killed her,' howled Victor. 'If we hadn't used her like we did, she wouldn't have jumped and—'

Montgomery thumped Victor hard on the arm. 'Keep your voice down, you idiot. This is no one's fault. And if she didn't make it, then she's a tiny price to pay for what we will gain.'

The knot in Victor's stomach seemed to rise and press against the base of his throat.

Montgomery leant forward in his seat. 'Come on, Fulcanelli,' he urged in the direction of the ambulance. 'Let's see our prize.'

The paramedic and nurse had rolled the first stretcher out of sight into the hospital. The second paramedic was helping the other nurse lower the end of the second stretcher. Feet first covered in a yellow blanket. The trolley slipped out into the protection of the covered entrance way.

Victor couldn't breathe.

Like the stretcher before it, this one was covered fully with a blanket. Head to toe.

'No! How's that possible? How can that be?'

Montgomery threw open the door of the Citroën. It juddered as he clambered from his seat.

Victor and Carter tumbled out too, pulling Montgomery back. 'Sir. Sir. We can't be seen. The rope. We mustn't get involved.'

Montgomery pulled against the hands that held him as the second stretcher was wheeled into the hospital. He saw the nurse turn before she disappeared from view. But the signs on the wall made it clear where she was going. She was following directions to the morgue.

DEATH CERTIFI

DEATH C
CITY

FULL NAME
Unknow

ADDRESS (Str

SEX	RACE
F	W

CCUPATION

ME OF FAT

SEN NAME

VE OF DEAT

FULL NAME OF DECEASED (First)
Unknown

ADDRESS (Street and Number)

SEX	RACE	MARITAL STATUS	DA
M	W		

Deathe
Decay

NOT

AUSE OF
respira
leading

N   OF PHYSICIAN
Alexandra Piros

PLACE OF BURIAL OR REMOVAL

UNDERTAKER

INFORMANT

I hereby certify the above to b
in this office.

(Date Issued)

82-158 (Rev. 6/82)

hereby
in this of

(Date Iss

82-158 (Rev. 6/82)

CATE

LISTED DOES NOT APPEAR

(Middle)

E OF BIRTH (Mo., Day, Yr.) | AGE
--- | 16 Yrs.

BIRTHPLACE

BIRTHPLACE

BIRTHPLACE

DEATH
tory impairment
to asphyxia - drowning

ADDRESS

BURIAL DATE

ADDRESS

ADDRESS
---

e a correct copy of a Death Certificate filed

COMMISSIONER OF RECORDS

(Registrar)

200820

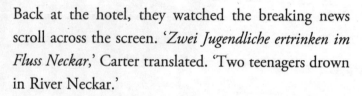

DAY 56
24th April

Back at the hotel, they watched the breaking news scroll across the screen. '*Zwei Jugendliche ertrinken im Fluss Neckar,*' Carter translated. 'Two teenagers drown in River Neckar.'

Even by the time there was a correspondent at the hospital, showing pictures of the Old Bridge and talking to passers-by who claimed to have seen the fall, the news had not sunk in.

'How?' groaned Montgomery. 'Tell me how? We saw him take the poison.'

There was only one answer and Carter was the one to voice it. 'We were wrong,' he said quietly. 'The poison must have worked later. Or the river was finally too much for him. He just wasn't Fulcanelli.'

Jed tugged the blanket from his face and sat up.

The paramedic had steered the stretcher into the mortuary and was locking the door behind him. A man in a white coat rushed forwards. '*Was tunsie? Wersinddiese Leute?*'

The paramedic waved him away. 'I'm trying to win a little time. These people are with me.'

The white-coated man didn't look satisfied with the answer, but the paramedic gesticulated defensively. 'Leave us. Please. I'll explain everything later. But you tell no one, understand? That's important.' He kept his hands raised a second longer than was necessary.

The man didn't need telling twice. He hurried out into the corridor and the paramedic locked the door behind him.

Jed jumped down from the stretcher and rushed across to where Kassia was lying. He tugged the blanket free. 'You OK? Are you OK?' His words tumbled over themselves like water over rocks in a stream.

She grabbed his hands and sat up tentatively. 'I'm fine. Honestly.'

'I seriously doubt you're fine,' said the paramedic, hurrying forwards. 'Your body has gone through an immense shock. It needs time to recover. You need to be monitored. You need to be kept—'

Kassia turned quickly to face him. 'I'm fine. And we need to get away from here.'

The paramedic was obviously surprised by the determination in her voice, but less so than he'd been when she'd concocted their escape plan in the back of the ambulance. 'I don't understand,' he'd pleaded. 'I get that you're scared of someone and whatever happened on the bridge wasn't good. But pretending to be dead? What's with that? You need to call the police. Whoever's after you needs to be caught.'

Jed turned now and tried to make his voice calm and balanced despite the panic swelling inside him. 'It's not that simple. The people who are after us must think we're dead otherwise they'll never stop chasing us.'

'But the police. They could protect you. Help you.'

Jed shook his head. River water dripped from his clothes and pooled at his feet. 'This is bigger than your police. We can't involve them.' He could see the man wasn't buckling. He agreed to their crazy plan in the ambulance to buy them time, but now he wasn't so sure. If he weakened one bit; if he gave them away, then everything was over. NOAH would close in and it would be finished.

'We were in witness protection,' Jed blurted. 'Back home in England. New identities. A new start. We can't mess that up. You have to let us go.'

The paramedic was thinking. He was glancing at

the door. He was chewing on his lip.

Kassia moved nervously forwards. 'Please. They can't know the truth now. It would destroy us.'

The paramedic plunged his hands deep into his pockets. 'You should be monitored. Your heart stopped. I could lose my job.'

'We could lose our lives!' begged Kassia.

'Our social worker,' cut in Jed. 'Ring him. He'll explain everything. Tell you why we've got to pretend we died in the river.' He gestured to Kassia. 'She has a phone. You can ring him.'

Kassia pulled the mobile from her pocket. It cried river water from a shattered screen on to the mortuary slab beside them. 'I can tell you his number,' she offered. 'His name is Jacob. He'll make it all clear.'

'I can't leave you alone here!'

'Is there a phone in the office? You could ring from there? We won't go until you've checked things out.'

The paramedic took a deep breath. He stared at Kassia, assessing her recovery. 'You feel OK?' he said. 'No pain. No racing heart?'

Kassia shook her head. Jed could tell she wasn't being entirely honest but it did the job.

'So what's his number?'

Kassia struggled to remember and for a second Jed feared the paramedic was changing his mind. 'Here.'

She grabbed a pen and clipboard from the mortuary table and scribbled the phone number next to a pre-printed diagram of a dead body. The paramedic took the paper and hurried into the office. 'Two minutes,' he called over his shoulder.

Finally, Jed and Kassia were alone.

Jed stood in front of her and took her hands in his. The rope had cut lines into her wrists. 'You were so brave.'

'Hey. I was just making sure I could get away,' she said, but her voice was shaking.

'Seriously. I can't believe you did what you did.'

'Yeah, well, I can't believe you did what you did either. The poison. Getting me out of the water . . .'

He squeezed her hands and she flinched a little. 'I'm so sorry,' he said.

'What, for squeezing too tight or for getting me involved in this?'

'For all of it.'

He looked away for a moment, down at the mortician's silver table. The surface was polished to a shine. It reflected his face like a mirror.

'Hey,' she spoke softly and he looked back at her. This time he could see the raised red weals on the skin below the base of her throat where the paddles had fired her heart back to life. 'It's going to be all right.'

'Is it?'

'Look. I know I took my time to get on board and to be sure. But it's both of us now and we'll find a way through all this. And we know now. For sure I mean. About who you are.' She turned her head to look around, and for the first time Jed took in the detail of the room they'd been brought to. There were lines of tall silver cabinets extended along the walls. Each cabinet was numbered. And locked.

'This is where they bring you,' Kassia said quietly. 'At the end. When it's over and the life has gone. But it's not over for us. It's just beginning.' This time she reached out and took his hands and squeezed them tight. 'Whatever happened all those years ago in a laboratory in Paris changed this. You discovered something that could make all this go away.' Kassia stared hard at him. Her wrists were bleeding, her chest burned, but her eyes were steely bright.

Jed didn't know what to say. Nothing seemed to be enough. 'I shouldn't have left you when we came out of the castle.'

'But you came back. That's what matters.'

His stomach twisted. He should tell her. What he'd seen in the Apothecary Museum. His mouth was dry. His lips cracked. But as he opened his mouth to speak, the door from the office swung open. The paramedic returned. 'Your story holds out,' he said. 'That Jacob guy supported what you said. I can't pretend to have a clue what's going on here but I can see you're involved in something big. Bigger than I can get my head round.' He passed the paper with the phone number back to Kassia. 'I think I believe that handing you over and making you come clean about what happened, even if we involve the police, could harm you. And I think I might lose my job if I let you go. But I think it's the right thing to do.'

'So you'll cover for us? Make the world think we're dead?'

'I'll do it. But there's something I need to know first.'

'OK.'

'You're the boy from the river back in England, right? The boy from the Thames?'

Jed nodded awkwardly.

'Man, this must be some complicated story you've got going here.'

'It is.' Jed took a deep breath. 'You'll still cover?'

The paramedic nibbled at his lip again. 'As far as I'm concerned I was too late to save either patient from the effects of water inhalation. It was a tragic accident. Both died in the ambulance.'

Jed smiled his thanks.

'But you'll make it worth it, right?'

Jed thought for a moment he was asking for money but the look on the paramedic's face showed he meant something more than that.

'You'll do whatever is needed to make this right?'

'We intend to,' said Kassia.

Victor carried the cans of drink in from the corridor and put them down on the unit inside the door. Carter and Montgomery were still on the sofa, focused on the television.

'Anything new?'

Initially they'd been grateful for the twenty-four hour news from the UK streaming straight to the hotel. They'd flicked back and forth now and then to check they weren't missing anything on the local German news, but this way they could at least understand what was being said. Now Victor was finding it frustrating. There were no new details. Just a soggy and rather disgruntled German correspondent stationed outside the hospital going over the same parts of the story again and again.

Suddenly, the reporter in the studio pressed his finger against his ear piece and looked knowingly at the camera. 'We go now to our special correspondent in Heidelberg who has news on the identity of the two

British travellers brought into the hospital early today.'

There was a slight time delay on the feed. The picture pixelated a bit, suggesting to Victor the report was being made on a camera phone and that they hadn't had enough resources in place yet to get a proper crew in position. Back in the hotel room, those seated on the sofa moved forwards to get a better view.

'Yes, thank you, Hugh. The hospital has just confirmed that one of the two British teenagers reported dead this evening after apparent misadventure in the River Neckar was believed to be the boy tagged as River Boy by the British Press a few months ago. The boy escaped from the River Thames, but wasn't able to remember anything about who he was or why he was in London. It seems this same boy got into difficulties in the Neckar River after falling from the Old Bridge in Heidelberg. There's no news yet on the identity of the person found with him, though reports suggest she was a teenage girl.'

The correspondent's face pixelated again and a library image of the boy from the Thames filled the screen. Montgomery punched his fist against the arm of the sofa. 'He was Fulcanelli!'

'No! We were wrong!' groaned Carter. 'We wanted him to be Fulcanelli. He was just a mixed up kid who wasn't safe around water.'

'But the symbol he drew?'

'A hollow sign.' He looked across at Victor, trying to pull him into the conversation. 'We've been chasing unicorns so long that when we think we've found one, we lose all reason. And that's because they're out there. Fulcanelli *is* out there. We just have to keep searching until we find him.'

'And how do we do that?' Victor sat on the arm of the sofa.

'We pull in all the surveillance footage we can from beside the river and outside the hospital,' said Montgomery forcibly. 'We get people in London crawling all over this, looking for anything that doesn't sit right. We get documents and papers. Someone from that hospital has to register the deaths and I want to see the evidence.'

Carter's face was pained. 'Sir, the boy in the river wasn't Fulcanelli. We have to let it go.'

Something about the way Montgomery looked at him made it clear he had absolutely no intention of doing that.

Jed was holding on to the pocket watch. The glass had steamed with water from the river but the mechanism still ticked. It was made of strong stuff. 'You're shaking.' Kassia reached across and steadied Jed's hand.

'I'm fine, honestly.' Jed was trying to sound like he meant it, but his hand was trembling like it had back in the Spanish farmhouse, when he'd crushed the glass, and like it had when he'd left the castle laboratory. 'Don't say anything or that paramedic will never let us go.'

That paramedic was back in the office making phone calls. He'd promised to arrange a way for them to leave the hospital without being noticed. Jacob and Dante were going to meet them en route.

'But why are you shaking?'

They'd changed out of their wet things into hospital issue clothing the paramedic had found for them. Jed was trying not to think about who the clothes had come from or why they no longer needed them. He was also trying not to think about his hand, but the convulsions were getting stronger. The pain was pulsing up his arm and his fingers felt like they no longer belonged to him. He pushed the watch into his pocket and hid his hand.

'Jed! Answer me!'

'I don't know. It's been happening for a while now. Since we came to Spain.'

Kassia looked at him. Her face was ghostly white. 'You do know, don't you? Before, you were going to say something. And the paramedic came back and you stopped.' She bit her lip but it was quivering. 'What aren't you telling me?'

So this was it then. Another line in front of them that once they crossed they'd never step back over. Why was this all so difficult?

'Jed?'

'It's to do with the elixir and the dragon and . . .' He paused for a moment. 'I don't even know if I'm right.'

'Tell me anyway.'

He took another deep breath. 'OK. It's the dates. Once the memories started coming back, I was sure there were these dates and they were important.'

'Like the date my dad died? We've been over this.'

'I know.' The night they'd talked while looking at the stars seemed a lifetime ago. 'There were five dates, and I kept telling you the dragon had six segments and how I was sure a date was missing. One I couldn't remember.'

'The perfect six?'

'Exactly. And then there were these other things I saw. And I knew they were important too. The height of St Paul's; the height of the O2; even the height of the clock tower up at the castle.'

'They all mean a year, right?'

'All of them. And when I saw that, something

happened. Like I was supposed to know a year was important.'

'OK,' she said tentatively. 'So supposing the sixth date's in a year's time. That would work, wouldn't it? Fit with all the clues.'

Jed felt the bottom fall out of his stomach. 'That's what I'm scared it means.'

'Why? What's so bad about a year being up?'

He ran his shaking hands through his hair and tried to compose himself. Knew it was important to say this all in one go. No stops. No hesitations. 'Up at the castle, there were six bottles representing the elixir. The guide explained the elixir made by the alchemists wasn't a one dose thing. It had to be taken six times to finally secure the change.'

'And what happens if it isn't taken a sixth time?' she pressed.

'The alchemist dies. Five doses takes the alchemist back to an age like I am now. Makes them immortal for a while. But a sixth dose fixes the change.'

'So what does that mean? For you?'

'I think it means I've taken the dose five times. I think it means I've got one more dose to take. And I think it means I've got one year to do it. Or . . .'

She put her hand against his lips. 'Don't say it. Please don't say it!'

He took her hand in his. 'Kassia, we have to face this. I might be immortal for a time. It's why the poison didn't kill me. But I have a year to find the recipe for the elixir and to make the change permanent. Otherwise it's over.'

'No! You're wrong!'

'I'm not, Kass.' Her hand was tight in his. 'You know I'm not. You've seen the signs just like I have.'

'But a year. It's not long enough! People spend their whole lives trying to find the elixir. How can we find it in a year?'

'We don't even have a year, Kass.' His hand was shaking violently now. 'We *had* a year *since* the river. That leaves us ten months.'

'But it's not long enough. It's not fair. It's not . . .' She couldn't finish her words. Her shoulders rounded as if all the air from her lungs had seeped away.

'It's what we've got, Kass. Ten months left to find answers.'

'So where do we start?'

He remembered Reverend Cockren on the steps of St Paul's and the answer he gave her was the same one he'd given the chaplain. 'I don't know.'

The door to the office opened and the paramedic came out. His face was grave. 'OK. I've pulled some strings, called in some favours. There's a van outside for you.' He smoothed his hair back and Jed noticed his cheeks were flushed a little. 'We call the van the death wagon. It takes people on their final journey. From here to the undertakers. Perhaps to the crematorium. It's for last journeys only.'

Jed nodded. He tried to speak calmly even though the words burned in his throat. 'How can we thank you? We don't even know your name.'

'It's Charlie Monalees. But if any of this goes belly up then you didn't know my name. Remember.'

'Sure.'

'And who exactly am I helping?' Charlie laughed. 'Seems we haven't done well on the introductions.'

'Kassia Devaux.'

'And your boyfriend?'

Kassia didn't say anything to correct him but her answer was a whisper. 'This is Jed.'

'Just Jed?'

'For the moment,' said Kassia. 'But maybe one day you'll know him as more than that.'

Charlie nodded. It was enough for now. Jed could tell he wasn't keen to press things and they could hear the purr of an engine outside the back door of the morgue.

Charlie passed Kassia a small piece of paper. 'Give

this to the driver,' he said. 'It's the address where your friend and brother are going to meet you.'

'I'm sorry if you do lose your job,' said Jed.

'I was missing America anyways,' quipped Charlie. 'And besides. I've made a pretty thorough effort to cover our tracks. You wanted to be dead and as far as the outside world is concerned, that's exactly what you are. I might get away with it!' He smiled. 'Look after her. She shouldn't have any stress. Her heart will need time to repair.'

'I'll look out for her heart,' Jed said, as he led Kassia to the door.

They stepped nervously out into the remains of the storm and clambered into the back of the death wagon as quickly as they could. The door with blacked out windows shut behind them. It was impossible to see where they were going. But they knew now they had exactly ten months left in order to get there.